CW01271725

The
PARROTS OF DESIRE

Also by Amrita Narayanan

A Pleasant Kind of Heavy and Other Erotic Stories

The

PARROTS OF DESIRE

3,000 YEARS OF INDIAN EROTICA

AMRITA NARAYANAN

ALEPH

ALEPH

ALEPH BOOK COMPANY
An independent publishing firm
promoted by *Rupa Publications India*

Published in India in 2017
by Aleph Book Company
7/16 Ansari Road, Daryaganj
New Delhi 110 002

Anthology Copyright © Aleph Book Company 2017

Introduction Copyright © Amrita Narayanan 2017

Copyright for the individual pieces and translations
vests in the respective authors and translators.

pp. 251 to 257 (Notes) are an extension of the
copyright page.

While every effort has been made to trace copyright
holders and obtain permission, this has not been
possible in all cases; any omissions brought to our
attention will be remedied in future editions.

All rights reserved.

In the works of fiction in this anthology, names,
characters, places and incidents are either the product
of the authors' imagination or are used fictitiously
and any resemblance to any actual persons, living or
dead, events or locales is entirely coincidental.

No part of this publication may be reproduced,
transmitted, or stored in a retrieval system, in any
form or by any means, without permission in
writing from Aleph Book Company.

ISBN: 978-93-83064-09-0

3 5 7 9 10 8 6 4

Printed in India

This book is sold subject to the condition that it
shall not, by way of trade or otherwise, be lent,
resold, hired out, or otherwise circulated without the
publisher's prior consent in any form of binding or
cover other than that in which it is published.

To the modern reader:
may reading, across time and language,
give you the companionship you need
to stay on the erotic side of the argument

CONTENTS

INTRODUCTION

THE EROTIC IN THE INDIAN IMAGINATION
To read centuries of voices writing on the erotic is to become keenly aware of a deep argument that exists in the geography of the subcontinent, an argument between literary romantics—who embrace the erotic for the gloss it adds to life—and religious traditionalists[1]—who caution against the erotic, for its disorderly nature and potential to cause chaos. While romantic and traditionalist voices are unanimous in their belief that the erotic holds an extraordinary power and attraction for human beings, each does something very different with that belief. Romantics are erotically positive: they believe life is made worthwhile by its erotic aspects, that the best life is one in which our understanding and awareness of the erotic are maximally enhanced. Traditionalists, on the other hand, are erotically anxious: they believe that a worthwhile life is one in which the four goals of life[2] are in balance; they do not favour the promotion of the erotic, worrying that if not tightly controlled, the erotic could undermine the other three goals of life. Aficionados of the romantic project used the arts as a vehicle of articulation; their literature, music, drama, even grammar, was thought to be imbued with the erotic and capable of enhancing our understanding of the erotic. Traditionalists used both religious writing and the social contract to articulate the dangers of the erotic, believing that the erotic must be kept on the sidelines, aside from its necessary use as a vehicle for reproduction. Romantics believe that coupling is a central life force, and they appreciate the energy that comes from all couplings, whether man-woman, woman-woman, men who identify as women (and are fantasizing about male gods), or (wo)men with God. Traditionalists believe in the notion of an 'ideal couple': heterosexually and monogamously married, with children and extended family in the foreground and a willingness and ability to keep the erotic in the background.

To further understand the argument between traditionalists and

---

[1] I chose the word traditionalist and not puritan because of the historical origins of puritanism that are not pertinent to India. However I thought it worth mentioning that the traditionalist argument is close in nature to the puritan argument. Here puritan is used in the sense of *against pleasure*, see for example, H. L. Mencken, who sardonically defined Puritanism as 'the haunting fear that someone, somewhere may be happy'.

[2] The four aims of life (purusharthas): artha (wealth), kama (desire), dharma (duty) and moksha (salvation from the cycle of life and death).

romantics, consider a brief history of the time that traditionalism and romanticism have held sway. The purview of this anthology begins about 1000 BCE in ancient India. For the first 800 years or so of this time period, that is, beginning with the Vedas, traditionalist sentiments prevail. During this time, the destabilizing dangers of the erotic are far better articulated in the literature than are its pleasures. From the Vedas onwards, traditionalist literature, which is largely in the form of religious texts, is squarely articulate on the need to manage the destablizing potential of the erotic. Beginning in 200 BCE, however, and continuing for several centuries, literary voices sang the glories of the erotic and their dedication to it—in Tamil, Sanskrit, and Maharashtrian Prakrit. From the second to the sixth century, an Indian literary-erotic-nature idiom was spelt out from Tamil Nadu to Maharashtra and up to Madhya Pradesh. Here the poets embraced the erotic along with its problems, accepting that though the erotic often brought anger, grief and shame, it was still worth embracing for its pleasures. During this medieval period emerged the Tamil Sangam poets and the Maharashtrian Prakrit *Gāthā Saptaśatī*, the prose and poetry of Kālidāsā and Bhartrihari, as well as the *Kama Sutra* itself. After this golden age of the Romantics, puritanism once again holds sway and the next major erotic work—at least the one that has survived—is the collection of romantic poems known as the *Amaruśataka*, written in Sanskrit in the seventh or eighth century and attributed to King Amaru of Kashmir. From the eighth century onwards there is again a long period in which very few important works have survived, the next set being from the Bhakti poets who compose discontinuously from the ninth to the fifteenth centuries in praise of erotic love with God himself. The fact that Bhakti poets praise erotic love only in language that involves a deity suggests that this was considered the most elegant and refined expression of romanticism at that time. Alternatively, perhaps, the social climate—which by this time included both Hindu and Muslim puritans—did not support an articulation of a more explicit person-to-person erotic love. The taboos on self-expression of erotic love might have impinged particularly on women poets and the re-direction of this love to the divine might have spared them the censorship that might have otherwise been forthcoming. Another way of thinking about it is that, dispirited with the limitations of romantic love between humans, some of these poets were able to find a more elevated idiom with the gods.

Following the Bhakti period, the proliferation of the Urdu language and the culture of refinement associated with Islamic courtly love played an important pro-romantic influence; but as the Hindu and

Muslim puritans were joined by the British puritans in the seventeenth century, one has the sense that romanticism was very much in the dark ages. Nevertheless, important works continued to emerge in a more scattered fashion. Amongst these individual works are those written by courtesans, such as the Telugu *Radhika Santawanam* (The Appeasement of Radhika) by Muddupalani, in the eighteenth century. Another is the erotic proponent of the Lucknow school of poetry, Qalandar Bakhsh Jur'at, known for his bawdy yet spiritual imaginings of women in sexual union. As the reader advances towards and past the twentieth century, individual writers offer an exploration of contemporary erotic problems alternating with the past. Contemporary Indian writers who match and build on the efforts of their ancestors write in, among other languages, English, Tamil and Malayalam, and continue to shed profound light on the erotic. In this anthology the contemporary writers I have chosen include those who have made a searing commentary on the relationship between kama and society: Perumal Murugan, Kamala Das; those whose reverential treatment of the erotic couple recalls the glorious medieval period: Pritish Nandy, K. Satchidanandan, Tarun Tejpal; writers like Manto and Ambai whose erotic-nostalgic writings make us feel lustful and tender at once; modern Bhakti poets like Arundhathi Subramaniam and Kala Krishnan Ramesh; and those who have treated in great depth the extraordinary conflicts that the erotic poses for an individual life: here found in the works of Mridula Garg, Deepti Kapoor and Ginu Kamani.

IN DEFENCE OF SEX AND MODERN MEANING: THE TREATMENT OF ANCIENT TEXTS IN THIS ANTHOLOGY

As excavator of this anthology spanning 3,000 years, my sympathies have been with the condition of the modern reader who is, among other things, constantly trying to find—or make meaning of—her, his or others' erotic life or lives. Therefore, instead of trying to depict the past pure and simple—if indeed that were possible—instead of attempting a chronological perspective on how ancient and modern literature from the Indian geography view the erotic, I have chosen instead to concern myself with gathering an anthology organized in a way that offers the most meaning to the modern reader grappling with twenty-first-century erotic life. Another way of thinking about traditionalists and romantics could be to think of two kinds of readers. Romantics read poetry and literature; they periodically feel as if they are living inside a poem, they relish the lived experience of the novel. Traditionalists are cautious about literature and poetry, they are more interested in the truth of reality than in the truth of fiction; they may see literature as a potentially corruptive influence that undermines structures and safety. This anthology is dedicated to modern romantic readers who identify with the joys and problems of the erotic and are passionate about keeping their lives erotic—whether by sex, literature, art or music.

As a reminder of this anthology's dedication to the modern romantic reader, its title, *The Parrots of Desire*, is a reimagining that implies a heterodox Kama, the god of desire. The parrot is a reference to Kama's vehicle, but the use of the word parrots in the plural is a stand in for modern references that may still be cloaked under traditionalism and therefore not invented when Kama was. From a single parrot on which a green-skinned boy rides around, shooting with his sugarcane bow and arrow, Kama's parrots are a contemporary shorthand for 'that upon which desire is borne'; these parrots become a stand-in for all that might bring us to the erotic life and all that the erotic life brings to us. With this twist, the reputedly 3,000-year-old Kama is still relevant because desire is still relevant. In the kind of modernity that many of us inhabit—in which we spurn religious consolation—we might still remember with a wry smile Voltaire's thought, that if God did not exist, man would have had to invent him. Gods after all, were amongst other things, imagistic shorthand for things that could not otherwise be singly captured. If Kama was invented as a shorthand for desire in all its complexities, then might we not still have access to this invention as modern, though perhaps religion-avoidant, readers?

In an effort to render modern meaning, *The Parrots of Desire* selects renditions of ancient texts that enhance our understanding of the erotic. Prior to the Tamil Sangam arounf 200 BCE, these are few and far in between: for most ancient texts are fraught with erotic anxiety rather than erotic wisdom. At times I found myself slicing slivers of erotic wisdom present in a text and serving it up like fruit, while still knowing that the tree from which they were picked erred, as do many of the ancient Indian texts, on the side of caution rather than Kama. Yet I felt no misgivings doing so, for the erotic anxiety present in the Vedas has been more than adequately nurtured over time. Even a text like the *Kama Sutra*, published well past the first 800-year period of intense erotic traditionalism, still gives a nod to traditionalism, suggesting that a limitation be placed on pleasure lest the other aims of life (artha, dharma, moksha) be disrupted. The modern reader who is ineluctably anxious about sex has no doubt had a surfeit of hearing about the dangers of the erotic life, for this kind of advice is implicit in the functioning of the Indian family. Since caution and anxiety about the erotic have already been given adequate social and political voice, I have used my role as editor to limit the anxious portions in order to present the erotic wisdom that lives amidst the anxieties and that might be of use to the modern reader.

Consider in this vein the short opening excerpt, 'You are Your Desire', from the Brihadaranyaka Upanishad. The verse is excavated from the context in which the tale was originally told: as spiritual advice from an older man to a younger one. Read in its original context, in which the older man directs the younger one towards living for the afterlife, we hear 'you are your desire, so better channel your desires to self-realization'. Read alone in a modernity that typically rejects the consolation of an afterlife, the verse becomes existential advice grounded in the present-life; we hear instead, 'You are your desires, what will do with your life?'

Another example of the decision to dedicate this anthology to the modern reader is the choice of the 'earliest' sampling. From the Rig Veda, the excerpt 'Why does Sex Exist?', written by Italian scholar Roberto Calasso and translated into English by Tim Parks, has a foot in history, but lays claim less to historical accuracy than the plight of the modern reader who may be half in awe, half disillusioned or even wholly rejecting of the gods, but is curious nevertheless of what the gods might have said about sex.

It is worth excavating the erotic wisdom from the ancient texts because buried amidst the anxiety about sex are liberating ideas about sex that are very difficult to access in the modern idiom. Despite being laced—or at times suffused—with erotic anxiety, traditionalist texts nevertheless touch upon what I believe to be the core of Indian erotic philosophy which develops over the next many hundreds of years. This 'core' is the notion that the erotic, like the human imagination itself, is an inspired realm—powerful, beautiful and valuable to human civilization.

In Calasso's rendition from the Rig Veda, the purpose of sex arises as a tale within a tale narrated by Atri, a sage and a prominent character in the 3,000-year-old text. The story is prefaced by the question: why does sex exist? Atri explains that the gods, having mastered the art of pleasure, congregate to ask their leader, Brahma, the purpose of this pleasure. Brahma answers that we need the erotic because without it the world is dusty—it lacks gloss. Ceding to pleasure, suggest the sages, is contributing to the renewal of the world's gloss.

KAMA LIVES (AND WE SHOULD CONSIDER
RESURRECTING HIM DAILY)
If pleasure is that which makes life liveable, then Kama, as a god of pleasure, might have been invented to allow people to worship the notion

of erotic gloss. The most popular story of Kama, of course, involves his death—our classic Indian traditionalist nod to the dangers of erotic life. Kama is killed for being a nuisance, but nonetheless resurrected, as if to say: though a nuisance, the erotic should be allowed to flourish—an idea that the modern reader might find herself agreeing with.

The echo that it is the erotic that makes life tolerable runs through erotic literature and is captured centuries later by the Anglo-Indian writer Laurence Hope, in her poem 'The Garden of Kama' (1901):

> We know not life's reason,
> The length of its season,
> Know not if they know, the great Ones above.
> We none of us sought it,
> And few could support it,
> Were it not gilt with the glamour of love.

Because the traditionalist and romantic positions are and always have been in argument, the modern-day reader may think of Kama as perhaps less a god than a symbol for the Indian romantic movement, a symbol who is alternately honoured, captured and burned, but eventually left alone as a delightful nuisance. In erotic literature, Kama is also a fictional companion for the romantic, a deity who provides reassurance—as with the invention of any god—that we are not alone in our erotic forays. An example of the supportive role that Kama plays in the imagination is seen in a conversation from the eighth-century *Amaruśataka*, when an older woman asks a younger woman who is setting off on an erotic adventure,

> 'But my child you're alone.
> Tell me why you aren't afraid.'

> 'No doubt the God of Love,
> armed with feathered arrows,
> will escort me.'

The presence, named or unnamed, of Kama as shorthand for the erotic-as-nuisance, as an inevitable companion, and as an essential way of making life beautiful, is one of the continuous threads in this anthology. Traditionalists in the pre-Common Era writings on the erotic may remember Kama for his dangers, for the story in which he is burned to death; however, from the Common Era onwards, we see the romantic movement focus on Kama's survival through representations of desire and its seasons in the natural world. From the argument between traditionalists and romantics comes a dialectic about Kama: 'though he is dangerous and unruly, let us spare Kama, for erotic gloss enhances life'.

IN DEFENCE OF NATURE

Perhaps as a way of circumventing the argument, or as an argument itself, the Indian romantic movement is characterized by nature as evocative of human sensuality. The natural world, the poets seem to say, is writ large with potential for humans in an erotic frame of mind. From 200 BCE onwards the first major wave of pro-erotic poetry, in what would be called the medieval period, appear in what is arguably the world's first group of romantic poets: the writings of the Tamil Sangam poets and the Maharashtrian Prakrit writers of the *Gāthā Saptaśatī* who make a sweeping curtsey to nature as a part of desire.

Pre-dating the romantic movement in Europe by thousands of years, these poets imagine life—and a lifestyle—with nature and the erotic at its centre. We do not find here echoes of the didactic tone of the European Romantics ('Let Nature Be Your Teacher') nor the wistfulness of the American Romantics ('I Think That I Shall Never See a Poem Lovely as a Tree'). The voices of India's romantic nature poets are unique in a unified perspective of humans and nature. Desire is enhanced and celebrated as a shared geography of (wo)man and nature, a microcosmos to a macrocosmos. This is accomplished via the extensive and at times codified use of nature metaphors: in the Tamil Sangam poems, sprinkled throughout this anthology, each erotic mood is associated with a different landscape. For example, mountains are associated with lovers' quarrels and wives' irritability (ku-unji) and the ocean with long separations (neidal).

The nature metaphors, arising concurrently with the celebration of the erotic in the Indian subcontinent during the several centuries of the medieval period, present the modern reader with both an aesthetic and a problem. Aesthetically, we might look—as our romantic ancestors did—towards nature for giving meaning to the seasonal nature of erotic love: the nuanced and fluctuating nature of erotic love was defended in the ancient romantic literature by nature references. But in the current Indian urban landscape that rushes away from rather than bends towards nature, we might wonder about nature's impact on our relationship with our own and our lovers' bodies.

Sample this verse from Kālidāsā's *Ṛtusaṃāram*, also from the medieval period, translated by Mani Rao:

Like immodest women unrestrained

Rivers   speedy agitated currents
            felling trees on banks as they
rush
to the sèa

In Kālidāsā's time we may have more easily read the rivers as our own
agitated bodies, eager for union with lovers; today the modern reader
might wonder what it is we rush towards—traffic comes to mind—when
we are 'speedy agitated currents'. Likewise, Kālidāsā's clouds and rivers
make us even more aware of the polluted waters and air of our urban
landscapes; while the Vedic texts signal us to not get lost in pleasures,
the medieval texts highlight the pleasures we might have lost.

If we were to read the medieval romantics for a lesson, it would
perhaps be: 'Stay erotic, stay close to nature'. In the *Kama Sutra* excerpt
'Lifestyle of the Man-About-Town'—which would today apply equally
to the woman-about-town—the person interested in a life of sexual
pleasure must choose a home 'in a house near water, with an orchard'
and keep around the bedroom 'oils and garlands...a pot of beeswax, a
vial of perfume, some bark from lemon tree and betel'. Likewise, teaching
parrots and mynah birds to talk, arranging flowers, cooking soup and
preparing wines are some of the nature-oriented activities suggested
to put men and women in the mood for sex. The chief protagonists of
the *Kama Sutra*, the Courtesan-de-Luxe and the Man-About-Town are
schooled for a life of sex and sensuality, engaging in the kind of lifestyle
and activities that in today's urban landscape are available at best on
vacation, to the wealthy, an India of heritage hotels that is enjoyed by
the privileged and performed by hired help.

Yet desire continues even as the natural ecology disappears. Kama,
after all, is infinitely resurrectable. As a counterpoint to Kālidāsā, consider
the searingly hot, dry, air-conditioned, hyper-urban, trafficked-up twenty-
first-century Delhi that forms the backdrop to the excerpt from Deepti
Kapoor's *A Bad Character*. Infused with a kind of emptiness that seems
to characterize the modern urban Indian landscape, the city and the sex
seem to share something in common, and what appears to have been
lost in the natural world has been gained in good whisky.

THE IRRESISTIBLE DISCONTENTS OF EROTIC LIFE
From making life meaningful using sex and sensuality, to making sex
and sensuality meaningful through nature and culture, the anthology
gravitates to where eroticism eventually takes us, that is, to despair. For
if lovemaking helps the world renew its gloss (from Calasso's Rig Veda
or Laurence Hope's 'The Garden of Kama'), then those who cannot make

love are those who are perhaps most hopeless. Here the contributions of modern Indian literature are salient, and in the excerpt from Tarun Tejpal's *The Alchemy of Desire* (2005), we can watch the downward spiral of the protagonist, who has built a life of meaning on a bedrock of sexuality. The narrator, who is infused with a desperate meaninglessness when he wakes up one morning without a libido, plunges from his engagement with a life of passion to a state of erotic despair where he has neither artha nor kama; in doing so he invites the reader into passionate conversation about the raptures and despairs of romantic love and a deeper contemplation of the question that was foreclosed by the Vedic writers: is erotic love worth its despair?

Numerous excerpts in this anthology build on the theme of a sexless life as a lifeless life; another example, is the excerpt from *Ek Pati Ke Notes* (A Husband's Notes, 1967) by Mahendra Bhalla. Translated by Harish Trivedi, the excerpt is a first-person narrative of a night of miscalculated signals and empty, forced sex that leaves 'The Husband' feeling not only bereft of gloss, but feeling like an inauthentic human being.

A unifying aspect of erotic literature is the notion that jealousy, bitterness, anger, ennui, even regret, form *part* of the experience of erotic love. This is no revelation to the poets, but might be balm to a love-weary reader who, forgetting the dark underbelly of passionate love, wishes only for its peak experience, the elation and the bliss. Though love includes disaster, being human means relentlessly courting it nonetheless; thus the notion of the erotic as a valuable nuisance continues. In the words of the ninth-century Tamil poet Manikkavacakar:

> Unyielding, as they say,
> as an elephant's jaw,
> or a woman's grasp, was love's unrelenting
> seizure.

ENDLESS FASCINATIONS: SPIRITUAL SEXUALITY
AND WOMEN'S SEXUALITY

Perhaps it is in awareness of the shame and pain involved in the erotic life that the oldest texts seem to counsel the inclusion of a third: what one might call a spiritual component to sexuality. There is no doubt that one of the most longstanding and unique contributions of Indian erotic literature is what could be called a spiritual—or at the very least, soulful—element. An example of soulful sexuality is hinted at in the Shvetashvatara Upanishad, in the excerpt entitled 'The Firesticks of Love'. Here the self or as the Upanishads translator Eknath Easwaran writes it, Self with a capital S, includes the notion of soul. Erotic union is Self joining Self, soul joining soul and the body between. Is there something in the body, the verse seems to ask, that takes us closer to our Self (with a capital S)?

It's a thread that gets picked up centuries later in the period of medieval texts such as the *Hatha Yoga Pradipika* and the Tantras, both of which enjoined readers to use the body, even sex, for the purpose of self-elevation to the level of soul. Building upon this notion is the erotic poetry of the celibate 'saints' of the Bhakti, Hatha yoga and Tantra traditions (produced discontinuously between the ninth and fifteenth centuries) poetry with rippling romantic and sexual metaphor, but often without the poets themselves having had a physical engagement. The lack of physical engagement seems to leave the erotic insights of these poets undiminished. It seems that the physical pleasures of sex may be given up while a highly sexual inner world is still retained. Perhaps it does not matter then, whether or not Kannada poet Mahadeviyakka has physical knowledge of a man; in her poems it is clear that her yearnings towards a divine figure are clearly erotic:

> Riding the blue sapphire mountains
> wearing moonstone for slippers
> blowing long horns
> O Siva when shall I
> crush you on my pitcher breasts?

Such fantasies of women when on their own form such an important part of the Indian erotic literary tradition that a whole section of this anthology is devoted to them. Here—as elsewhere through the text—you'll find verses from the *Gāthā Saptaśatī* (200 BCE–200 CE), the Tamil Sangam (200 BCE–200 CE) and the *Amaruśataka* (900 CE) as well as selections from the Bhakti period, from Āntāl and Mahadeviyakka (900–1100 CE), that describe women's fantasies of men (whether human or godly) and of other women. What stand out in these fantasies across time are the pleasures and beauty of sex-in-solitude. There is also the enjoyment of repetition, for as Freud liked pointing out, much of what we find pleasurable in masturbation is not the new but the old.

Consider the theme of memory and repetition in the excerpt from Krishna Baldev Vaid's female voice, Nasreen, translated by Harish Trivedi:

> Whenever I am alone and feeling low and have had a drink or
> two I sit down to replay my first night with you and can never
> decide where to begin and find myself beginning at a new point
> each time—sometimes at the Kala Bhavan, sometimes with the

The Parrots of Desire

first drink we had together or with our first kiss or with the first spark ignited by our gazes meeting or with some antic of yours at Reva's party or something you said there. I then try to bring back moment-by-moment the entire duration from the Kala Bhavan up to that very last moment we shared that night. Without forgetting a single thing that was said or done or thought or even the silences.

Men speaking in women's voices, as Vaid did, also has a longstanding tradition in Indian writing, particularly in erotic writing. Reading the number of poems across time written by men in women's voices suggests literary proof of the idea postulated by India's first psychoanalyst, Freud's contemporary, Girindrasekhar Bose, who famously wrote in a 1929 letter to Sigmund Freud that it was not penis envy but its opposite, the unconscious wish of the Indian man to be a woman[3], that drives the Indian psyche. Why Indian men might wish to be women is read in Arshia Sattar's translation of an excerpt from the Mahabharata, 'Man or Woman?'. In this story, which explains the superiority of women to men when it comes to sexual pleasure, Bhisma tells Yudhishthira the story of Bhangaswana, a king cursed to become a woman who, when he has an opportunity for the curse to be lifted, chooses to remain a woman because 'in the sexual intercourse between man and woman, it is always the woman who obtains the greater pleasure'.

Writing in the ancient language of Maithili, the fourteenth-century poet Vidyapati chooses a woman's voice to describe the birth of Kama, which he says is equivalent to the birth of a young woman whose 'Restless feet, a blush on the young breasts, hint of her heart's disquiet'. Likewise, sixteenth-century poet Raskhan, though he addresses a divine God, picks up the imagery and the delight of being female to seduce God-as-lover:

Why should you go wandering into the garden, my love,
    For let me show you a garden right here.
My heels have the lustre of little pomegranates
    My arms sway towards you like boughs of the champa.
On my chest you'll find two lemons full of juice,
    I'll lift my veil to have you taste my lips like grapes.
Between my legs is a chalice of joy
    And I'll let you loot my flower of love.

Another poet, the eighteenth-century Urdu Sufi writer known as Jur'at, translated by Saleem Kidwai and versified by Ruth Vanita, enjoins her

---

[3]G. Bose, quoted in S. Kakar (1989). *The Maternal-Feminine in Indian Psychoanalysis.* Int. R. Psycho-Anal., 16:355-362.

lover to forget men for 'those wretched husbands have made our lives a misery' and give in to the joys of two pairs of lips rubbing together:

> Let us play at doubled clinging, why sit around, better
> labour free.
> To the enjoyment of this clinging what other pleasures can compare?
> This rubbing above below, is intercourse wondrous rare
> Making love with one's own likeness is a strange, delightful thing

ON THE EROTIC ROAD: SUSPICIOUS HUSBANDS, BORED WIVES, VIRGINS, LOVERS' QUARRELS AND CONFUSION

Much of the anthology has been arranged around the theme of erotic states of mind that explore questions and experiences relevant to each state. Taken together, they represent a range of emotions that form the erotic experience—from the trepidation of the first time to the delirium and delicious rapture of the subsequent ones; from the anguish of being abandoned to the ennui of steadfast fidelity. Above all, I believe the tremendous value yet extraordinary vulnerability of living an erotic life prevails.

In the section on suspicion—too often a rapid successor to the gloss of the erotic life, consider the helpless agony—translated from its original Maharastrian Prakrit—of the second-century poet, writing in the *Gāthā Saptaśatī*, of her relentlessly suspicious husband:

> What can I do?
> we make love in the common position
> he calls it sedate
> but invent something new
> he asks where I
> learnt it

While that poet manages to coax a wry amusement from her feeling of being trapped by her suspicious husband, there is nowhere amusement, and everywhere horror in the damage wrought by infidelity in the excerpt from Perumal Murugran's *One Part Woman*, translated from the Tamil by Aniruddhan Vasudevan (2015). In the novel, a childless couple is encouraged to participate in a temple ritual that allows free sexual wandering and, therefore, a chance for a woman without children to become impregnated by a man other than her husband. Despite her misgivings, Ponna joins the ritual; in the first part of the excerpt we see how confusing it actually is for her to shake off her habitual lover Kali and take on another; the unknown lover shape-shifts in her imagination;

she seems to pretend at times that the unknown lover is actually a known one in order to get the confidence to proceed into love-making—hers is a dark, uncertain and yet lustful experience of betrayal.

Another experience of suspicion is of wanting to know the truth, but also finding this truth unbearable. The decision to choose a bearable fiction over an unbearable truth is beautifully observed in Kamala Das's (very) short story 'Sanatan Choudhuri's Wife'.

If a faithless lover is an agony so as much can a faithful one be. Ennui, or boredom, particularly in married life, is another agony of the erotic realm. Sita, the object-protagonist of Bhalla's *Ek Pati Ke Notes* (1967), is in abject pain while her husband seems keen on proceeding with the sexual act, despite his own boredom and pain, as if sex has the role of keeping him ignorant of the stiltedness in their marriage (a feint that fails).

While some married people seem keen on avoiding the truth of the inevitable moments or periods of boredom, others are painfully in touch with it: take the deep anguish about the absence of sex in this married woman's poem to her husband, from the eighth-century *Amaruśataka*:

How our bodies were one before!
Then they grew apart: you the lover,
and I, wretched one, the loved.

Now, you are the husband, I the wife.
What else could have made a stone of the heart
but this? A bitter fruit hard to swallow.

Twelve centuries later, have we evolved when it comes to boring marriages? Published in 1992, the 'little wife' in Kamala Das's *A Little Kitten*, finding herself 'without a glow' in the wake of her husband's marital infidelities, quickly finds a restorative revenge. Yet, in another work, her true-life poem about marriage, *The Old Playhouse*, Das's fictional fantasy of revenge rings less true—her tone is very much like the voice of the eighth-century stone-heart wife:

You called me wife. I was taught to break saccharine into your
tea and
To offer at the right moment the vitamins. Cowering
Beneath your monstrous ego I ate the magic loaf and
Became a dwarf. I lost my will and reason,
to all your
Questions. I mumbled incoherent replies.

Forgiveness: how it is wished for and how it is given is another problem whose resolution seems to be an unchanged recipe from the 200 BCE poems of the Tamil Sangam, to the poems of the eighth-century *Amaruśataka*, the nineteenth-century *The Appeasement of Radhika* or the twentieth-century poem by Pritish Nandy, 'At Midnight Resurrect Our Love'. These conditions are: the simultaneous existence of rage and longing; the wish that one—or both—of the lovers has for forgiveness; the wish to be chased, coaxed and desired again 'as it once was'.

Forgiveness in erotic love always includes the body. In this vein, there is the (literally) blow-by-blow account of what we might today call the finest example of make-up sex in history, the Telugu courtesan Muddupalani's *The Appeasement of Radhika*, beautifully translated by Sandhya Mulchandani. The excerpt begins with Radhika describing the blow to her ego and self-esteem from Krishna choosing a younger woman, and devolves to an actual kick when Krishna asks for forgiveness. Krishna responds—as perhaps befits a god—with the wished-for response of lovers across time, not anger but understanding and continued desire. Krishna, after being kicked, is not only unperturbed, he is undiminished in his sexual admiration:

> Dear maiden, (when you kicked me) your thighs thundered
> Your sari slipped, your breasts heaved
> And your anklets trembled,
> As your foot struck my head
> But my body trembled with ecstasy,
> How can I describe this euphoria?

Confusion—as in the scene above—along with its companion, nostalgia, reigns supreme in erotic life; this anthology has entire sections devoted to each. Given that present loves seem to have past loves contained in them, and given that humans are creatures of unconscious fantasy, can we really know who we are having sex with? In response to the question of unconscious fantasy in lovemaking, most readers can relate to remembering or missing one love while in the arms of another. In the section 'Nostalgia' readers will find the short story 'Smell' by Saadat Hasan Manto, in which the protagonist, Ranvir, cannot make love to his wife, craving instead the smell of the prostitute with whom he made love on a rain drenched morning in Calcutta. In 'Kailasam' by Ambai, a woman recollects a would-have-been lover, and 'writes' him her body long after he is dead.

Mridula Garg's *Chittacobra*, originally written in Hindi, is an extraordinary picture of the conflicts of a modern Indian woman, bubbling with both literary brilliance and kitchen smarts, tortured by

The Parrots of Desire

the veneer of her marriage, and her explosive affair with her fellow theatre player. Manu, the central character of *Chittacobra*, uses her brain as easily to dissect Kafka as to figure out the addition and subtraction problems presented by the preparation of koftas (some spicy and some not, to accommodate the taste buds of various in-laws). Housekeeping and intellectualism add to the confusion that mounts when Manu, besotted with her lover, nevertheless has ambivalent sex with her husband during which she comes into contact both with physical pleasure as well emotional deadness.

CODA

One of the most remarkable aspects of the Indian romantic project is that it has flourished amidst great anxiety. While the fear of the destabilizing power of the erotic is common to all cultures[4], it has been imagined as particularly threatening in modern India, where the traditional family structure—rather than the modern structure(s) given to it by the erotic couple—has remained, for the majority, the centre of social life. Perhaps it is the way that traditionalism has, until recently, captured—or held captive—the imagination of the Indian family that accounts for the still skinny ratio of erotica writing to time evident in this anthology.

An excavation of the sort required for an anthology spanning 3,000 years, like the archaeological metaphor the word evokes, is bound to be inexhaustive. The filters for my excavation were for well-written—or orally handed down—pieces, about or upon the subject of the erotic in the Indian literary tradition. By well-written, in this case, I mean writing that is aesthetic and sensual, as well as offering some illuminative truth about erotic life. The collection that you have in your hands covers thousands of years of time, and an array of Indian languages including Sanskrit, Tamil, Malayalam, Urdu, Hindi, Bengali, Gujarati, Maithili (a spoken language in Bihar and parts of Nepal), Brajabuli (a Bengali literary vernacular), Marathi, Maharashtrian Prakrit. Of the notable omissions are the tantric texts which exist largely in the oral form and for which I was not able to find any suitable translations.

Another possibility for the short number of pieces is my own somewhat stringent proclivities of what I consider 'worthwhile' writing. Between the selection criteria, the works that have survived time, and the language limitations, the sample might suggest that truly worthwhile pieces of erotic writing emerge less than once in a hundred years;

---

[4]Ancient Greeks, for example, also grappled with this question, see for example Socrates' idea for the communalization of women and children in Plato's *Republic*.

however, that is more likely due to the above limitations than to some external truth. Even if the harvest is incomplete, it is still rich. I imagine that there is something for everyone, and I invite you to read as ruthlessly, asking, as does the protagonist of Kala Krishnan Ramesh's poem:

What's in your wares-basket today?
(Is there anything at all?)

If
it doesn't grab my attention,

I swear I'm going to
to that other trader across the
rivers, on
that other hill—the libertine,
in whose stock are jars
full of intoxicants.

If you do find something in this wares-basket, if you even find yourself looking, then you have already gravitated to one side of the ancient argument, identifying in some way as a romantic, someone who lives as if a sensual body is a wonderful thing to have or share. As such a reader you further contribute to the the argument of traditional versus romantic through the very pleasure you take in reading; you relive the wisdom of sage Vasistha in the Rig Veda excerpt by Calasso: 'every time you cede to pleasure you contribute to the world's erotic gloss'. For the notion that what we read might enhance our understanding of the erotic experience is as old as our history. And, amongst the *Kama Sutra*'s list of the sixty-four kalas (arts), that enhance an erotic lifestyle is one to which I hope you succumb while immersed in this anthology: *read out aloud*.

—Amrita Narayanan
Goa
July 2017

The Parrots of Desire

Why Bother With Sex?

.... ~ ....

YOU ARE YOUR DESIRE

Brihadaranyaka Upanishad

You are what your deep, driving desire is.
As your desire is, so is your will
As your will is, so is your deed.
As your deed is, so is your destiny.

—Translated from the Sanskrit by Eknath Easwaran

WHY DOES SEX EXIST?

Ka: Stories of the Mind and Gods of India by Roberto Calasso

Thus recounted Atri: 'Why does sex exist? In the beginning we didn't even know what it was. Born-of-the-mind of Brahmā, accustomed to the multiplication of fleeting images, we were bewildered when Brahmā announced that it would be our task to initiate a new mode of creation. And he said something about the female body. The wedding feast was drawing to a close, and we still hadn't touched Dakṣa's daughters. Soon we found ourselves lying in our beds, and for the first time we were not alone. With great naturalness and gravity, we discovered—and they too discovered—what it was we must do. Brahmā hadn't even mentioned the pleasure. It took us by surprise.

'A few thousand years went by. We had become masters of pleasure. One day when he had called us all together, we asked Brahmā: "What's this pleasure for?" Brahmā smiled a somewhat embarrassed smile, as when he had called us to Dakṣa's house. He answered: "To preserve the world's gloss." We asked no more, because the gods love whatever is secret. But we began to go around and around those words in our minds. "Pleasure is *tapas* of the without," said Vasiṣṭha, the most authoritative among us. "The world is like a cloak we must put on, otherwise it would grow dusty. If *tapas* always drew us back, to the formless place from whence we came, the world would wither too soon. It is well that our wives trouble us, it is well that kings put their daughters in our beds, it is well that the Apsaras come and make fools of us, play those tricks of theirs, at once so infantile and so effective... Every time we give in to them, we help the world to refresh its gloss".'

—Translated from the Italian by Tim Parks

The Parrots of Desire

The Garden of Kama: And Other Love Lyrics from India
by Laurence Hope

The daylight is dying
The flying fox flying,
Amber and amethyst burn in the sky.
See, the sun throws a late,
Lingering, roseate.
Kiss to the landscape to bid it good-bye.

The time of our Trysting!
Oh, come, unresisting,
Lovely, expectant, on tentative feet.
Shadow shall cover us,
Roses bend over us,
Making a bride chamber sacred and sweet.

We know not Life's reason,
The length of its season,
Know not if they know, the great Ones above.
We none of us sought it,
And few could support it,
Were it not gilt with the glamour of love.

But much is forgiven,
To Gods who have given,
If but for an hour the Rapture of Youth.
You do not yet know it,
But Kama shall show it,
Changing your dreams to his Exquisite Truth.

The Fireflies shall light you,
And naught shall affright you,
Nothing shall trouble the Flight of the Hours.
Come, for I wait for you,
Night is too late for you,
Come, when the twilight is closing the flowers.

Every breeze still is,
And, scented with lilies,
Cooled by the twilight, refreshed by the dew,
The garden lies breathless,
Where Kama, the Deathless,
In the hushed starlight, is waiting for you.

THE GIRL AND THE WOMAN

Vidyapati

The girl and the woman
bound in one being:
the girl puts up her hair,
the woman lets it
fall to cover her breasts;
the girl reveals her arms,
her long legs, innocently bold;
the woman wraps her shawl modestly about her,
her open glance a little veiled,
restless feet, a blush on the young breasts,
hints at her heart's disquiet:
behind her closed eyes
Kama awakes, born in imagination, the god.

—*Translated from the Sanskrit by Edward C. Dimock Jr.*

GIRL WITH BRIGHT THIGHS

Amaruśataka

Where to
girl with bright thighs?
There's no moon tonight.

Out to my lover.

Not afraid, young in the darkness
to travel alone?

Can't you see—at my side
with lethal arrows the
love god?

—*Translated from the Sanskrit by Andrew Schelling*

THE FIRESTICKS OF LOVE

Shvetashvara Upanishad

Meditate and realize that this world
Is filled with the presence of God.

Fire is not seen until one firestick rubs
Against another, though the fire remains
Hidden in the firestick. So does the Lord...
Remain hidden in the body until
He is revealed through the mystic mantram.

Let your body be the lower firestick;
Let the mantram be the upper. Rub them.
Against each other in meditation.
And realize the Lord.

Like oil in sesame seeds, like butter
In cream, like water in springs, like fire
In firesticks, so dwells the Lord of Love,
The Self, in the very depths of consciousness.
Realize him through truth and meditation.

The Self is hidden in the hearts of all,
As butter lies hidden in cream. Realize
The Self in the depths of meditation,
The Lord of Love, supreme reality,
Who is the goal of all knowledge.

This is the highest mystical teaching;
This is the highest mystical teaching.

—*Translated from the Sanskrit by Eknath Easwaran*

DELIGHTFUL

Bhartrihari

Delighted are the rays of the moon
as are grassy forest tracts;
the pleasure of meeting noblemen is
delightful and so too are stories told in verse.
Delightful also is the face of the beloved
glittering with tears of anger.

Everything is delightful if you agree not to
think even a little of how transient it all is.

Should I settle on some sacred river's bank
to practice austerities?

Or should I be the gentleman and wait
upon women of high qualities?

Or I should perhaps drink from scriptures'
streams or maybe taste the nectar of vibrant
poetry?

How do I decide which to do when life
is here only for the twinkling of an eye?

—*Translated from the Sanskrit by Kala Krishnan Ramesh*

The Parrots of Desire

The Art of
Seduction

THE LIFESTYLE OF THE MAN-ABOUT-TOWN*

Kama Sutra

When a man has acquired learning, he enters the householder stage and begins the life of a man-about-town with the wealth that he may have inherited from his ancestors, or received as a gift, through conquest, trade or wages[1]. He should take a house in a city, or large village, or in the vicinity of good men, or in a place which is the resort of many persons. This abode should be situated near some water, surrounded by a garden, and also contain two rooms, an outer and an inner one. The inner room should be occupied by the females, while the outer room, balmy with rich perfumes, should contain a bed, soft, agreeable to the sight, covered with a clean white cloth, low in the middle part, having garlands and bunches of (natural, garden) flowers upon it, and a canopy above it, and two pillows, one at the top, another at the bottom. There should also be a couch, and at the head of this a sort of stool, on which should be placed the fragrant ointments for the night, as well as flowers, pots containing collyrium and other fragrant substances, things used for perfuming the mouth, and some bark of the lemon tree. Near the couch, on the ground, there should be a pot for spitting, a box containing ornaments, and also a lute hanging from a peg made of the tooth of an elephant, a board for drawing, a pot containing perfume, some books, and some garlands of the yellow amaranth flowers. Not far from the couch, and on the ground, there should be a round seat, a toy cart, and a board for playing with dice; outside the outer room there should be cages of birds,[2] and a separate place for spinning, carving and such like diversions. In the garden there should be a whirling swing and a common swing, as also a bower of creepers covered with flowers, in which a raised parterre should be made for sitting.

Now the householder, having got up in the morning and performed his necessary duties, should wash his teeth, apply a limited quantity

---

*This term would appear to apply generally to an inhabitant of Hindoostan. It is not meant only for a dweller in a city, like the Latin *Urbanus* as opposed to *Rusticus*.
[1]See Wendy Doniger and Sudhir Kakar, *Kama Sutra* (New York: Oxford University Press), 2009, fn 2, p. 17: 'If he is a Brahmin, he gets his money from gifts; a king or warrior, from conquest; a commoner, from trade; and a servant, from wages earned by working as an artisan, a travelling bard, or something of that sort.'
[2]Such as quails, partridges, parrots, starlings, etc.

of ointments and perfumes to his body[3], put some ornaments on his person and collyrium on his eyelids and below his eyes, colour his lips with red lac, and look at himself in the mirror. Having then eaten betel leaves, with other things that give fragrance to the mouth, he should perform his usual business. He should bathe daily, anoint his body with oil every other day, apply a lathering substance[4] to his body every three days, get his head (including face) shaved every four days and the other parts of his body every five or ten days. All these things should be done without fail, and the sweat of the armpits should also be removed.[5] Meals should be taken in the forenoon, in the afternoon, and again at night, according to Charayana. After breakfast, he teaches his parrots and other birds to speak, passes his time by going to cock-fights, quail-fights and ramfights. A limited time should be devoted to diversions with libertine, pander, and clown, and then he should take a midday nap.[6] After this the householder, having put on his clothes and ornaments, should, during the afternoon, converse with his friends. In the evening there should be singing, and after that the householder, along with his friend, should await in his room, previously decorated and perfumed, the arrival of the woman that may be attached to him, or he may send a female messenger for her, or go for her himself. After her arrival at his house, he and his friend should welcome her, and entertain her with a loving and agreeable conversation. Thus end the duties of the day.

---

[3]Doniger, Kakar, *Kama Sutra*, fn. 5, p. 18: 'He uses oil in small quantities, because he is no man-about-town if he uses large amounts. He colours his lips with a ball of moist red lac and fixes it with a small ball of beeswax. He puts a ball of sweet smelling mouth-wash in his cheeks and takes some betel in his hand to use later. He does what needs to be done to accomplish the three goals of human life.'

[4]This would act instead of soap, which was not introduced until the rule of the Mahomedans.

[5]Doniger, Kakar, *Kama Sutra*, fn. 6, p. 18: 'He has hair shaved from his hidden place with a razor every fifth day, and then every tenth day, has his body hair pulled out by the roots, because it grows so fast. The sweat that breaks out after any activity must be constantly removed with a rag, to prevent a bad smell and a consequent lack of sophistication.'

[6]Noonday sleep is only allowed in summer, when the nights are short.

SIXTEEN DAILY STATIONS IN THE BODY OF YOUR GAZELLE-EYED LADY

Koka Shastra

On the first day, the lover brings his girl to orgasm by embracing her neck, pressing kisses on her head, pressing both her lips with his tooth-tips, kissing her cheeks, ruffling up her hair, making gentle nailmarks on her back and sides, plucking softly at her buttocks with his nailtips, and softly making the sound 'sit'.

On the second day, she comes to orgasm if, lovesick from handling her breasts, you kiss the edges of her cheeks and her eyes, pull on her two breasts with your nailtips, suck her lips, tickle her armpits with your nails, and embrace her closely.

On the third, you will have her in season by holding her fast, ruffling the hair in her armpits, lightly nailprinting her sides, putting your arms around her neck and savoring her mouth and teeth, and giving the 'click' nailmarks in the region of the breasts.

On the fourth day, lovers reckon to hold a woman tighter still, pull the two breasts hard together, bite the lower lip, mark the left thigh with the nails, make the 'click' several times in the armpits, and polish the body of Lady Lotus-Eyes with the water that comes from the spring of her own love-juice.

On the fifth day, hold her by the hair with the left hand, bite her two lips, and set her hairs on end with a sinuous nail stroke starting at the nipple—then passionately kiss both breasts.

On the sixth day, bite her lips—when she will begin to tremble all over, start with the 'click'* at the navel; then as if drunk with love, mark the rounds of both thighs with your nails.

On the seventh day, bring her gently into condition by rubbing the house of the Love-God with the hand, kissing inside her mouth, running the nails around neck, breasts and cheeks, and so preparing the theatre of the Deity for the performance.

On the eighth day, embrace her with an arm around the neck, nailmark her navel, bite her lips, make gooseflesh on the rounds of her breasts and kiss them; press her hard in so doing.

On the ninth day, let your hand play with the cup of her navel, bite her lips, pull on her breasts, set a finger in the Love-God's house, and mark her sides with your fingernails.

---

*Acchurita, a light touch given with all five nails.

On the tenth day, you can make love by kissing her brow, nailprinting her neck, and running your left hand around her buttocks, breasts, thighs, ears and back.

On the eleventh day, she will come for nailmarks about the neck, tight holding kisses within her mouth, a sucking kiss on the brow, a few blows over the heart given in jest, and a hand that plays with the lock of the Love-God's prison.

On the twelfth day, with an arm around her neck, kiss both cheeks and open her eyes with your fingers, give the sound 'sit', and bite her within the mouth.

On the day of the Love-God (the thirteenth), she will come quickly to orgasm by kissing her cheeks, pulling upon her left breast, and slowly scratching her neck with the fingernails.

On the day of the Love-God's Enemy (Siva), kiss her eyes, play with your nails in her armpits, thrust your hand elephant-trunk-wise into the strongroom of the Love-God, and over her whole body.

At the New Moon and at the Full Moon, a woman becomes passionate if you run your nails over the flat of her shoulders and handle her yoni and her nipples.

—Translated from the Sanskrit by Alex Comfort

WHO ARE YOU HAVING SEX WITH?:
THE PHYSICAL TYPES AND THEIR SEASONS

Koka Shastra

THE PHYSICAL TYPES OF WOMAN

The gazelle (mrgi) has a shapely head, thick curling hair, a slender body with plump buttocks, little nostrils, flashing teeth, beautiful lashes, red lips, rosy hands and feet, delicate well-proportioned arms, oval ears, cheeks, and throat, hips and thighs not overgrown, neat ankles, the swaying gait of a mighty elephant. She is full of desire: her breasts are high. She is tender and easily moved as a stalk of bamboo; of moderately hot temper, greedy for lovemaking, eats little, has a love-juice that smells of flowers; her fingers are even, her speech slow and tender, her yoni is deep-set and six fingers in breadth and in depth. She is straight-grown and amorous.

The mare (vadava) holds her head half-bent. She has strong, smooth, supple hair, mobile as a lotus leaf; oval ears, neck, and face; prominent teeth; long lips, tight well-filled breasts, very charming plump arms, a slender body, and hands soft as lotuses. Her breastbone is broad; she has an attractive staccato speech; is restless with desire. Her navel is deep and quite round; she has fine hips, even, smooth thighs, powerful buttocks, a deep-waisted figure, a lazy, rocking gait, pink, well-proportioned feet, and a fickle heart. She loves sleep and eating; she is affectionate. Her love-juice, which flows readily in intercourse from start to finish, has a pleasant odor like sesame meal and is yellow. She is fit at any moment for the love-struggle, and has a nine-finger yoni.

The elephant (hastini) has a broad brow, broad cheeks, ears, and nostrils, short plump fingers, feet, arms, and thighs, a short, strong, and slightly bent neck, teeth which show, and strong black hair. She is perpetually sick for lovemaking; her voice is in her throat and deep as an elephant's; her body is strong; she has a broad pendant belly and lips. Her love-juice is abundant; she is red-eyed, quarrelsome, with a genital odour like the 'tears' of a rutting elephant. She commonly has many secret vices, is unusually full of faults, can be won by brute force, and has a twelve-finger yoni, which is the number ascribed to the Sun.

THE PHYSICAL TYPES OF MAN

The hare (sasa) has big red eyes, small even teeth, a round face; he dresses well, has well-shaped, soft, pink hands with narrow fingers; is well-spoken, volatile in mood; soft-haired. His neck is not too long; he is lean about the knees, thighs, hands, genitals and feet. His appetite is small, his manner unassuming, and he is not much given to copulation. He shines with cleanliness; he makes money easily, success inflates him; his seminal fluid has a pleasant odour—he is attractive to women and affectionate.

The bullock (vrsa) has a strong, erect head, a very broad face and brow, a stout neck, fleshy ears, a rounded tortoise-shaped body; he is stout, with deep armpits, long dangling arms, red hands and lips. His eyes are like a lotus-leaf, red in the corners, which have fine long lashes and stare straight at you. He is spirited, with a swinging free gait, soft-spoken, tough, generous, inclined to sleep long, broadminded, tall but gangling, passionate in coition, capable of repeated orgasm, phlegmatic, well-preserved in middle age, inclined to be over-corpulent, happy with any woman, and having a penis nine fingers long or less.

Stallion (asva) is the name given to him who has a very long, but not lean, face, ears, neck, lips and feet, fatty armpits, fleshy arms and strong, soft, thick hair. He is violently jealous; he has arched feet, bowed knees, good fingernails, long fingers, large mobile eyes; he is powerfully built but lazy. His voice is deep and pleasant; he walks fast; his thighs are plump. He is fond of women, talks loudly, is overendowed with both bony and seminal matter, and tormented by lust. His semen is salt[y], yellow like fresh butter, and very abundant. He has a twelve-finger penis and a bulging breast-bone of the same length.

We may also encounter individuals where the size of the sexual organs diverges from these standards. These represent very extreme or very poor examples of their type. Mixed types are also encountered, with intermediate attributes. In dealing with these, the expert will go by the sum total of characters present.

—Translated from the Sanskrit by Alex Comfort

WAYS OF EXCITING DESIRE

Kama Sutra

If a man is unable to satisfy a Hastini[1], or woman with a great sexual appetite and fierce sexual energy, he should have recourse to various means to excite her passion. When he begins to make love, he should rub her between her legs with his hand or fingers, and not enter her until she is wet. This is one way of exciting a woman. Oral sex kindles the passion of a man who is of dull sexual energy, past his prime, too fat, or exhausted from love-making.[2] Or use sex tools, made of gold, silver, copper, iron, ivory, or buffalo horn, or ones made of tin or lead, which are soft, cool the semen, and produce a violent effect during the sexual act.

Or, he may make use of certain Apadravyas [sex tools], or things which are put on or around the penis to supplement its length or its thickness. In the opinion of Babhravya, these sex tools should be made of gold, silver, copper, iron, ivory, buffalo horn, various kinds of wood, tin or lead, and should be soft, cool, provocative of sexual vigour, and well fitted to serve the intended purpose. Vatsyayana, however, says that they may be made according to the natural liking of each individual.[3]

The following are the different kinds of sex tools: 'The armlet' (Valaya) should be of the same size as the penis from the inside, and should have its outer surface made rough with globules.[4] Two of such armlets form 'The couple' (Sanghati). Three or more, up to the full length of the penis, form 'The bracelet' (Chudaka). 'The single bracelet' is formed by wrapping a single string of beads around the lingam, according to its dimensions.[5]

The Kantuka or Jalaka is a tube open at both ends, with a hole through it, outwardly rough and studded with soft globules, and made to fit the size of the yoni, and tied to the waist. When such a thing

---

[1]See p. 15, 'The Physical Types and Their Seasons' from the Koka Shastra.
[2]See Wendy Doniger and Sudhir Kakar, Kama Sutra, fn. 3, p. 166: 'A man whose passion has arisen but who does not start to make love because his penis is not hard, may kindle his passion with oral sex, which gives rise to the delight of ejaculation. For the penis of an old man or a fat man stands up only with difficulty.'
[3]Ibid. p. 167: '[The] ones made of wood more closely resemble the original.'
[4]Ibid. fn. 8, p. 167: 'It should be as wide as the erect penis, hollowed out inside, and fastened securely on the erect penis, like a second surface.'
[5]Ibid. fn. 11, p. 167: 'Wrap around a string of beads made of something such as lead, as much as the circumference of the penis will allow.'

cannot be obtained, then a tube made of the wood apple, or tubular stalk of the bottle gourd, or a reed made soft with oil and extracts of plants, and tied to the waist with strings, may be made use of, as also a row of soft pieces of wood tied together.

The above are the things that can be used in connection with or in the place of the penis.

The people of the South think that true sexual pleasure cannot be obtained without perforating the lingam, and they pierce a boy's penis just like his ears.[6]

Now, when a young man pierces his penis, it should be done with a sharp instrument, and then he should stand in water so long as the blood continues to flow. That very night, he should engage in sexual intercourse, even with vigour, so as to keep the hole clean.

After this he should continue to wash the hole with astringent decoctions, and increase the size by putting into it small pieces of cane, and the Wrightia antidysenterica (tellicherry bark), and thus gradually enlarging the orifice. It may also be washed with liquorice mixed with honey. After that, he enlarges it by inserting a lead tube with a protruding knot at its the end, and lubricates it with the oil of Semecarpus anacardium (marking nut).[7]

In the hole made in the penis a man may put sex tools of various shapes, such as the 'round', the 'round on one side', the 'wooden mortar', the 'flower blossom', the 'armlet', the 'bone of the heron', the 'elephant's tusk', the 'collection of eight circles', the 'lock of hair', the 'place where four roads meet', and other things named according to their forms and means of using them.[8]

---

[6]Ibid. fn. 16, p. 168: 'Someone skilled pulls back the foreskin to expose the glans, holds it back, and then cuts through the glans sideways so that there is an opening on both sides. Standing in the water stops the bleeding.'

[7]Ibid. fn. 21, p. 168: 'He uses lead because it expands; and the lead knot, wrapped as if by a palm leaf, soon enlarges the opening.'

[8]Ibid. fn. 24, p. 168: The 'round' one has a little trough in the middle, in which a leather thong is attached; the 'round on one side' has, on the other side, a trough like an elongated eight-day old sliver of moon, in which a leather thong is attached; the 'little mortar' is narrow in the middle, where a leather thong is attached. Both the 'little blossom' and the 'thorny' should be inserted lengthwise; the 'eight circles' and the 'spinning top' should be inserted on an angle. Other objects may be used, too, and any means that give sexual pleasure. Attaching a leather thong to some of them prevents any harm from resulting from the act. As for individual preferences, one must determine the roughness of the vagina, according to its smooth, medium, or extremely rough quality, and choose a device of appropriate roughness; and, similarly, one must determine the softness of the vagina, and find devices appropriate to that softness.

THE ASCETIC OF DESIRE

Sudhir Kakar

It can happen that in pursuing profit, one ends with loss. A sexual relationship must be approached with prudence.

Kamasutra 6.6.1

It was almost the beginning of summer when I finally ventured into the forest next to the hermitage. In the countryside, the earth was heating up as if in a low fever. Bled dry by the rays of the sun, the cracks in the earth's baked surface had begun to widen ominously. The trees, robbed of their discoloured leaves, had begun to look as if struck by a wasting sickness, casting doubt on their capacity to survive the arid winds of high summer which would soon seek to grind them down with fiery sand.

That particular morning Vatsyayana had appeared listless. Dark smudges under his eyes accentuated the fine lines at their sides. As we sat in our accustomed places in front of the hut, he was unusually quiet. His eyes often glazed over and at times he seemed to be looking through me into the depths of the forest behind my back. Images of Malavika alone in the forest flashed through my head. I forced my mind back to the hut and the calmer vision of a guru instructing a reverent student. It was a struggle, though, and noticing my growing discomfort, he made an effort to pull himself together.

'I slept badly last night,' he said. 'After many years I again had a nightmare I used to have as a child.'

He lapsed into silence. After a few minutes, without my prompting, he began to narrate the dream, more to himself than to me.

'I am climbing up the gentle slope of a hill. It is just before sunset. The hilltop is bathed in a rosy light which drifts toward me in swirls. The lake at the bottom of the hill is a motionless sheet of water glinting with the colours of the setting sun. Suddenly it becomes dark. The hillside becomes pulsatingly alive. Tree branches extend toward me like twisted arms. The ground below me starts to heave like ocean waves. I cannot keep my footing. I am falling. I am falling into a lake of water blacker than any seen by a human eye, blacker than an ink spot in a pile of black beans.

'In childhood I used to wake up screaming from this nightmare. Whichever bed I was in—my mother's or Chandrika's—became a place of agony. The woman would try to comfort me but I shrank from her touch. The only person who could soothe me was our cook, Ganadasa. He had to be woken up, and would bring me a glass of hot milk with sugar, almond slivers and saffron. He would sit next to me while I drank the milk, quietly feeling his solid presence.

'And then?' I asked.

'Oh, nothing much happened after that,' he said. 'I would go back to sleep. On waking up in the morning I had to carefully wash my face to ward off the dream's baleful influence. I still do.'

Sensing his reluctance to go on, I put off asking questions about the text with which I had come prepared. I was content to wait. When he suggested that we talk later in the afternoon and that I spend the morning in the forest, I readily agreed.

Today I wonder whether it was his intention that I meet his wife alone since Malavika spent much of her day there. In any case, it was at his encouragement that I walked into the forest. Perhaps it is more exact to say that as I walked away from the hermitage I gradually found myself in the forest. Hermitages straddle the space between cultivation and wilderness and it is not easy to say where one ends and the other begins. There were a few markers, though. The initially wide and almost straight path narrowed and broke up into small crooked trails which meandered away from each other even as each in its own way followed the lay of the land, skirting thick scrub, a thicket of tall grass or a dense grove of trees. Except for the closely clustered bamboo trees with their slim spear-shaped leaves, indifferent to summer as they are to other seasons, the forest showed distinct signs of fading. Most sal trees had already lost the fresh green leaves of spring to a darker foliage. Grass was turning into clumps of dried stalks. At randomly chosen spots, however, the forest, as if bored with its different shades of bilious green and brown, had impulsively decided to break into flames through trees covered all over with orange and red flowers.

As I walked further into the forest, it became more dense. The foliage overhead straining toward the sun and perpetually hungry for light, allowed less and less of it through. The dun-coloured anthills, imitating sheer cliffs and needle-thin mountain peaks seen only in dreams, became rarer. Spotted and swamp deer gave way to antelope that bounded away at any close approach. Then, suddenly, I found myself in a clearing, exactly where Vatsyayana had said his wife would be.

Malavika was sitting on a grassy knoll that sloped down gently into a large pond. Half a dozen ospreys were lined up below her at the pond's edge, staring fixedly at the dragonflies skimming close to the surface of the water. Malavika took my intrusion more calmly than did the birds. As I sat down next to her, the indignant cries of the ospreys fading into the distance, she was at first very much the guru's wife, kind but reserved. I will not pretend that I was unaware of her physical presence. Much of the time I looked at her feet while we exchanged polite pleasantries. For more than a decade of their exile together, Lakshmana never once raised his eyes above Sita's ankles and hence could not recognize her necklace and earrings which had fallen off when Ravana carried her away. My own difficulty was that feet, especially those as shapely as Malavika's, can become the repository of all of a woman's beauty, a distillate of all her charms. The problem lies with the gaze, not its object. Given my strong attraction to her, conflicted and suppressed as it may have been, I would have even found Malavika's toenail irresistible. Only a few years older than me, yet she was absolutely unapproachable. As described by Manu, the punishment for intercourse with the wife of the guru, even if Vatsyayana, strictly speaking, was not my guru, is unambiguous...and chilling:

> The mark of the vulva will be branded into his forehead; he will be forced to embrace the red-hot iron image of a woman till he becomes pure by dying; or he may cut off his penis and testicles and taking them in his joined hands go on walking in the south-west direction till he falls down dead.

I discovered at our very first meeting that I could comfortably assimilate my different feelings for her. To my surprise, neither desire nor fear came in the way of my being at ease as we began to talk, impersonally at first and then with a mounting intensity and lack of reserve which is the singular blessing of youth. In the beginning, our conversation was mostly about trees. Malavika loved trees and flowers. She was never as animated as when she could tell me things about them which I did not know before. I knew that a sal forest of the kind we were in was sacred because the sal tree is associated with Vishnu in his incarnation as Rama. To convince a hesitant Sugriva to ally with him, Rama had demonstrated his strength by shooting an arrow which pierced seven sal trees standing in a row before it returned to his quiver. I did not know, till Malavika told me, that Lord Buddha was born under a sal tree. On her way to her paternal home for childbirth, Mayadevi, the Enlightened One's mother, rested in a grove of sal trees. As she stretched her hand upward to pluck flowers from a branch, the baby was born and the tree shed flowers on the newborn child.

Malavika described the erotic significance of the red dye made from the flowers of the flame-of-the-forest, and how at one place in the Kamasutra her husband compares the spring buds of the tree to nail marks made by a passionate woman on the body of her lover. There were yet other trees and flowers on whose significance we differed amicably. The five arrows of Lord Kama through which he excites the five senses and inspires passion, Malavika held, are made of flowers of the ashoka tree. I agreed that ashoka is indeed dedicated to the love god and is closely associated with women, especially forest nymphs. But I knew that the arrows of the love god are made of five completely different and much more fragrant flowers: blue lotus, jasmine, mango flowers, champaka and sirisa.

In all this talk of trees, flowers, gods and nymphs, time flew with the speed of Krishna's discus and it was well past noon by the time I returned to the hermitage, lightheaded with the fresh air of the forest. Observing my somewhat exhilarated mood, Vatsyayana gave me a quizzical look and only nodded when I told him about meeting his wife by the pond. I was happy to see that he had recovered a measure of his usual equanimity, although when he began to talk it became apparent that he was still engrossed in remembering his early life.

'I have often wondered whether my mother disliked me, not for what I was—for they tell me I was a sweet-tempered, plump and cuddly baby—but for what I did to her beautiful body. Barely thirty, in her youth she was renowned in lands far from our kingdom as the jewel of Kausambi, the incomparable Avantika.

'Your mother had no rival in all the kingdoms,' Ganadasa used to tell me. 'She knows by heart all the poems sung during a dance and has mastered the language of gesture by which the various moods of love are expressed. She knows how to play the drum and how to adjust the tightness of its skin to regulate the sound. She knows the flute, as also the art of playing ball. She can prepare dishes almost as well as I can, according to the recipes of the best cuisine. She is skilled in the manner of bathing, in the body's sixty-four positions of making love, in seeming reluctant and in anticipating men's desires. She knows how to write elegantly with a cut reed, to draw and paint. She knows the language of flowers and how to arrange magnificent bouquets chosen for their form and colour. She has studied astrology, mathematics and poetics. Very few people are aware that it was your mother who invented the well-trick which is now taught in the best brothels of the central countries.'

'The well-trick, Ganadasa?' I asked.

'Like any great innovator who gets a reputation by solving a longstanding problem in his field, what your mother did was to find a solution to the courtesan's dilemma.'

'Now, listen carefully. A good courtesan must make her lover believe that she is truly and passionately in love with him. Yet however much the man wants to go along with her pretence, he cannot quite forget it is a measure of the courtesan's skill to make him believe precisely that. Her loving glances, passionate cries and poetic declarations of love will never quite succeed in removing the last residue of doubt in his mind. That is, if the man is sensible, and generally men who amass riches are sensible.

'Many years ago, a wealthy merchant became your mother's lover. He liked her well enough, even after the initial infatuation had worn off, but looked sceptical whenever she professed her great love for him. "I would die if you ever left me, even for a month," she would say, but the merchant would only touch her arm and smile, as if humouring a child.

'One day, the merchant announced that he was going away on a business trip and would return to Kausambi after six months. Your mother wept, imploring him not to leave her. She tore at her hair and clothes, crying all the while that she could not bear the separation, but the man took it as a game and smiled his disbelieving smile.

'She clung to him as he was leaving, weeping piteously, and when he reached the gate she ran into the garden, crying, "I cannot bear it anymore! I want to die!" Suddenly, we heard a shout, "The mistress has jumped into the well!" All of us rushed toward the well. There was much confusion, with people milling round, women crying—Kanchanmata's wails were the loudest. A servant was lowered into the well by a rope tied around his waist.

After a few anxious minutes, we heard him call out, "It is a miracle! The mistress is alive!"

'Your mother was pulled up, soaking wet and only half-conscious. By this time the merchant was besides himself. He was rolling on the ground in his grief, crying, "Oh, my love Avantika! How could I have ever doubted your love!"

'After that, he was her slave, opening up his heart and his purse without reserve. Your mother left him after a year, much poorer and, I suspect, heartbroken. What your mother had done that day was to have a net secretly tied under the surface of the water to break her fall into the well. Of course, by now the well-trick is so well-known that a courtesan can only use it with a lover who is a stranger to the Middle Kingdoms, and even then she needs to be sure that the man is unaware of your mother's innovation.'

Somehow I did not like the end of the story.

'Why did she leave the merchant if he loved her?' I asked. 'Because he had become poor,' the cook was patient with me. 'A good courtesan would rather touch a corpse than a pauper, and your mother was the best. It is a very rare courtesan who is honoured by the king, as she was with the title "Lady of the Court". You should be proud of her.'

Well past the first flush of youth when he was born, Vatsyayana's mother had not taken well to motherhood. For all her accomplishments, she found it hard to reconcile herself to the loss of freshness in the beauty of her face and to the gradual blurring of lines in her sculpted form. What Vatsyayana remembered most clearly about his mother while he was growing up was her preoccupation with the rejuvenation of her fading looks. Two classes of objects increasingly claimed her full attention: those which held out the promise of enhancing her beauty— lotions, salves, oils, scents, powders—and those which reflected the results of these efforts, primarily mirrors, not only of the highly polished copper kind but also, and especially, the eyes of men.

'I can now imagine the strain the obsession imposed upon her, particularly when she was out among people on the street. Even at home my mother must have been uncomfortable when clients came for the evening entertainment where Chandrika was the star attraction. Letting her sister be at the centre of the stage while she kept herself in the background, my mother's desperate eyes must have scoured—without appearing to—the eyes of the assembled men, for a glimmer of that desire always sent a shiver of well-being coursing through her. Her search became more frantic with each passing year as the number of indifferent eyes, each capable of inducing a succession of small inner collapses, increased.

'Unlike Chandrika, my mother had no use for the eyes of a small boy, my eyes. The only men she granted access to her special world were those who could facilitate her obsession. Essentially, these were only two: the doctor who came in once a week with the herbal medicines of rejuvenation which Ayurveda prescribes for a person entering the thirties and thus the beginning of old age, and Ganadasa, whom my mother consulted for hours on the preparation of potions from fruits, vegetables and meats which served as her daily beauty draughts. The rascally doctor, with his dyed hair and beard, whose infallible science was ever at the service of profit, was well known for ogling his fairer patients, and though old in years and experienced in conspiratorial seduction, often played the young man for them. All my mother needed me for was to pluck out the gray hair that had begun to appear on her head, paying a cowry for every five I could find—a task I hated in spite of the cowries I began to accumulate. I feel sad about it now, but at that time I accepted her indifference to my existence as the natural way of a mother with her son. But my mother's indifference was more than mitigated by Chandrika, who welcomed me into her self-absorption. She was an altogether different goddess—who did not spurn my adoration.

'Just before I fell asleep last night, I remembered something else—the stretch mark on my mother's belly which she often told me was my 'gift' to her. It was the faintest of marks, a short thin line a shade lighter than the golden brown of her skin. Barely noticeable, it nonetheless looms in my memory like welts left by the blows of a cane on a thief's naked back. I remember that when she finished examining herself in the mirror, my mother would lightly rub her right palm against the mark I was responsible for. I imagined I could see the mixture of repulsion and duty as she did that, as if caressing the cratered face of a pock-marked husband one no longer loves, and I cringed along with her—I, the wrecker of her beauty. And then, as she put on her favourite long red skirt and tied the girdle high on her hip to hide the mark, I wished I could give her back the perfection of her beauty, her unalloyed pleasure in her body, give them back to all women.'

'Acharya,' I wanted to protest, 'you have given so much to so many women! You gave them permission to be active in love, encouraged them to be fearless in seeking pleasure. You unshackled their erotic life from prohibitions imposed upon it by generations of sages since the time of the epics. Is freedom any less important than beauty?'

I remained silent, receiving Vatsyayana's pain even as he masked it by carrying on his narration in a neutral, almost bemused voice.

'I know my mother would have preferred a daughter. What could she do with a son who was only a guest in her home for a few years? A son belongs to the father and she knew that when I turned ten he would take me away. She could not afford to love me with all her heart; it would have broken when I went away. With a daughter she need not have fought her feelings, not deliberately forced the fading of the glow in her eyes at the sight of the child. A daughter would have taken her place, inherited her profession. She could have remained a part of a daughter's life. She would have loved teaching the girl all she had learnt, prepare her for life with her own experience. What could she do with me?

'My mother's unhappiness touched with wintry frost what I otherwise remember as a lively house full of music, dance, laughter and the bustling flow of a stream of clients. There were no financial worries even though the expenses were considerable. The monthly wages of the musicians, maids, cooks, the mahout and the keepers of other animals, the gardener and the washerman, must alone have come to fifteen hundred *panas*. If I add to this the cost of animal fodder, food and clothes for the servants and all other household expenses, then the total amount we spent every month must have been over three thousand *panas*. That is sixty gold dinars in your Varanasi money. Yet money was never a concern, although Kanchan-mata constantly grumbled about our expenses and the need for thrift. Chandrika alone paid four hundred panas every month to the king's treasury, the amount which the tax inspector had fixed as being equivalent to two days of her income. For the wealthy and the powerful men of the city she was a prized trophy, universally accepted as the seal of great success. The fact of being her lover could be flaunted to arouse the envy of other men; after all, what good is success if it does not arouse envy?

'At the time of which I speak, between the fourth and sixth years of my life, she was living as wife to the jeweller Madansen, a man whose financial generosity was matched by his possessive jealousy. Not counting tradesmen, servants, musicians and dance teachers, the only male visitors Madansen tolerated were the chief of prisons and my father, who divided his occasional affections between the two sisters. The jeweller did not permit my father's visits out of sentiment but because my father was one of the most respected leaders of trading caravans throughout the central countries. "The great Sarathvaha of Kausambi", as he was often called, carried Madansen's more valuable consignments in his personal care. It also helped that since he was on the road most of the year, my father's visits to Kausambi were infrequent. Since my birth, or rather from the time I can remember and till the age of six my father visited us but four times.

'Why did my mother continue the connection with my father? It had nothing to do with me, their son. My father was wealthy, and brought expensive and exotic gifts for us from foreign lands. The copper mirror from Damascus was one of his presents. My father's continued liaison with us provoked Madansen to keep his own ardour and generosity at a high pitch, and prevented him from forming other liaisons.

'The chief of prisons, a small, plump and fussy man—his name was Nitigupta—came more often, perhaps once a month. I knew of his impending visit by the sight of Madansen's unsmiling face at the evening entertainment a few days before Nitigupta came to spend the night with Chandrika, and the solicitous attention my mother paid Madansen during these evenings. As a tradesman, however wealthy, Madansen was in no position to alienate the chief of prisons. His protest was confined to sulking, from which he had to be coaxed by the two women—both experts at the task of coaxing sullen men. On these evenings Madansen would refuse to stay over for the night, and a contest of wills took place between him and Chandrika to see how near the beginning or after the end of Nitigupta's visit she could seduce the jealous jeweller. Nitigupta too paid well, but of course not on the same scale as Madansen and even less than my father. The liaison with him was useful for reasons other than money: it protected us from unscrupulous tax collectors, avaricious policemen and the other human vultures who hover around the establishments of courtesans.

'Madansen made large presents of money as well as ornaments. The gold pieces came in beautifully embroidered silk bags tied with a red string and the jewellery in carved wooden boxes padded with dark red velvet. But, of course, as a courtesan it was a point of professional pride for Chandrika to see how much she could get out of him through her own artfulness. In my Kamasutra, this is one of the points where I hold a different opinion from previous scholars.

'What I say about money, however,' Vatsyayana continued, 'is for the ordinary prostitute, not for the most accomplished practitioner of the courtesan's calling. In Chandrika's case it was not the money that was important but the exercise of her professional talent. It was a matter of pride to extract as much as was possible from her lover. What she did was to excite Madansen's competitiveness with the most expansive, generous part of himself, not with other possible lovers. I remember overhearing their conversation one summer afternoon when they were in her bedroom. They were lying in bed and Chandrika had opened the window towards the veranda where I had been prowling around for a while waiting for her to do so, "Chandrika, what can I give you?" Madansen had asked.

'"Yourself, as you did just now," she replied.

'"But I want to give you something else too," he said.'

'"Whatever it is can never be more than you. I am sure that whatever you give will match my worth in your eyes. The preciousness of the ornament will reflect my value for you but will always be less than yours for me."

'The exchange I overheard through the bedroom window was perhaps not in such a serious tone, as I remember it now with the memory of an older man. The couple was young. They had just made love on a summer afternoon. Perhaps they giggled as they talked. Perhaps she tweaked his penis when she spoke of the "preciousness of the ornament".

I do not know. The next day, just before we were sitting down for our noon meal, Madansen's servant arrived with a silk-covered box. In it was a most exquisite filigree necklace, its gold reflected in the emeralds and green aquamarines like the afternoon sun in small forest pools.'

Ennui in Marriage

HOW OUR BODIES WERE ONE

Bhavakadevi

How our bodies were one before!
Then they grew apart: you the lover,
and I, wretched one, the loved.

Now, you are the husband, I the wife.
What else could have made a stone of the heart
but this? A bitter fruit hard to swallow.

—*Translated from the Sanskrit by R. Parthasarathy*

EK PATI KI NOTES

Mahendra Bhalla

The servant announced dinner and Sita and I went and sat opposite each other. The table was set for three guests too but just the two of us now sat there. One could feel the emptiness on both sides of the table. We ourselves seemed to be guests to each other. At least that was what I felt.

[Sita seemed still flushed from our impromptu dancing while we were waiting for the guests.] We ate as we listened to the wind.

'Listen,' she looked into my eyes and said, 'not tonight.'

'Why not?' I smiled.

'No, just not tonight.'

'So what shall we do then? What else is there to do?'

I gave her a look, a good long look. She wanted to be cajoled. For some reason I was annoyed at this vain trick of hers, this attempt at flirtatiousness. Perhaps because I could see through it.

'Ok, we shall have a good night's sleep then,' I said with some dry bitterness.

She looked at me, and I grew conscious that I was averting her gaze. I was pulling a face with distaste. I also felt a great uneasiness. She finished dinner quickly. I thought she ate less than usual. She got up and washed her hands, soaping them twice as always. She went off to the living room and switched on the radio. After a while she switched it off.

I came out of the house on to the street. I put a paan in my mouth and lit up a cigarette. There were hardly any passers-by. The wind was sharp and chill. A dog ambled slowly along.

I decided with keen bitterness that a man had best live alone.

When I returned Sita was crying. I stood in the doorway and watched her. She had her head between her knees, a shawl was draped round her back, and she was crying away. I felt that she could sense that I had come back. But she didn't raise her head. I sat on the sofa opposite her and carried on smoking and watching her.

When she had cried for the first time I had panicked. That was before we got married. Without paying any attention to the rhyme and reason of her crying, I just kept asking her why she was crying and telling her not to cry any more. And all this in a tone of contrite pleading. That's when we were truly callow, I thought. I also wondered whether it mattered at all.

'What is it, Sita?' I asked. Detecting my less than caring tone, she stepped up her crying. I sat silently and watched. After a while I got up and went to her and tried to sweeten her down. I put my arm around her shoulders.

'Ok dear, just calm down now.' I tried to raise her face, but she clenched it even harder between her knees.

'Sita, Sita, what is this, crying like a baby! What on earth is there to cry about?' As I said it I recalled that ghazal by Ghalib [which I had played earlier in the evening sung by Sehgal: 'My heart is not brick and stone, why should it not fill up with pain/ If someone treats me badly I'll cry and cry again.'] I tried to pull her towards me. But she remained quite stiff. In fact, she shook off my arm from her shoulders and said, 'Just don't come near me, you!'

I put my arm around her again. 'Ok, that's enough, now.' She shook off my arm again, this time in a bit of a temper. She wanted to be pacified and cajoled, I felt, and for quite a long while. The very thought seemed tiresome to me. I sat there as I was. Then I got up and went into the bedroom. As I was changing into night clothes, I said out to her, 'Right, I think I'll go to bed now. Do make sure to lock the front door when you get up.'

I switched off the light and lay down. After a short while I fell asleep.

In the depth of the night I somehow woke up. I reached out to feel for Sita. At once, though she seemed asleep, she grabbed hold of my hand. Tenderly. A warm wave surged through me too. I pulled her to me. Darkness often induces a softness of feeling. The thought had often come to me that had I been blind I would have loved her more. What I couldn't see wouldn't hurt me. But who knows.

Thus lying together at night it seems that we are the only two in the world. The rest of the world does not exist. It's a strange hour.

'What was it in the evening, Sita?' I asked. I shouldn't have asked this. But in the state I was I hardly knew what I should be asking and what I should not. She heard me and immediately stiffened. I tried to kiss her. She fended me off with her hands and arms and kept up the defence, with her body taut. I grabbed hold of her hands. She tried as hard as she could to resist and break free. But I forced her and her hands and arms grew slack. Bit by bit she grew limp. A doubt arose in my mind. Had she stiffened about whatever it was in the evening or to get me to force her? She sometimes liked that. While we now went about making love, that's what I kept thinking about. I woke up in the morning with an arm gone numb and with regret. I shrugged myself awake, as a dog does. I drew the curtains, and opened half the window to look out. The day stood still like an inanimate object. What had taken place seemed unreal and fraudulent. In fact I stood just where I was at the beginning. Virginal. Everything lay before me. No, neither before nor behind. Just where it was.

—Translated from the Hindi by Harish Trivedi

A LITTLE KITTEN

Padmavati the Harlot and Other Stories by Kamala Das

When they had finally settled themselves down after weeks of honeymooning in a small flat at Dadar, she told her husband that she felt miserable and lonely from eight in the morning to six in the evening while he worked in his insurance firm at the heart of the city. If only you could get me a pet, she murmured, nestling closer to his chest, a little kitten, even a kitten would be such a comfort... And, he threw back his head and laughed. What a sweet and innocent creature he had married! He tickled her until she rolled over on their double bed and screamed out for mercy. You are killing me, please stop, PLEASE STOP. Then, he began to lick her toes, mumbling, you see, I am your kitten, I am your little kitten.

After three months of ardour, they began to quarrel. Nothing very serious, of course. Just a few probing queries regarding his relationship with Miss Nadkar, his secretary, and his mysterious silences that would last for hours. Speak to me, I cannot bear these silences. Leave me alone, he would say and disappear into the bathroom.

One day, she climbed upon a stool and peeped into the bathroom through the ventilator. He was seated on the edge of the tub, frowning. What are you doing there, she shouted at him. He got up and pulled the ventilator shut. It nearly snapped off her fingers. No wonder she was angry and frustrated.

When they were on the best of terms she used to take a bath in the evening after tea and buy a jasmine strand from the flowerboy to hang from her long plait. She had naturally pink cheeks but on tiring days when she saw herself pale she cheated a little with a touch of rouge which she kept hidden away. When Miss Nadkar was unwittingly drawn into the orbit of their life together, she stopped taking the evening bath. The flowerboy went away disappointed.

Even the old Maharashtrian woman who used to wash the vessels for her in the morning began to wonder what had gone wrong. She had lost her bridal freshness. There was a new crease on her brow which sliced the red bindi in two halves. Pimples began to form on her cheeks. She found herself worrying about her digestion.

Then, one day he came home dead drunk after attending an office dinner. She tore her wedding saree into shreds. She grew frighteningly hysterical. Would you like to visit your parents for a month, he asked her. You look as if you need a change. She was alarmed. She went to look at her face secretly in the bathroom mirror. He was speaking the truth. She had lost the glow which she had before she settled down at Bombay. They were living close to a mill. She felt that the smoke from its chimney was darkening her skin. Yes, I need a change, she told him. But you will have to come with me...

He gave for the first time a birthday gift to his secretary because he had begun to compare her with his petulant little wife. Miss Nadkar was serene. In fact, he had once heard the clerks teasingly calling her Her Serene Highness. He thought it clever of the clerks. When he gave her an ivory figurine on her birthday, Miss Nadkar blushed very nicely and murmured: You shouldn't have spent so much money on me... He had done it on an impulse. After all, he was not the demonstrative kind. And she was Miss Nadkar to him although once she had asked him to call her by her name, Indira. I heard that you were planning to leave us, soon, Miss Nadkar, he said. The office will miss you. She blushed again. The marriage will take place only in December, she said. My fiancé will come from Canada in October. Still four months to go. And looking up into his eyes, she flashed a smile, a gleaming jet of a smile that made his stomach quiver.

That was their first evening together. They went to dark, smoke-filled restaurants and always took the corner table where they could sit half-concealed behind potted cacti. At home, his wife sulked and lost her looks thinking unkind thoughts incessantly. Once or twice, she put all her silks inside a trunk and decided to go back to Dharwar, but he dissuaded her. What will your parents say, he asked her.

One day, when he came back home, warily crossing the hall to go to their bedroom, he found his little wife seated before her dressing table brushing her wavy hair. She turned her face to smile at him. He was taken aback. She looked so pink and healthy. There was a gleam in her dark eyes, a secret message for the male. He rushed forward to embrace her. You look so pretty, he said. So pretty and happy. Then he saw above her breasts a long red scratch What happened, he asked her. Did you find yourself a kitten? He looked around. Perhaps, it was hiding somewhere in the kitchen. Is it a stray, he asked her. She kept silent. She was looking over his head to a spot in the dusky sky. What are you staring at, he asked her, I don't see anything there but some clouds, some smoke...

TWO ON MARRIAGE

Gāthā Saptaśatī

The bride's mother
Was pleased at the sight
of tooth mark seen
on the thigh revealed
when her daughter's skirts
were lifted by the wind,

as if she'd seen the mouth
of a jar full of treasure.

◆

When her friends asked the young wife
Who was pregnant for the first time
What she craved most
She simply looked at her husband.

—Translated from the Maharashtrian Prakrit by Andrew Schelling

Rapture and Longing

THE SEASONS

Ṛtusaṃāram by Kālidāsā

SUMMER

1.
My Love,
Summer's here burning

Sun a scorching scourge
Moon desirable

Rainwater pools for anytime-dips

Dusk agreeable
  Kāma mellow

18.
A frog jumps tortured by sharp sun-rays
out of a dirty pond

sits under the parasol-
hood

of a thirsty cobra

22.
A keen forest-fire crop-shoots withered

Fast furious winds dry leaves flung up

In the sun's heat all around shrunken waters
Watching at forest-edges
  High Anxiety

23.
Birds pant
on dry-leafed trees

Tired monkeys take
to mountain shrubs

Bulls roam everywhere

Want water

Elephants extend trunks
into water-wells

RAIN

1.

My dear,

Cloud Misty's here
The love of lovers

A rather high and mighty entry
like a King

Thunder drums
Lightning flag

Ruttish elephant

7.

Like immodest women unrestrained
Rivers   speedy agitated currents
        felling trees on banks as they
rush
to the sea

8.

Fresh rainwater
   full of termites dirt grass
   sallow
snakes   downwards

A snake-y crooked gait

Frogs watch
worried

19.

flow	Rivers
rain	Clouds
roar	Ruttish elephants
shine	Forest-edges

remember	Parted lovers
dance	Peacocks
shelter	Monkeys

SULTRY SEASON

2.
Bleached

Earth	by	Kāśa blossoms
Nights		the moon
River		waters swans
Lakes		lilies
Forest-edges		flower-laden Saptacchadā trees
Gardens		Mālatī blossoms

7.
Night matures
  like a wild young girl
day by day

She wears
      choice jewellery star-clusters
      silken moonlight

      Moon-face freed from cloud-veil

22.
Surpassed!

Women's graceful gait
  by swans

Radiant moon-faces
  by full-blown lotuses

Eyes
  by blue lotuses

Eyebrow-coquetry
  by nicely rippling waves

FROST

1.

Here
Grain-sprouts shot up delightful
Full-flowered Lodhrā tree
Paddy ripe n' ready
Dew dropped
Wilted lotuses
The frost-season's arrived

5.

Women prep for sex fests
Smear turmeric on limbs
Etch leaf-designs on lotus-like faces
Perfume hair in black-aloe smoke

14.

Some young woman
prettifies her lotus-like face.
       in the mirror
       in the morning sun

scrutinizes lips her lover sucked
his teeth-tip bites

15.

Another
      body weary from too much sex
      lotus-eyes red from waking all night
      hair awry loose around her shoulders
      tries to sleep
      warmed by a mild sunray

WINTER

1.

Hey choice-thighs,
The earth   covered reverberates
        heaps of paddy   a krauñca-bird warble
        and sugarcane   someplace
Lots of passion
Women love it!

hear,
winter's here

2.
Now's when
People   shut windows
                    stay in
go to
fire sunrays sweaters nubile women

3.
Not   moonlight cool sandalpaste
           terraces cool as autumn-moon
           winds chill with fresh snowflakes
Now
           none of these
appeal to people's minds

4.
The nights
        cool from thick dew-fall cooled by moon-rays
        decked in bright star-clusters
No use to people

SPRING

21.
All over
        Kiṃśuka forests' hanging blossoms like
        wind-shaken fire-flames
The earth glows
        Like a new spring-sprung bride in red robes aṃśuka

Why does this cuckoo try
                with melodious warble

to steal the minds of youth?
Are they not already
Loaded   by pretty faces
poked   by Kiṃśuka (why-parrot) flowers
             the colour of parrots' beaks

Rapture and Longing   45

seared   by Karnikara (*ear-piercing*) blossoms

23.
Happy vague warble of male-cuckoos
Murmur of tipsy buzzing bees

Disturb
even   the hearts of
brides   bashful and timid

though in their husband's home.

—Translated from the Sanskrit by Mani Rao

MY BARE LEGS

Gāthā Saptaśatī

My bare legs flung apart after love
how could I
forget him
tasting each crease in my
body
as the climax
subsided

—*Translated from the Sanskrit by Andrew Schelling*

SOIL MY BED WITH INDIGO FOOTPRINTS

Gita Govinda of Jayadeva

Sung to Rāga Vibhāsa

'Soil my bed with indigo footprints, *Kaminī*,
Lay waste the grove
savage it with your petal-soft feet.

'I take your feet in lotus hands, *Kaminī*,
you have come far.
Lay these gold flaring anklets across my bed.

'Let *yes yes* flow from your mouth like *amṛta*.
From your breasts, *Kaminī*,
I draw off the *dukūla*-cloth. We are no longer separate.'

Sung to Rāga Rāmakarī

*She sings while Krishna plays, her heart drawn
into ecstasy—*

'On my breast, your hand Krishna
cool as sandalwood. Draw a leaf wet with deer musk here,
it is Love's sacramental jar.

'Drape my loins with jeweled belts, fabric and gemstones.
My *mons venus* is brimming with nectar,
a cave mouth for thrusts of Desire.'

Reckless, inflamed, she presses forth
to the urgent campaign
of sexual love,
flips over and mounts him,
savors the way he gives in...

...later, eyes lidded,

The Parrots of Desire

loins cool and no longer rippling,
her arms trail like vines.
Only her chest continues to heave.
Is climbing on top
what brought her victory?

Reader, open your heart
to Jayadeva's well-
crafted poem. Through it
Krishna's deeds have entered your own memory-stream—
amṛta to cure
Kali Yuga's contagion.

—Translated from the Sanskrit by Andrew Schelling

MORNING CHILL

The Alchemy of Desire by Tarun Tejpal

Love is not the greatest glue between two people. Sex is.

The laws of school physics will tell you it is more difficult to prise apart two bodies joined at the middle than those connected anywhere near the top or the bottom.

I was still madly in love with her when I left her but the desire had died, and not all the years of sharing and caring and discovering and journeying could keep me from fleeing.

Perhaps I recall it wrong.

Strictly speaking I did not leave. Fizz did.

But the truth is she did—as always—what I wanted her to, what I willed her to. And I did what I did because by then my body had turned against hers; and anyone who has stretched and plumbed both mind and body will tell you the body, with its many nagging needs, is the true engine of life. The mind merely steers a path for it, or consoles it with high-sounding homilies when there is no path to be found.

The ravings of the puritans and the moralists are the anguished cries of those whose bodies have failed to find the road to bliss. When I see clergy—Hindu, Muslim, Christian—rail against the instincts of the body, I see men who are lost and angry and frustrated. Unable to locate the glories of the body, unable to locate the path to surpassing joy, they are resolved to confuse all other journeymen. Those who fail to find their sexual synapse set our mind and body at war against each other.

I agree there are the truly spiritual, just as there is the one-horned rhino, but they are few and far between and easily identifiable. For the rest of us, the body is the temple.

The truth is godhead is tangible.

Smellable. Tasteable. Penetrable.

The morning I woke up and felt no urge to slide down her body and inhale her musk I knew I was in trouble.

INFINITE

K. Satchidanandan

*I want to do with you
what Spring does with cherry trees*
—Pablo Neruda

1

The last drop of summer rain is
trickling on to the fallen mango leaf
pining beyond the window.
I am trying to unravel your mystery,
gathering your letters, nail marks
and the odours of your body
like a Sherlock Holmes decoding
fingerprints, rose petals,
manuscripts and poison vials.
I recreate your contours
like a drunk driver sighting a rainbow
across the distancing glass.
In the end, with irrepressible fervour,
I hug everything I come by:
The moist robes of rutting autumn,
the half-blossomed bunch of rajanigandha,
Kafka's letters to Milena,
Lorca's ballads,
*Ramanan,**
Mona Lisa.

2

It was a summer evening.
You quietly placed your palm on mine
like God polishing a rainbow
and placing it in the azure sky.

What did the promise mean?
—that we will walk, rain-drenched,
splashing water from the puddles

---

*A popular pastoral elegy in Malayalam by Changampuzha Krishna Pillai.

along the side-lanes of a childhood spring
that we failed to share?
—that we will, through an electrifying kiss,
transmit to each other the whole
uneasy history of our past travails?
—that your ears will emit the scent of jasmines
As my lips turn into an intense breeze
and murmur, 'love is an eternal quarrel with an angel?'*
—that, through the night, flinging
our robes of shame into fire,
we will taste the wild honey of
nocturnal flowers with our eager tongues?

3
You are that lean eleven-year-old,
fleeing the bomb in Vietnam.
As the dry-leaved lanes of your village caught fire,
You ran naked, leaving your blazing body
to the wind and the sun.
It was to my breast which had lulled
hunger to sleep you came.
Among the scars of many battles,
I had set aside for you
A barrel of words to quench the fire,
A drop of honey for your burnt heart
And a sunflower seed for tomorrow.

Don't say we are on two planets,
that our dancing feet are shackled.
Don't say it is from within the rocks
that we dream of leaves and birds.

You were mine since you were born.
I grew these thorns waiting for you.
Yet only the springs deep beneath the sands
can fill the dates with sweetness.

4
Lulled by the rose-like caress of a cool breeze,
we walked by the dreaming lake

---

*Jaroslav Seifert: 'Struggle with an Angel'.

The Parrots of Desire

that lay like a peacock feather.
Your heart throbbed in my hands
in the blushing memories
of a night of honey and acid.

My lips had four rainbows;
and your breasts, four clouds.
The strands of your hair
scribbled on my pillow: 'Your scent, dear,
I will carry to my garden.'
My tongue whispered to your tiny belly:
'I long to sprout inside you,
I want to be born in a war-free world.'

You sobbed over the children
massacred in Baslan; I fell in fragments
into the last vineyards from the
blown roof of Baghdad.
A cigarette-butt, flung by God,
winked at me: 'You have
three more nights to celebrate your survival.'

5
You place a red *manchadi* seed on my brow.
I roll a pearl along your navel.
I rub your nipples with
the honey of banana blooms.
You place a purple *manganari* flower
On my lips and blow
a couplet of Tukaram onto my breast,
I worship your eyes with a leaf from
The poetry of Ezhuthacchan.
I say: Matisse
You say: Beethoven
I say: Van Gogh
You say: Mozart
I say: Picasso
You say: Stravinsky
I say: Brecht
You say: Kumar Gandharv
I say: Vallejo

You say: Ramanathan
I say: Love.
You say: Love.

I raise you to the moon like a goblet.
Then we kiss, toasting the whole creation.
You come back, a rainbow
round your neck, a star in your hair.

You say: Sky
I say: Sea
Blue envelopes us.
Blue music. Blue moonlight.
Blue you. Blue me.
Blue ecstasy.

6
I am reading to you the lines of Ritsos:
'I know it is very late now. Let me come
because for so many years I've remained alone.'*

I thought you would speak of
Rilke's lion or Mallarme's swan;
but you were thinking of love,
that fairest of gods.

7
Why were you born so late?
In which star were you, in which water?
In which sunrise, in which fear of mankind?

No, love never comes late;
it annihilates years and ages,
falls like lightning at the centre of Time.
Then sitting on tombstones
It murmurs the nostalgic lines of Celan:
'Your golden hair, Margarete,
your ashen hair, Shulamith...'**

---

*Yannis Ritsos: 'Moonlight Sonata'.
**Paul Celan: 'Death Fugue'.

O, your straight hair drives me mad.
like the greedy soldiers back home
from the warfront, driving their vans
again and again along the countryside,
my fingers grope lustily
along those black lanes
for a broken bangle-shard,
a drop of moonlight,
a forgotten lullaby.

Your bubbling lips drive me mad.
I return to them over and over
like a drunkard to his wine.
I come back to your firm breasts
Like a devotee to the marmoreal idol
of his household goddess.
I come back to your burning navel
like the offering to the sacrificial fire.
I am the offering, the first man.
You are the fire, the first woman and the last,
limitless and timeless.
You are Gauri, Aruna, Bhargavi, Medini.
I am the hibiscus blossoming in the tribal hamlet
chanting your thousand names,
aching to attain your lap.

8
I have been travelling to you
through many half-lit births.
You have many names: Radha, Urvashi,
Laila, Anarkali, Leela, Chandrika:
each one a sunflower in half-bloom.
I do not want Juliet nor Cleopatra;
I want the thorny one, one like me,
flowering in the desert,
remembering everything, sharing everything:
pain, madness, words, thoughts,
body, soul, everything.

Daughter of legends, carry me ,
away from this world

growing dreadful day by day
for those who are not yet blind
into the moonlight of *ranjini*,*
the valley of pianos.
Look, Bob Dylan has turned into moonlight;
each tree swaying in the breeze, his guitar.

9
Where did you bury that red mark
my teeth had left on your right breast?
Did you lend it to the evening sky?
All the birds criss-crossing the sky grow red.
Leaves, flowers, streams, hills, all red.
A red moon bends over a red sea.
Tomorrow's sun will be red too.

How a bedsheet turns into
Vatsyayana in a single night![1]
Love too is meditation,
in twenty-four postures.

10
'Like the red earth and the pouring rain...'
a simile steps out from
the pages of the *Kurunthokai*.[2]
We are so mixed and kneaded
no drought can separate us.
I am there in your each drop,
and you in my each grain.

You are a bamboo bush.
As I blow through you,
each of your pores exudes Chaurasia's music.

You are a palette. My mad fingers
spread your colours on the canvas
like a Paul Klee painting.

---

*ranjini: a raga in Carnatic music.
[1]Remember Vatsyayana's Kamsootra, dealing with postures in love.
[2]Kurunthokai: an anthology of Tamil classical poetry

Your anklet resounds in all my words;
The flapping of your wings
echoes in all my seasons.
This moist book you have kept open for me,
Is it *Geetgovind* or *Gathasaptasati*?[1]

11

There are many birds in your throat.
One, a parrot, another a mynah.
When you sleep, they return to the woods.
When I see you sleeping in the nude,
I recall Hiroshima. I remove
the glass shards from your flesh
and wipe away the clotted blood.

You are every woman, the one
abandoned in the forest, the one
buried in backwaters, stoned on the street,
burnt at the stake, poisoned, exchanged,
beloved, bride, widow, whore.

Let me kiss your contended body
for all the flowers that failed
to blossom on earth, for lovers and refugees.

O, my Magdalene,
I who am no Jesus.

12

Now half-asleep, we are listening to Kabir.[2]
Rama relinquishing the throne
puts his arms on our shoulders
and sings of the body free of insignia
and of unqualified love.
He invites us to the Infinite.
I peer into the nightsky of your eyes.
where a crescent moon plays violin.

---

[1]Geetgovindam, a fourteenth century erotic-devotional poem in Sanskrit by Jayadeva, Gathasaptsati, an anthology of erotic love poetry in Prakrit collected by King Hala.
[2]Kabir, the sixteenth century devotional poet, weaver by profession, a critic of status quoist religion.

Come, let me lie in your lap this moment.

I wish to hear the sea billow like
Kumar Gandharv singing Tukaram's *abhang*.[3]

13

You are reading poetry from the dais,
with the same lips I had drunk from last night.
My hands become a breeze caressing your hair.
Each emerging word carries a kiss's wet seal.
We don't see the audience.
Let the world vanish; your words are only for me.
How everyone's language becomes
ours alone in certain moments!
Every noun becomes an olive branch extended to me,
every adjective, a wing, every verb ticks
like a clock measuring the span of love.

Ask the synonyms to leave us alone,
let us talk straight.

In the madness of odours, I jump into you.
You are the wildest of rivers,
the ever-billowing sea, the journey of the salt
beyond Babel, the vigil of the spark
beneath the ash.

14

Tell the sun not to rise tomorrow.
Tell the door not to open into the world's hurry.
Tell the bed not to betray us to the daylight.
Your cheeks are red like an arch on flame.
I see you as a tiny girl in a little white skirt,
in plaited hair, with a tender coconut-leaf
in your hand, on your way to the church
holding your mother's hand.
I see you taller in full skirt, waiting for the bus

---

[3]*Abhang* is a verse form popularized by Tukaram, the seventeenth century Marathi
saint-poet.

The Parrots of Desire

in the village square. Had you noticed me then,
fluttering about you as a butterfly?
A sparrow I had watched you
from the window-sill of your college class room.
Every step you took was towards me.

I am scared. Night will come tomorrow too.
O, the night of blood and devils,
in hell, without you.

Before we part, pour into my words:
that mixed fragrance unique to you, of
white lilies and hot chillies;
that rare voice of swallows twittering
over the rushing rainwater below;
that touch of your long fingers that passes
to each follicle the message of a cyclone;
that taste of your secrets, of *champa* blossoms
or of the pink flesh of pomegranate,
I will never know.

Then I can look straight at the solar eclipse
of this terrible century: until there remains
in my blinded eyes only, only,
your beloved image.

The First Time

THE CURE

from *Junglee Girl* by *Ginu Kamani*

It all started when I began to grow. My mother watched me closely. Very closely. She couldn't believe I was destined to be a giant. Every day the tile around my room door was scratched with heel marks. Every night the keyhole to my room was smeared with lipstick.

I didn't mind my mother breathing heavily outside the room. I felt sorry for her, so I let her watch. I spent a lot of time sitting at my desk. I marked how my legs had grown to such a length that my knees scraped painfully against the underside of the desk. I clearly remembered my legs dangling high off the ground at that same desk. I would lean forward over the table and lay my arms out in front of me on the big pink blotter. My fingers touched the wall behind the desk with ease. I remembered when I had to pull my body over the table up to my stomach in order to touch the wall behind the desk. I liked to sit there at my old desk and imagine how small my body had once been.

I also spent time looking at myself. I now had to stand far back to see my full frame in the cupboard mirror. My face was no longer in line with the top of the mirror when I stood flush against it. I could no longer lean against the cool surface and see my twin face joined wherever I desired, at the cheek or at the nose or at the tip of my tongue.

My mother blamed herself for allowing me to wear her heels when I was younger. She was convinced that my height signalled that I was meant to be a boy. Her ill luck at having produced a daughter meant she would suffer in her next birth. 'At least you didn't turn out a *blackie* on top of it,' she muttered in consolation.

My parents nervously watched me grow and grow, until I was so tall that my father was embarrassed to stand next to me in public. My father stopped speaking to my mother as he no longer believed that I was his child. He also felt that no man in his right mind would marry a giantess like myself and resigned himself to the fact that I would remain an unmarried dependent for life.

Every day my mother recounted to me sadly how much she used to love me, and how she wished she loved me still. Until the age of eleven, I was the apple of my mother's eye. I was also a carbon copy of her. She was small and fair, with large eyes and a perfectly straight nose. At the age of eleven I began to grow, and my small fair body became a looming tower that stooped forward over everyone. My limbs were long and thin, but my mother said I was obviously eating too much.

She cut out sweets, snacks and soft drinks from my diet. She fed me milk of magnesia every night, to help 'flush out the excess body matter'.

For two years my height increased at a steady pace. There seemed to be no end in sight. She asked all her friends what to do about her 'jumbo child'. The women suggested ice packs to shrink the flesh, and gas-forming foods to keep my long frame bent over double. They wanted mother to take me on a pilgrimage, because I was obviously too proud, standing tall over all men, my elders, the gods and all. Mrs Mishra suggested sending me to a doctor. Why not? These days doctors have a cure for everything.

◆

The driver Ramdass was my constant companion. He didn't care that I was too tall, in fact it had never even entered his consciousness. To him, I was still 'Baby', still the young child of his employer. Even though he was on 'house duty', Ramdass referred to himself proudly as 'Ramdass, office driver'. He had a crew cut of gray hair and sweat stains in the armpits of his starched uniform which he wore unbuttoned in the Bombay heat.

In the evenings, after picking me up from school, Ramdass was at my disposal. We could take a drive anywhere we wanted to. Every evening without fail, I would heave my schoolbag onto the front seat, climb into the back and stretch my legs out along the seat.

'Worli, *direct!*' I would announce to Ramdass, and he would speed through the crowds of schoolgirls, hawkers, laborers and office workers to get me to Worli Sea Face. How diligently he coaxed the big blue Ambassador, elegantly turning the wheel with sometimes languid, sometimes rapid gestures while dancing from the knees down as he alternated pressing the foot pedals. He swayed from side to side, his body completely absorbed into the motion of the car. Ramdass would watch the traffic and I would watch Ramdass. His front-seat ballet would make me drowsy and I would lie back with eyes half-closed.

Eventually we would turn off the main road onto the wide sweeping curve of the Sea Face road. Ramdass would break into a smile as he shifted gears and raced the car down the usually empty road. The breeze would whip up my hair like a shredded black flag. At the end of the sea wall, Ramdass would pull to the side and park. He and I would step out and walk toward the raised sea wall. It was a few feet off the sidewalk. I would walk quickly along the narrow wall, swaying from side to side to keep my balance. Ramdass would march alongside with one hand ready to grasp me in case I lost my balance. The waves would glide in to the bottom of the wall, breaking softly without spraying me. In this way we would walk the length of the wall, first in the direction away from the car, and then back toward it.

Every evening as dusk settled onto the city, we returned to where the car was parked and waiting for us was the man we called the *Suitwallah*. He was always there for our return, seated on that sea wall as though he had been sitting forever. We never saw him coming.

The Suitwallah had a long thin face and long thin hands. He always wore a three-piece suit. He looked like a schoolmaster. He sat facing me with his hands placed on his thighs. He would watch me without a word, until I finally broke his gaze by walking past him. Then he would nod at Ramdass, who would courteously nod back. He never turned his face to follow us as we got into the parked car and drove off. Sometimes I had Ramdass wait a few minutes before turning on the car, just to see whether Suitwallah would turn around to look at the car, but he never did turn around, as though we had disappeared from existence once we stepped around him.

One afternoon, when Ramdass came to pick me up from school, my mother was in the back seat. She watched me glumly as I bent down to half my height in order to climb into the car. She sniffed disdainfully as I sat sideways on the seat to provide my long legs with extra room. 'Lady Doctor!' my mother ordered the back of Ramdass' head. Ramdass looked at me frantically from the corner of his eye, waiting for me to confirm the order. He sensed that something was very wrong. I waved him on.

♦

The lady doctor shrieked as I entered her office. She pulled the spectacles off her nose and stared at me in a rage. She waved her arms about, as if asking the universe to explain my presence. Finally she recovered her voice.

'Oh you poor thing!' she exclaimed and rushed to embrace my mother. My mother's composure crumbled entirely and she began sobbing in the doctor's arms.

'Oh, it must be so hard for you!' the doctor groaned sympathetically, wiping my mother's tears and kissing her on the head while motioning irritatedly for me to take a seat.

My mother wiped her nose with the end of her sari and covered her face with her hands, sobbing like a little girl. The lady doctor steered my mother toward the examining table and helped her onto the padded surface. My mother sat slumped over like a rag doll. The lady doctor paced up and down the room, frowning and gesticulating in silence. Then she stopped in front of me and straightened her stethoscope.

'Fundamentally over-sexed!' hissed the lady doctor, pointing at me. 'Danger to society. Sex hormones out of control. Shameless and uninhibited. Look how she tempts!'

The lady doctor marched over to where I sat sprawled in the armchair, grabbed my thighs and pressed them tightly together until they were sealed shut. She held them that way until I crossed my legs.

She turned back to my mother and grasped her hands, squeezing and releasing them while shaking her head dumbly to and fro. My mother leaned forward with quivering lips as the lady doctor frowned and searched for the right words.

'Just take it, madam,' she exhaled at last, 'that your suffering in this lifetime will be limitless...'

My mother cried out in shock.

'...unless you take my advice.' The lady doctor marched to her desk and quickly wrote out a prescription. She tore it off the pad, then wrote down some more information on the back. The lady doctor pressed the buzzer on her desk and instantly her office attendant walked in.

'Next!' the lady doctor ordered the attendant, and he nodded and closed the door. Our time was up.

The lady doctor steered my mother outside the office to where Ramdass was parked, and I followed. The doctor pressed the paper into my mother's hand.

'My dear lady, here is a tranquilizer prescription for you. I can see you haven't been getting much sleep.' My mother whispered grateful thanks.

'And on the back is the name of a doctor I know.' The lady doctor dropped her voice to a whisper. 'He is a licensed *sexologist*.'

The lady doctor paused, and stiffened her back.

'You will understand everything,' she announced haughtily, 'when I ask you: "Can one woman ever really know another?"' She sniffed and looked me up and down.

'This girl needs to be cured by a proper *man*. Dr Doctor is the one for her.'

◆

I bit into the glass of milk until my teeth hurt. Suddenly the glass cracked. The broken piece came away in my mouth and the milk spilled onto the table. My mother looked at me tiredly from across the dining table. The tranquilizers were keeping her groggy all day long.

'Good,' she said yawning, 'one less thing for you to eat. Anyway, milk is meant for a growing child, not for a demoness.'

We were waiting at the dining table for the arrival of Dr Doctor. The name, he had assured my mother on the phone, was genuine and not to be worried about. His ancestors for generations had been doctors, and doctoring was in his blood.

The bell rang sharply and my mother sat up. Lakshman, the servant, could be heard running quickly from the back of the house, through the kitchen, and out into the reception area to answer the door. After some discussion, the servant stuck his head in the dining room, peevishly snapped, 'Doctor sahib,' and retired to the kitchen.

Dr Doctor entered the dining room, and I gasped. He stopped in shock as he recognized me. He dropped his medical bag onto the carpet.

'So we meet at last,' he murmured,

Standing in front of me was the Suitwallah from Worli Sea Face. He was even thinner than he appeared while seated. His face was hollow-cheeked with dark slashes for eyes and mouth. His legs were no thicker than bamboo poles and his cadaverous frame stooped forward, as though unable to support his narrow torso. His eyes gleamed and his eyebrows froze into lopsided arches. I was facing him and he marched toward me. My mother's small body was almost entirely hidden in the plush swivel chair and Dr Doctor spun her around to face him. He stood over her, his thin lips curling with a mix of eagerness and impatience. He stuck out his hand. It was long and pale and hairless.

'At your service, madam,' he rumbled in a surprisingly deep voice.

My mother cautiously touched her hand to the doctor's, then swiveled around to face me.

'She's the one,' my mother pointed. 'Cure her.'

Dr Doctor looked at me and smiled. He already knew me well. What had he thought of me all those hundreds of times he had locked his eyes with mine.

'I am well acquainted with her case,' the doctor said pleasantly. 'I have been watching her development for years. Certainly a rare specimen.'

My mother puzzled over the doctor's statements.

'Excuse me, doctor, but do we know you from somewhere?'

'Your daughter's height is a topic of much discussion in Bombay. We were bound to meet sooner or later. I have already made notes on her case in anticipation of this event.'

My mother's face crumpled at the mention of my height.

'Won't you stay for tea?' my mother cried as she rushed to the kitchen shouting 'Lakshman! Chai!' to cover up her tears.

Dr Doctor motioned for me to stand up, then he walked all around me, sighing and clucking his tongue.

'Hunh...' he hummed with wonder, 'hmm...now, let's see...uh-huh...'

When my mother returned with the tea, he took a chair next to her.

'Madam, in all my years, I have seen nothing like this. Breathtaking opportunity. Once in a lifetime chance! I would be interested even in taking her on as a charity case.'

My mother reached forward fearfully and clutched the doctor's hands. 'Please, I insist on paying you *highest* fees. You are a specialist of *great repute*. Find a cure, that's all I ask. Turn her back into my innocent darling.'

Dr Doctor whipped out his calling card and turned it over. He wrote out the time of his next visit.

'You see, madam, it looks like a *grave* imbalance...' the doctor paused, irritated by my mother's ingratiating smiling and nodding.

'This is not to be taken lightly, madam! It is a one-in-a-million imbalance of the...uh...of the...ohhhh...feminine *fluids*, let us say. I must monitor this condition by taking *regular* samples of her female waters. Do you get my meaning? It is a complicated process but you have no cause for alarm because I will come to *her*. Best to see such once-in-a-lifetime cases in their own homes, madam, so they feel at ease.'

My mother sniffled gratefully and placed a many-folded hundred rupee note in the doctor's palm. He patted my mother's arm and leaned forward intimately.

'I know what it is like having daughters of disposable age, madam. Your pain is mine, madam. I will bring all my knowledge to this case, madam. You can count on me.' He collected his doctor's bag and stood up to leave.

'I strongly recommend that you absent yourself for the duration of my weekly visit, madam. Only to make it less *painful* for you, madam, being the girl's mother and all.'

I looked at the card he had dropped on the table. Dr Cyrus Rustom Doctor, M.D., F.R.C.S. Son of Dr Ardeshir Mehli Doctor, M.D. Grandson of Dr Kekoo Naoroji Doctor, M.D.

I looked at Dr Doctor and his face was suddenly stern.

'I will see you next *in your own house*,' he warned.

'Don't expect us to meet on *any other path*.' Then he winked, waved his arm in a wide circle and left.

◆

I didn't tell my mother that the doctor and I actually knew each other well. There was no other way to describe our countless daily meetings: my great anticipation at seeing his form slowly materialize as I walked along the sea wall; the long length of time over which we stared at each other without discomfort. I could tell from the way he was accustomed to looking at me that he knew me as a person, not just as a child.

I was curious to see whether I had correctly understood his words as he left the house. I had Ramdass drive me to Worli Sea Face the next day. I walked along the sea wall as usual, but the staring, seated form of the doctor did not appear. He had meant his words. We were now destined to play a different game.

◆

The day before Dr Doctor was due, I cleaned my room with great excitement. I knew my mother was watching through the keyhole, but I didn't care. The following morning, I rushed down to the car and jumped in breathless next to Ramdass.

'I have a friend coming today!' I sang to him. 'Finally, someone to see *me*!'

Ramdass was ecstatic. 'A friend for Baby! It is very good. We must buy some sweets to welcome this friend.'

Ramdass stopped outside a sweet shop. The shop owner recognized him and waved. Ramdass shouted out an order for a kilo of mixed sweetmeats. When the shop boy came running up with the neatly packaged box, Ramdass paid for it with his own money.

I got home and readied myself for the visit. I tied my hair back, to keep it out of the way. I trimmed my fingernails and toenails, so as to not scratch him accidentally. I brushed my teeth and scraped my tongue clean.

What would the doctor want me to wear? I decided on a dress which could be unbuttoned fully from the collar to the hem, like the gowns in hospitals. When I tried it on, I realized that the hem was higher than the last time I had worn it. My body was continuing to grow.

The house was quiet. My mother was out shopping and our servant Lakshman was out smoking with his friends. The front door was wide open. In my room there was a sealed envelope pinned to my cork board, marked PERSONAL AND CONFIDENTIAL and addressed to Dr Doctor, M.D. Below the letter, on my desk, I placed the wrapped and ribboned box of sweets.

◆

Dr Doctor entered the room. He was wearing a brown three-piece suit with a maroon tie. His oiled hair was as black and sticky as shoe polish. He wiped the sweat off his brow and neck and locked his gaze on me. The hair on my arms rose in waves.

'Will you have something to eat?' I asked.

'No, no,' he waved like an orchestra conductor. 'I have not come to a restaurant. I am here to diagnose the aberrance of your maidenhead, a task that undoubtedly increases my thirst. Water is all I ask.'

I went into the kitchen and opened the refrigerator. There I found chilled coconut water in a glass, neatly covered by a lace cloth weighted down on the edges with beads. When I returned to the room, Dr Doctor was looking through my closet.

'You wear men's clothes?' he asked, pointing to my collection of trousers. I looked at the doctor's trousers. They were drainpipe-narrow in the leg and tight and creased across his hips.

'My pants all button on the side.' I emphasized

'Oh-ho!' the doctor chuckled. 'So you are indeed a woman.' He motioned me towards him, put his hands on my shoulder and turned me in one direction and then the other to see what I was wearing.

'Ah, good," he cried, 'you are wearing a dress. This delicate procedure, you see, requires that I...well, that uh....a dress is very good.'

The doctor sat at my desk and opened his doctor's bag. His long fingers lazily pushed aside instruments and papers until he found what he wanted. He pulled out two thin glass slides wrapped in tissue paper and laid them gingerly on the desk, flicking away specks of dust. His eye caught sight of the envelope my mother had pinned to the cork board. He held the envelope up to the light, saw that it contained a hundred-rupee note and stuffed it into his coat pocket. He noticed the box of sweets and turned to me in surprise.

'Is it your birthday today?' He quickly unwrapped and opened the box and thrust a sweet into his mouth. 'Now come here,' he commanded and patted his knee. I walked over to him, wondering if he would feed me a sweet as well. He put his hands on my hips and looked up at me.

'Good, good,' he said, squinting at my face. 'You are too tall for your eyes to be a distraction.' He took the hem of my dress in his hands and tugged on it as he spoke.

'Listen carefully now. I have to perform this procedure, which will take place in the lower half of your body. It might take a few minutes, because you are young and not accustomed to such manner of contact. You don't even know it, but there is a special kind of fluid in you, that I must have to make my diagnosis. At the appointments I will need to test this fluid and I cannot stress enough how important it is that you simply learn to relax!'

Quick as a whip, Dr Doctor reached under my dress and pulled down my panties. They fell to the ground, and I stepped aside and kicked them away.

'Now bend a little at the knees,' he murmured, then steadied his head against my stomach. He placed one hand around the back of my legs and brought the other to his mouth. He licked the index finger front and back, then reached between my legs. His hand was ticklish on my skin. I leaned my arm against the cork board to keep my balance.

'It's like finally meeting a pen pal,' I whispered to myself.

'You're such a big girl,' the doctor responded, leaning intently against my hip. I could feel his thumb and two fingers pushing against my thighs. The other two fingers were pushing inside me, but I couldn't quite understand where. Was he trying to find my stomach from the inside? His pushing made me sway. He held tighter around my legs to keep me still. His fingers made me more ticklish and I laughed. Deep inside me he had found a pouch of skin! It felt like what the pouch of a kangaroo must be like, only on the inside.

'This will take time,' he murmured into my hip.

I couldn't stop laughing. The doctor also smiled.

'When you were ready to be born, the doctor put his fingers inside your mother like this to tickle you and wake you up. That's why you're so ticklish.'

I could feel his fingers slowly, gently, going round and round and up and down inside my pouch of skin. The rest of my body seemed to be floating away into the air. I looked down from the ceiling at the sight of the doctor bent over and clasping me, as though asking my forgiveness.

Suddenly the tickle inside became very strong, burning me, and I had to put a hand on the doctor's head to keep from falling. I couldn't keep my legs bent any more, they were trembling. The doctor could feel my shaking.

'It's okay, it's okay,' he groaned, thumping karate chops on the backs of my thighs and forcing my knees to remain bent.

'I'm going to...I have to cross my legs or I'm going to...' I could barely speak.

'Nothing is going to happen!' the doctor snapped. 'Just stand still till I've finished.'

My breathing was out of control. I couldn't understand whether I should inhale or exhale. I was going to wet his hand any second if he wouldn't let me go to the toilet.

Then I coughed and choked and my thighs shut tightly around Dr Doctor's fingers. He screamed. I screamed.

'Let go of my hand!' he shouted in panic. He beat on the back of my thighs to get me to open up my legs. I lost my balance and fell on top of him. The chair crashed to the ground. I hit the funny bone in my elbow and screamed again, shaking with laughter. My thighs released their precious cargo. The doctor pushed my body away, straightened his suit, and jammed my legs open with his knees. The sensations in my funny bone and the tingling between my legs felt like one and the same. I couldn't stop laughing.

'Crazy female!' the doctor panted, reaching up to grab one of the glass slides. He pushed my thighs further apart, almost tearing the muscle, then dug his finger again and again into my pouch of flesh and wiped his finger on the slide each time. Finally the doctor let go of my legs and I rolled over onto my side.

'Look!' commanded the doctor, pushing the slide under my nose. 'I have captured your essence. Now we will get to the bottom of your too-tall self. They don't call me Dr Doctor for nothing!'

He placed the second slide carefully over the first, sealing the secret of my too-tall body under the clear glass. He gulped down the coconut water, popped another sweet into his mouth and straightened his tie.

'Next week,' he admonished, 'you must do better. You must practice, practice, *practice*, until you learn to relax.' Dr Doctor slapped his palms together in prayer. 'These are the fingers of a skilled surgeon,' he hissed. 'I cannot have you breaking them!'

I sat up slowly and looked around for my panties. They were under the desk. I grabbed them and slid them on. Dr Doctor watched me while he popped another sweet into his mouth. His oily hair was plastered onto his forehead and his ears were bright red.

'What about my pouch of skin...'

'What's that?' snapped the doctor in irritation. 'What did you say?'

'Inside. First it tickled, now it burns.'

'Hmmm...' said the doctor, munching on more sweets. The box was now empty. He mashed the crumbs of sweets onto the end of one finger and licked it clean.

'Let it burn. No harm in it. You're a big girl now. You must learn to bear your pain.'

Dr Doctor brushed off his suit one last time, picked up his bag and walked out of the house.

◆

The Parrots of Desire

I wondered whether I should tell my mother about this first session of treatment. At least now I knew what a *sexologist* did; I was certain that my mother did too. She must have known what female waters are, and how they affect a girl's height. She must also have known about the pouch of skin from where the female fluid flows. I resolved to tell her everything if she asked me, but the questions never came.

Perhaps she would get some hint of what was going on by spying on me through the door. The doctor had said to practice relaxing. I stood with my legs bent at the knees and tried to do what the doctor did. I tired quickly and achieved nothing. If my mother saw any of this through the keyhole, she made no mention of it.

A few days later, the doctor sent my mother his *diagnostic notes*, written out in beautiful handwriting:

INDICATIONS:
The patient has a tendency to immodesty and nakedness.
The patient displays no resistance to contact with her female chamber.
The patient produces fluid in overabundance, a condition normally seen only in Red-Light Women.

DIAGNOSIS:
Coitus or other sexual stimulation will be deleterious to the patient's health.

URGENT RECOMMENDATIONS:
Lifelong celibacy, supplemented by dedication to social causes.
Early sterilization in case of accidental penetration.
Further fluid samples from the patient for an ongoing, comprehensive evaluation.

My mother stirred from her stupor. The tranquilizers kept her drowsy but her unhappiness penetrated the fog. Dr Doctor's diagnostic notes mentioned nothing about a cure. My mother wanted results. She showed the doctor's letter to her friends. They were mildly disturbed at the extent of my problem, but were absolutely appalled at the recommendation that I remain unmarried and forcefully infertile. The sin to any woman of having an unmarried daughter in the house was just too much to bear.

Push for *results*, they told my mother. Don't get bullied into accepting his way of thinking. After all, he is a man, and cannot know what pain we go through. My mother decided that the doctor could test me three more times, and no more. Then she would take a look at his findings and send him on his way.

◆

On the second visit, Dr Doctor wore only an old short-sleeved shirt and floppy pants. Without his three-piece suit, he looked unimaginably thin. He rolled up his sleeves and smoothed back his hair, then looked around.

'Ah...no sweets for the doctor today?' he sighed wistfully.

'Water, if you like,' I offered. The doctor was uninterested.

'How do you expect me to drink anything when I have to wrestle with you?' he retorted. 'Have you been practicing how to relax?'

'I can lie down on the bed,' I suggested. 'That way we won't fall down.'

'Hmph!' said Dr Doctor. I removed my panties and lay back on the bed.

The doctor bent my legs at the knees, then pushed my thighs wide apart. I watched him pulling and pushing my body.

'Don't look at me!' he warned. He pulled a doctor's mask out of his pocket and slipped it onto his face, covering his nose and mouth.

'Have to be careful in unhealthy environments,' he muttered, then bent down.

The doctor hunched down between my legs, digging in so hard that my belly danced in and out.

'I want to do it myself,' I whispered, tracing his tense fingers with my own.

'Hmph!' he snorted and pushed my hand away. He resumed tickling me. I tried to bring my legs together, but he jammed his shoulder against one leg and stuck his elbow into the other.

'Relax!' he commanded. 'I must do my job.'

I could feel his fingers all the way to the knuckles, burrowing in me like worms. They were inside the pouch of skin, which was buried inside the mound of my belly, which was sunken inside the bag of my hips, which was buried inside the arms of the doctor. He was almost sitting on top of me.

The pouch of skin was like a fizzy Coke bottle. When he shook it, the fizz shot up and bubbled and spat and came sliding down into the bed and stained the sheets and wet the doctor's fingers. I could see the trail on the glass slide as he coated it with skin bottle fizz over and over again. As soon as he had finished, Dr Doctor pulled off his mask, dropped the slides into his bag and snatched his payment off the cork board. He paused at the door.

'I am a licensed doctor, not you. God has given me these hands as tools, not you. It is my *duty* to stimulate your fluids! Disregard any inclinations towards contradicting that.'

◆

Ramdass found out from Lakshman that my mother had left me alone in the house with a stranger. Ramdass was anxious at the news and pressed me for details. Who was the man? Where did he come from? What did he do?

I chided Ramdass for being so stupid. I told him it was our *friend*, the one we saw every day when we went for the drive. Ramdass didn't know who I was referring to. He didn't remember ever seeing any man at Worli Sea Face. He blamed himself for buying the sweets without checking whom they were for.

'I thought Baby had invited another *baby* friend!'

I pointed out to Ramdass that he was my friend and *he* certainly wasn't a baby. Ramdass cried out in alarm at my words. He assured me that he was only the company driver, and if I went around calling him my friend, he would surely get into trouble.

When I got out of the car at the end of the day, Ramdass requested me to give him this Dr Doctor's address. He said he would find out what kind of doctor-man he really was.

◆

The doctor came for his third visit. By now he was dressed in tennis shorts and a t-shirt. His legs were like match sticks. He was as thin as a poor laborer.

I lay back on the bed and bent my knees. I opened them wide. Dr Doctor nodded his approval.

'I've been thinking about our meeting,' I volunteered, as he licked his fingers one by one and thrust them into me. I winced as I felt a jagged fingernail digging in at the opening.

'What's that?' he gasped, pressing his head between my legs. I could see only the back of his neck.

'I've known you for so long. Did you know that one day we would meet? Perhaps we were suddenly separated in a past life...'

My head swam as the doctor probed. I could feel the wetness through which his fingers slid like snakes. My knees folded in around the doctor's face and he jabbed me in the thigh.

'Pay attention!' he barked. 'I don't have all day.'

His fingers made me uncomfortable. His voice was too harsh. He was breaking the spell of our intimacy. I sat up suddenly, and his fingers slid right out. He looked at me in astonishment.

'I'll get the sample for you,' I announced bravely.

'You are a *guest* in this house. This is too much work for you.'

The doctor opened his mouth to contradict me, so I repeated, 'You are a guest in this house. You must rest.'

The doctor looked at me nervously. He wiped the sweat off his brow and stood up. I licked my finger and touched the opening of my pouch of skin. How unusual and soft it felt. I slid the tip of the finger through the sticky fluid spread all over between my legs. Everywhere I touched, my mouth let out a soft cry, like the meow of a cat. I was suddenly confused to be doing the doctor's job. I closed my eyes so I wouldn't see him frowning at me.

Soon my legs were trembling and shaking and the skin of my finger felt numb and puckered as though it had fallen asleep in a swimming pool. All in a rush, the mountain of skin rose up through me and pushed me down into the mattress. I could not move; the force of the moment sucked every ounce of strength out of me.

The doctor pushed away my useless hand and dug out the fluid. My skin burned where he touched me and my arms and legs jerked like puppets. His touch was too hard. I couldn't bear the pressure. I rolled over and shut my legs tightly. The feeling was very different now that I had done it. The doctor packed up his slides and left without a word.

I wondered whether I should tell my mother that I could now do to myself what the doctor was supposed to. She probably wouldn't care. She was busy looking for alternate solutions.

◆

Ramdass quickly closed the car door for me, then slid into his seat. He pulled out onto the road with great speed. He spoke rapidly. 'This doctor of yours, he lives all alone at Worli Sea Face. No one visits him there. He sees all his patients in their homes. All of them are memsahibs and girls of good family like you. Many of them have remained his patients for ten, fifteen, twenty years.'

I remained silent, so Ramdass turned to me in alarm.

'Don't you see, Baby?' he pleaded. 'This man is good-for-nothing. What kind of doctor keeps his patients sick forever?'

'Tell my mother,' I replied casually.

Ramdass stepped hard on the brakes and I fell forward against the seat. He pulled over to the side of the road and turned to me.

'Please, Baby, I am a good man. I come and go quietly every day. I do my job properly and I respect your father and mother. Please don't get me into any trouble. I cannot speak directly to your mother or anyone else in your family. All blame will fall on my head. I am a man and I know how men are. I am simply telling you what I have found out.'

I imagined Ramdass as a detective, sneaking around the doctor's office with his peaked driver's cap pulled low over his eyes, looking furtively through the files, coaxing information out of the building lift man, bribing the doctor's peon to spill his secrets. I smiled with satisfaction. Ramdass was a true friend.

'Very good, Ramdass,' I said in my stiffest memsahib tone. 'You are a good worker and I will recommend you for a raise.'

Ramdass shook his head sadly and put the car into gear.

'How will you understand, Baby. I don't care about the money. You are still young. I have done what I can. Now I leave it to god.'

I listened to the concern in Ramdass's voice. He was such a loyal companion.

'The doctor knows something about me that you don't,' I confessed to Ramdass. 'You didn't find out anything about that, did you?'

Ramdass frowned into the rearview mirror.

'No,' he finally admitted. 'I didn't.'

'Did you enjoy being a detective?' I asked.

Ramdass's sad face suddenly twitched and then he burst out laughing.

'Yes, Baby, I really did enjoy myself!' Ramdass paused, suddenly thoughtful. 'I looked everywhere in his house, but only one thing I didn't find was his doctor's bag. That man must keep evil things in his bag, I just know it.'

I thought of the slides sitting wrapped in the doctor's bag. What would Ramdass make of them? He would look at them over and over, puzzling over them, turning them this way and that. Would he finally lift off the top slide and smell the liquid? Would he finally realize what it was and cry out, *Baby*?

The thought of it made me smile.

◆

My mother waited out the doctor's third visit, then on a school morning she called up and informed the principal's office that I would be absent from lessons that day. She took her time dressing me up in one of her silk saris, tied my hair back in a bun, applied some lipstick to my face and splashed me with perfume. I inspected myself in the mirror. I had been transformed! I looked like a grown woman. How did I get this way? My mother solemnly fixed her hair and straightened her sari, and we left the house.

Ramdass paled as he saw me walk toward the car. He looked nervously from me to my mother but said nothing. He got into the car and started the engine. When he looked back at me through the rearview mirror, I could tell he was frightened. I shrugged as if to ask him *What?* and he looked even more unhappy.

We drove to the Taj Mahal Hotel. Ramdass let us off in front and we walked up the steps into the dazzling lobby. The chandeliers glinted and sparkled in the midday sun. The hushed tones of foreigners filled the large carpeted space. There were Arab men in long white robes, blond giants in jeans and t-shirts, chic Indian women in heavily embroidered silk suits. Different perfumes mingled in the cool air. My mother had me sit in the first empty seat, so that my height wouldn't cause too many heads to turn. She left me there as she went to find the person we had come to meet.

Two European men watched my mother cross to the front desk, then turned to face me. They looked at me and smiled. Immediately I lowered my eyes, but then I wondered why. Why couldn't I look at a tall blond man? I had stared into the doctor's eyes for years. I had looked at Ramdass all my life. These men were no different. Green eyes instead of brown, that's all. Why should anyone stop me?

I looked up in triumph and the two foreigners immediately stood up and came over. My mother came racing back across the lobby.

'Watch out!' she shouted in warning.

The two men stepped back as my mother came to a stop by my chair. They scowled in defeat and walked away.

'You see,' my mother breathed conspiratorially. 'Everyone thinks you're a grown woman. That's why I've brought you here. Mrs Engineer will fix up something for you.'

My mother couldn't find an empty seat near me, so she sat on a sofa across from me, glaring at all the men who sauntered past my chair.

We sat in the lobby and waited for Mrs Engineer to come down from her room. She was getting her massage. She came to Bombay twice a year, by appointment only. She always stayed at the Taj. She traveled to all the big cities in India, and also to London, New York and Toronto.

A large woman wearing a shimmering sari of white and gold silk waddled out of the lift. She had short curled hair and beamed from ear to ear. My mother jumped up and waved at her. Mrs Engineer nodded and came bouncing towards us. My mother stood by my side and clasped my shoulder tightly.

'Aha!' Mrs. Engineer beamed by way of greeting. 'What have we here!' She tugged on my hand to get me to stand up, but my mother pressed down firmly on my shoulder.

'Later,' my mother whispered nervously. 'You can see her deformity when we leave.'

Mrs. Engineer took my mother's hand and chided her gently. 'Do not use that word, madam. Each of us is one of god's children. I give you my oath that we will find a suitable match for her. Our service has been very successful, as you know. How else could I afford to stay in this hotel?' Mrs. Engineer swept her arm across the majestic lobby. My mother nodded glumly.

'In India, no one needs to be left out of matrimony. We guarantee a match. Now I will tell you all the groups we work with day in and day out.' Mrs. Engineer took a deep breath.

'We have married,' she sang at the top of her voice, 'the blind...the deaf...the frigid...diabetics...amputees...midgets...mental patients...black-skinned girls...alcoholics...women of the night...and also giants, like your daughter.' Mrs. Engineer had a twinkle in her eye.

'All this, of course, as long as you are willing to pay.'

Mrs. Engineer burped contentedly and looked from my mother to me.

'For an extra fee, very small really, we can teach your daughter how to cook, clean, sew, give her husband massage and other womanly things. We guarantee marriage for your child, but cannot promise a servant in the house to do the work for her!'

My mother blanched and gripped the chair.

'You mean...my darling...'

'I assure you, madam, we will arrange for your daughter to marry as far from Bombay as possible, and you need never see the man or the conditions in which he lives. Soon your daughter will adjust because, after all, she will be a respectable married woman and have children and a husband to take care of. Our service has a ninety percent success rate, especially when you send some extra money each month to guarantee that the husband treats the girl well.'

'But...but...but...' My mother was agitated by the thought of me down on my knees, scrubbing the floor, bending over the well, drawing up buckets of water, blowing on the coals between gusts of smoke, coughing over a cooking fire.

Mrs. Engineer clapped her hands to silence the whimpering.

'Mrs. Mehta!' she barked. 'Let us not mince words. Your daughter has a visible *deformity*. The whole world can see it. Nothing you can do will change her problem. I am very disappointed by your attitude.

As her mother, it is *your duty* to get her married. I leave Bombay at the end of the week. I expect to see sufficient down payment delivered to my room before then. Now goodbye!'

Mrs. Engineer stood where she was, glaring at us. My mother hoped she would walk away, but the matchmaker wanted a glimpse of my height. My mother took her hand off my shoulder and walked quickly out of the lobby. I stood up and straightened my sari. The hem fell short, brushing at my ankles when it had stretched down to my toes on arrival. My body had increased in length yet again. Mrs. Engineer watched me wiggle my body as I slid the sari lower down around my hips. She clapped her hands together in glee and chuckled.

'Take good care of yourself,' Mrs. Engineer warbled. 'You are worth your *height* in gold to me.'

◆

The next morning Ramdass drove me to school. I started crying in the back seat and Ramdass immediately pulled over to the side of the road. He bit his lips, scratched his head and wrung his hands.

'Baby,' he said softly, 'very sorry, Baby. You are in pain? You want to go home?'

I shook my head. Ramdass sat in silence, watching me stretched out on the back seat with my face in my hands.

'No. Don't do anything. Don't go anywhere. You're my only friend. Just stay with me.'

Ramdass smiled nervously and shook his head.

'What kind of friend can I be? I am stupid, only a driver. Who is friends with a fool like me?'

Ramdass turned off the engine and we sat in silence, listening to the cars rushing by. I looked at Ramdass as he stared out of the window. He had the kindest face I had ever seen.

'Where are you from?' I asked him.

'Very far away, Baby, my village is on the other side of India.'

'Where is your wife?'

'She has gone to heaven, poor woman, so many years ago. I left my children with my mother and came to this city to find work.'

'You have a house in the village?'

'It is only a hut. We are simple village people.'

Ramdass turned to face me, uncertain about my inquiries. In all the years he had worked for us, I had never asked him any personal questions. He let his hand hang over the back of his seat.

I took his hand in mine. He gasped and tried to pull away but I

The Parrots of Desire

clasped his hand hard. His skin was smooth with calluses.

'I am going to marry you, Ramdass. You don't have to treat me in any special way and we don't have to have children. You don't even have to make a woman of me: I know how to take care of all of that. We will go back to your village and live with your family. My parents will send lots of money which will take care of all of us.'

Ramdass cried out as though I had struck him and jerked his hand away. He shrank back against the steering wheel, then jumped backwards out of the car as though his seat were on fire. He put his arms around his body and shivered miserably. He squatted on the ground and clasped his head between his hands. He was very afraid.

I hadn't stopped to think that Ramdass might not want me. He *had* to save me! Didn't he care for me? He had known me since I was a child, and must have always loved me. Now he simply had to learn to love me as a *wife*.

It struck me that I might yet get Ramdass under my spell. I reached forward and honked the horn. Ramdass stood up slowly and brushed off his uniform. He got into the car and sat slumped over the wheel. I tapped him gently on the shoulder.

'If you won't marry me,' I whispered, 'at least stop the doctor from stealing my essence. You don't want him to keep me sick forever.'

Ramdass stiffened and lifted his head. 'Why do you let him into the house? Call the police! They will arrest him.'

'Ramdass, you know that no one listens to a young girl. If you do it my way, we won't get into any trouble. This evening after the doctor leaves our house, follow him. As soon as you can, open his bag and take everything out carefully. There you will find what he steals from me. He seals it between two pieces of glass. You will recognize what it is. Bring it back to me.'

Ramdass breathed deeply and his shoulders relaxed. He started the car engine and nodded thoughtfully. He was back to being his old self.

'That bad man has stolen something of yours. Ramdass, company driver, will bring it back!'

◆

Twenty minutes before the doctor's fourth visit, I pulled off my panties and lay down on the bed. I could feel that my female fluid was already leaking out. I slowly massaged the loose skin all around my pouch of skin. By now I knew that what I felt down there was not ordinary, even though this was simply my body touching my own body.

When the doctor walked in, the skin fizz was already spread out and cooling between my legs. He saw from my face that I had finished his job. I stretched my glistening fingers toward him. Without a word he gave me the glass slide.

Is this what kept his other patients sick for ten or twenty years? Letting him take their fluids week after week, touching them where no one else ever did. I turned away from him and reached in to wipe up the fluid with my fingers. I could feel his eyes burning into my side. I could no longer look into the doctor's eyes with the old thrill of anticipation. I could no longer match him stare for stare. I suddenly realized that it didn't matter if I never saw him again.

I loaded up the slide with the familiar sticky liquid, but then saw with surprise that there was a curly hair mixed in. I felt around with my fingers and realized that I hadn't even noticed that there was hair growing between my legs. Where had it come from!

I put the wet slide on Dr Doctor's palm. He placed the second slide on top of the first, wrapped the two in tissue paper, tossed the bundle into his bag and snapped it shut. The envelope with his payment remained pinned to the cork board.

'You don't have to come back here anymore,' I murmured.

The doctor turned sharply at my words. His eyes were wide with anger.

'What exactly do you mean? Does your mother know what you've decided?'

'It's my mother who doesn't want you here.' I shrugged. 'She has another plan for me.'

The doctor smoothed his hair back and snarled. He pulled his payment off the cork board and tore the envelope in half.

'Ungrateful ignorant women,' he muttered hatefully. 'You won't get rid of me so easily.' Dr Doctor marched out of the house.

I ran to the window that overlooked the spot where Ramdass was parked. The doctor hailed a taxi on the street, and Ramdass slowly pulled out behind him. The chase was on! I crossed my fingers tightly and wished the driver best of luck.

All that evening I thought about Ramdass. We would get married, but he would surely want me to complete my schooling. Perhaps he could continue as a driver for a few more years, or perhaps there was a good school in the village where he lived.

If Ramdass's house was small, then he would have little furniture. Ramdass, his mother, his children and I would all sit cross-legged on the ground and eat out of metal plates. What kind of food did he like? He probably loved chilies, and I would have to learn to like them as well.

Would his mother choose to change my name, giving me a new identity as the lucky young bride? Would she lock our bedroom door from the outside for our first night as was common with a newly married couple?

I saw myself lying on the bed next to Ramdass, both of us buried under mounds of nuptial flowers. From the corner of my eye I saw that Ramdass was afraid. I heard him excusing himself for not touching me. After his wife's death he had made a vow before god that he would never touch another woman again. I heard myself telling Ramdass not to worry, I already knew how to touch myself and didn't need him for any of that. I saw Ramdass relax at those words and put his palms together in gratitude. I teased him that he could watch me if he wanted, and he laughed with delight. I heard him say that he always knew that Baby was a clever girl.

It was close to dinnertime. Perhaps the doctor was out for a stroll or visiting friends for a meal. Ramdass would make his move, enter the doctor's house and search out the medical bag. He would carefully pull out the contents one by one, puzzling over each one of them as he had no familiarity with a doctor's tools. Out would come the stethoscope, prescription pad, cotton wool, syringes, face masks, gloves. Stuffed in the middle would be empty sweet wrappers, calling cards, pens, pencils, notebooks. And there to one side would be the slim package of glass slides wrapped in tissues.

Ramdass would think about this. The other items in the bag were solid, functional. This item was wrapped. It was different. He would unroll the tissue and pull out the slide. He would see the smear of liquid, but not feel any wetness on the top or bottom. Turning the slides on their side would reveal that there were two joined together. Ramdass would carefully slide a nail between the slides and pry them apart. There would be a soft sucking noise as the slides came clear of each other.

Ramdass would stare at the bottom slide cautiously, then bring it to his nose. He would smell my fluid and gasp. He would recognize the smell as belonging to me. It would take a while for him to understand that he was now under my spell. But then he would draw in my aroma once again and declare his love for me.

There was a sudden banging on my bedroom door.

'Get up, come out, the doctor is here!' shouted my mother. I jumped off my bed and unlocked the room door with shaking hands. I pulled the door open. Ramdass stood sobbing in front of me, utterly defeated. I screamed and withdrew into my room. Dr Doctor gave a grim smile and stepped in after me. My mother followed him in, her eyes flashing with rage.

Dr Doctor walked up and down the room, lost in thought.

'Sit, sit,' he told my mother and me. We sat on the bed. Dr Doctor pulled Ramdass into the room and pressed him down to the floor until he collapsed cross-legged. Dr Doctor wiped his hands on his jacket and cleared his throat.

'I encountered this man in my house. I asked him who he was and what he wanted. I shouted at him to get out, but he gave no response. He had spread all the contents of my medical bag onto a table and was standing over the mess crying wretchedly. In his hand was the fluid sample I had collected in this very house a few hours earlier.'

Dr Doctor paused, and looked at me. I looked back at him, trying to ascertain how much he really knew. My mother couldn't believe what she was hearing.

'Ramdass broke into your house? But he would never do such a thing. He doesn't even know where you live!' The doctor ignored her interruption.

'I took this wretch aside and I asked him what the devil he thought he was doing. He started babbling about someone named Baby. He said he had to find her a good husband, that he couldn't marry her, he just couldn't do it, he kept babbling about not doing it.'

Ramdass had given me away!

My face burned with horror. I looked at the driver, willing him to lift his head and deny everything, but of course Ramdass didn't understand any English.

'When I asked him why the devil he was in tears, he pointed to the specimen slide, which has, of all things, a pubic hair on it. He said that he couldn't live with himself now that he had seen Baby's nakedness. Imagine, a grown man crying over a pubic hair!'

My mother stood up unsteadily and tried to form some words but her mouth wouldn't obey. She walked to the window and leaned her ashen face on the glass. The doctor looked at her witheringly and continued.

'I figured out that this chap was your driver and that Baby is none other than your specimen daughter. I realized that some plan involving marriage is obviously afoot, against my better recommendations. I can see however that you don't have any great ambitions if you're going to marry her off to this...this driver!'

At the word 'driver', Ramdass looked up. He looked directly at me with his kind eyes and spoke sadly.

'Baby, I cannot make you happy in this world. I am a poor man who knows nothing. But this Doctor sahib, he is a good man who can treat you with honor. Why not let him take care of you? He has a big house, a good job and no wife. How could I ever compare with him. I am a man and I know how men are; he will make a better husband for you.'

'Ramdass!' my mother screamed out his name and looked at him in amazement. I covered my ears, anticipating a torrent of rage directed at the driver. But my mother was speechless with a different emotion: gratitude. Her lips quivered hopefully and her eyes brimmed with joy. She turned to Dr Doctor.

'Doctor...' She groaned, her hands forming question marks in the air. 'Could it be true?'

My mother bit her tongue as soon as the words came out, but she willed herself to continue.

'Would you really marry my daughter? Can god in heaven be so kind?'

Dr Doctor looked at me triumphantly from the corner of his eye. He opened his arms expansively and then joined his hands in humble prayer.

'I took an oath as a physician. It is my duty to heal. Where I cannot change the ways of nature in mending your daughter's body, at least I can offer my humble self as husband and protector of her womanhood.'

I could not believe what was being said in front of me. My mind was playing tricks on me.

The driver spoke with my mother's voice.

'Oh doctor,' he gushed, 'god will bless you for accepting this deformed girl as your wife.'

The doctor spoke with my mother's voice.

'She should consider herself lucky. She may be too tall, but after all she isn't a *blackie*.'

My mother spoke with the driver's voice.

'A husband for Baby! It is very good. We must buy sweets to welcome him into our home.'

My head rang like a vibrating metal gong. My skin crawled as though covered with ants. My face burned as though too close to a fire.

My mother swayed back and forth while crying with relief, squeezing the doctor's palm with one hand and brushing off the driver's uniform with the other. She told Ramdass how time after time she had defended him to her husband, insisting that the driver be maintained in their employ as he was such a trustworthy fellow. She told Dr Doctor how she had sensed right from the beginning when given his name that he was the man for her daughter.

My limbs suddenly itched. My skin felt like it was stretching. My body was going to reach farther away from the people of the world and grow taller right there and then, even though I was already bigger than everyone I knew. They called me jumbo and demon, giant and mutant. I was not one of them! I was not one of them and I never had to be.

'Stop!' I screamed at my limbs and at my mother.

'Stop it now!' I cried to my bones and to the driver.

'Don't you dare do it,' I spat vehemently at my body and at the doctor.

I felt the pressure ease in my joints and a relaxing of my skin. 'None of you can decide for me. None of you. I know what I am. Not you.'

I felt the tautness release in my bones and a slackening in my flesh. 'I am not an animal. I do not belong to you. I am not a slave. I am not scared of you.'

I felt a warm glow light up my body and a cool breeze fan my brain.

'Don't you understand that I'm bigger than all of you? Get out of here. Get out at once. Get out!'

I knew right then without a doubt that my body would no longer grow.

ON CREATING CONFIDENCE IN THE GIRL

Kama Sutra

For the first three days after marriage, the girl and her husband should sleep on the floor, abstain from sexual pleasures, and eat their food without seasoning it either with alkali or salt. For the next seven days they should bathe amidst the sounds of musical instruments, should dress well, dine together, and pay attention to their relations as well as to those who may have come to witness their marriage. This is applicable to persons of all castes. On the night of the tenth day, when they are alone, the man should begin to speak to her with soft words, and thus create confidence in the girl. Some authors say that for the purpose of winning her over he should not speak to her for three days, but the followers of Babhravya are of the opinion that if the man does not speak to her for three days, the girl may be discouraged by seeing him spiritless like a pillar, and, becoming dejected, she may begin to despise him as a eunuch. Vatsyayana says that the man should begin to win her over, and to create confidence in her, but should abstain at first from sexual pleasures. Women being of a tender nature, want tender beginnings, and when they are forcibly approached by men with whom they are but slightly acquainted, they sometimes become haters of the sexual connection, and sometimes even haters of the male sex. The man should therefore approach the girl according to her liking, and should make use of those devices by which he may be able to establish himself more and more into her confidence. These devices are as follows: He should embrace the upper part of her body, because that is easier and simpler. If the girl is grown up, or if the man has known her for some time, he may embrace her by the light of a lamp, but if he is not well acquainted with her, or if she is a young girl, he should then embrace her in darkness.

When the girl accepts the embrace, the man should put a 'tambula' or screw of betel nut and betel leaves in her mouth, and if she will not take it, he should induce her to do so by conciliatory words, entreaties, oaths, and kneeling at her feet, for it is a universal rule that however bashful or angry a woman may be, she never disregards a man kneeling at her feet. At the time of giving this 'tambula', he should kiss her mouth softly and gracefully without making any sound. When he has won her over he should get her to talk, and so that she may be induced to talk he should ask her questions about things of which he knows or pretends to know nothing, and which can be answered in a few words. If she does not speak to him, he should not frighten her, but should ask her the same thing again and again in a soothing manner. If she does not then speak he should urge her to give a reply, because as Ghotamukha says, 'All girls hear everything said to them by men, but who do not themselves sometimes say a single word.' When she is thus urged, the girl should reply by shaking her head, although if she has quarrelled with the man, she should not even do that.

When she is asked by the man whether she wishes for him, and whether she likes him, she should remain silent for a long time, and when at last importuned to reply, should give a favourable answer by a nod of her head. If the man is previously acquainted with the girl, he should converse with her by means of a female friend, who may be favourable to him, and in the confidence of both, and carry on the conversation on both sides. On such an occasion the girl should smile with her head bent down, and if the female friend says more on her part than she was desired to do, she should chide her and dispute with her. The female friend should say in jest even what she is not desired to say by the girl, and add, 'she says so', on which the girl should say indistinctly and prettily, 'Oh no! I did not say so', and she should then smile and throw an occasional glance towards the man.

If the girl is familiar with the man, she should place near him, without saying anything, the tambula, the ointment, or the garland that he may have asked for, or she may tie them up in his upper garment. While she is engaged in this, the man should touch her breasts in the sounding way of pressing with the nails, and if she prevents him doing this he should say to her, 'I will not do it again if you will embrace me,' and should in this way cause her to embrace him, While he is being embraced by her he should pass his hand repeatedly over and about her body. By and by he should place her in his lap, and try more and more to gain her consent, and if she stops him he should threaten her by saying, 'I shall impress marks of my teeth and nails on your lips and breasts, and then make similar marks on my own body, and I will tell the story that it was you who did it. What will you say then?' In this and other ways, as fear and confidence are created in the minds of children, so should the man gain her over to his wishes.

On the second and third nights, after she is more trusting of him, he should caress her entire body, and kiss her all over; he should also place his hands upon her thighs and if he succeeds in this he should then shampoo the joints of her thighs. If she tries to prevent him doing this he should say to her, 'What harm is there in doing it?' and should persuade her to let him do it. After gaining this point he should touch her hidden parts, should loosen her girdle and the knot of her dress, and turning up her lower garment should touch her gently where her naked thighs join her torso, but he should not at that break his vow and begin having sex. After this he should teach her the sixty-four arts, should tell her how much he loves her, and describe to her the hopes which he formerly entertained regarding her. He should also promise to be faithful to her in future, and should dispel all her fears with respect to rival women, and, at last, when she is no longer a virgin, he should begin to make advances to her in a way that doesn't frighten her. That is how one creates confidence in the girl. There are, moreover, some verses on the subject:

A man acting according to the inclination of a girl
should try and gain her over so that she may love him
and place her confidence in him.
A man does not succeed either by implicitly following
the inclination of a girl, or by wholly opposing her,
and he should therefore adopt a middle course.
He who knows how to make himself beloved by women,
as well as to increase their honour and
create confidence in them, this man
becomes an object of their love.
But he, who neglects a girl
thinking she is too bashful,
is despised by her as a beast
ignorant of the working of the female mind.
Moreover, a girl forcibly enjoyed by one
who does not understand the hearts of girls
becomes nervous, uneasy, and dejected, and suddenly
begins to hate the man who has taken advantage of her.
When her love is not understood or returned,
she sinks into despondency, and becomes
either a hater of all men, or, hating her own man,
she has recourse in other men.

MIRA YAGNIK NI DIARY

Bindu Bhatt

6 JANUARY

At seven in the morning, I was in the warden's service...she herself was in the Lord's service...absolutely 'up-to-date'...the hairdye, lotion and lipstick and impeccably ironed and starched sari, peeping through all this were fifty years spent in solitude...

My heart went out to the warden who seemed to be making desperate attempts to put back the clock. I was surprised though that her love for colour had not disappeared!

The warden is friendly with all the gods, but she is particularly close to Saibaba, who is like a family friend. Every Thursday, without fail, there is a *bhajan* at the hostel. The girls attend the *bhajan* to curry favour with the warden. I could not have managed that. Instead I plucked all kinds of flowers from the Botanical Garden behind the hostel, carried a neat bunch as an offering to the warden and began the saga of Vrinda:

'Madam, she is my friend. She is doing her M.A. at the moment. She used to live with her brother here, but last month the brother got transferred to Rajkot. Poor thing, she still has two more months to go before her examination. If you would allow her to be my guest, I'd be awfully obliged to you, always...' etc. etc.

To tell you the truth, I have made a positive impression upon the warden, so there was no hitch. But madam still retained the divine weapon 'If there is an order from above, she will have to leave immediately. And also, she cannot have a separate room of her own. She will have to make an advance payment for one month's guest-charge and mess-bill. With today's girls, one can never tell. Eat, drink and abscond! She will have to follow hostel rules regarding visitors and outings. Do inform your friend, I am very strict. And yes, *No boyfriend business I...*'

So much for your rules...on the one hand she prevents you from cooking in the room and on the other she lands up in Usha's room to eat pudding!

For Vrinda's sake, I had to swallow my anger, but what kind of person is she! Paints all with the same brush...I felt so small...as if I had been publicly undressed!

Now I understand why Ruchi's wheat-complexioned face so often looks withered and wilted! How can that girl be cheerful and exuberant in a house where she has to constantly breathe an air of suspicion and surveillance? That shuttered look on her face is in fact her pent-up anger. The warden ruined my morning and this heartless Vrindadi my evening. I waited for her all of this evening. Our lady calls up at nine—I'll come tomorrow morning, she says. *Bhai* and *bhabhi* have gone to see a film, and have left Bunty with her; but what about this Mira who remained hungry waiting for you!

7 JANUARY

It's 11.30 in the evening. Vrinda is sleeping in my room, on my bed and yet I can't believe that she's actually here! We have often wanted to live together, and it has finally happened

When she came this morning, she said, 'I have come to a student for *guidance*.' I retorted, 'Am I still only a student to you?' She didn't say anything. Quietly she held my hand. Vrinda looks worried, rather sad but I don't want to ask any questions. She'll tell me on her own. No point in probing. I may get some response, but not the truth.

8 JANUARY

This was the first time that I slept with someone other than my mother. Sleeping with mother, I would rest my hand on her stomach and she would turn away in disapproval. But did I ever listen to her, stubborn that I am!

I did the same thing again last night when out of habit, I put my hand on Vrinda's stomach. She immediately hugged me. For a moment I didn't know how to react! The body found itself in a strange state of confusion. When she saw my confusion, she gently disentangled herself. Was she offended?

9 JANUARY

I had expected Vrinda's presence to fill my days with joy. I thought we'd read poetry, talk about books...every evening return together from the library and walk towards the hostel. We would walk by the path that has dark, shady trees...admire the flowers on that ancient tree in the compound, feel the scarlet rays of the setting sun, drink in the joy of lovers...I had thought we'd wait for the shirish flowers to bloom by our windows, but...

But this Vrinda is lifeless. I asked her this morning if she wanted to come along to the library, but she refused. I was taken aback. The library had been her constant haven in school. When I returned that evening, I found her sitting in a chair with a book lying on the table in front of her and her eyes staring at nothing. She hadn't even realized that I had come in. Before I could steal up to her and surprise her, someone yelled out for me from no. 38. It was Ujjwala and she is maddening. She makes constant demands on me: this time she asked me to fasten her bra clasp. She was getting ready for her boyfriend and cursing the servant woman in the process. Initially I used to feel inhibited, but how many times she must have dragged me to the bathroom to soap her back... 'What is this? This is as bad as those village women who bathe by wells and rivers,' I would say and she would retort 'Absolutely, that's the way it should be. If I had my way, I would campaign for nudism. We sacrifice health and beauty at the altar of clothes.'

Ujjwala is quite right. By constantly covering it with clothes, we are unable to think of a woman's body in 'normal' terms.

In a short while the clock will show a new day.

Vrinda is asleep on the bed. Her hand seeking me lies next to her. How much I asked her to eat this evening but she just wouldn't listen. I swallowed a few morsels myself to avoid acidity and entered the room to find that *deviji* had spread her sari on the floor and was sleeping on it! It's so cold, you can hardly put a bare foot on the floor and look at her! I was about to lose my head, but I then I suddenly remembered that yesterday I had asked her not to bother with a mattress.

Very gently I lay down beside her and turned her face towards me. She submitted her body to me. Though her eyes were closed, she was not asleep. I gently ran my fingers through her hair. After a while, with a mischievous grin, she said, 'That feels nice.' Wicked! I was about to get up but she caught my hand and brought me down onto her body. She kissed my earlobe and quickly got up saying, 'Come, let's go to sleep.'

10 JANUARY

There are many things I accept (I think), but not the misuse of my name. Today I realized that there are alternative ways of using a research cabin in a library! For the last few days I'd had a feeling that my cabin in the library was being misused in my absence. I constantly felt some one else's presence there. This afternoon at three when I went to the library I found the remains of salted nuts, blown-out ends of matchsticks and smoke in the air in my cabin. So when I am not around from twelve to three every day... I went straight to the librarian who did not seem in the least bit surprised. With an indifferent air he said, 'Give it in writing. We will investigate.'

In the mess this evening, when I was talking about this to Vrinda, Usha from the opposite table intervened, 'Ever since Adarsh Hotel, the solitary restaurant in the university area has been under repair, many student-lovers have taken the library peon into confidence.' But how does Usha know that?

Ujjwala laughed, 'Did your boyfriend also...'

Usha was infuriated. She snapped, 'Of course not, love is not a clandestine matter in Germany. In any case, if peons can sit on stacks of books and smoke *bidis*, librarians can manipulate the purchase of books, students can tear off pages, is it surprising that that a library turns into a restaurant or a hotel?'

Usha is a very committed research student of philosophy. Her involvement with Indian philosophy is so deep that she even changed her name and Indianized herself completely. Coming from a different country, culture and society, there are things that Usha notices that we don't. I felt bad about suspecting her. *I am really sorry, Usha.*

11 JANUARY

It was my illusion that Vrinda and I were close friends. She suffered such pain and I did not have the faintest notion of it! Why didn't she tell me? Did she feel so vulnerable talking about her misery or was she protecting me from her sorrow?

When I returned from the library this evening, the warden gave me two letters. A brown envelope with Vrinda Parekh written on top and another, an inland letter from Mummy. Mummy and the folks arrive tomorrow morning at the Sabarmati Ashram. I hurriedly climbed the stairs and practically ran to the room only to find Vrinda dead to the world. My spirits climbed down a little and I said, 'Here, letter for you.' She sat up immediately, but froze on seeing the brown envelope. Almost out of a sense of duty, she read its contents and put it away. As I was going into the bathroom to change, I asked her, 'What is it?' She put the letter in my hand and left.

Vrinda has resigned! She didn't even tell me? Did something happen in the school? I came out of the room looking for her. She was nowhere to be found. Was she in the balcony or in the bathroom then? I turned around to check if she was on the terrace. She stood out there staring out into the void. I went up close to her and put my hand on her shoulder. She fled to the room, put her head on the table and began sobbing violently. It seemed as if her tears, frozen for years, had now begun to flow. I let her cry. After a while I gave her water. She washed her face and said, 'Come, let's walk to the university.'

On the way there she began to talk about everything.

When she was in the tenth standard, Kamani Saheb had just joined as the principal of the school. He taught mathematics very well. Vrinda was always interested in math and she used to visit his house for math lessons. She followed Kamani Saheb's advice and acquired a diploma in tailoring in order to join the school as a teacher. Apart from tailoring, she also taught languages and mathematics. When I came into the eighth standard, Vrinda had been teaching for two years.

Later, she took training as a junior in the National Cadet Corps. School became her central focus because she loved Kamani Saheb. He was married but his wife was at her mother's house, because Kamani Saheb's widowed sister stayed with him. The husband and wife must have lived together for barely a year or two. They have a daughter. His wife also taught in some school, away from the town. Saheb had to make a difficult choice between his widowed sister on the one hand and his wife and daughter on the other. Because of his feelings for Vrinda, he made no attempt to either seek divorce from his wife or to reconcile with her.

I couldn't understand why the two of them didn't marry even though they loved each other. Vrinda's reply to this was, 'Marriage can happen only if Saheb is divorced. This means I can become a wife only after depriving another woman of her rights, not to mention their daughter. I cannot commit that sin, as a woman, I simply can't. As to what it is to be an abandoned and single mother, ask your own mother about it!'

Vrinda, you've touched a raw nerve!

We were out of breath by the time we came to the room, weighed down by a huge baggage of silence.

When she seemed somewhat better, I asked her, 'But why did you resign? Didn't Kamani Saheb stop you?'

'He gave in his own resignation three months ago.' She gave a letter to me:

Vrinda,
I looked for ways of addressing you all these years, but you weren't helpful. I am leaving now, taking voluntary retirement. There's my brother's motel in London I'll help him in his business.

I can't help saying something at the end. There is a lot you gave up to safeguard a woman's rights, but only after inflicting pain upon me. You have Mira as your support. But I? I will try to find happiness in my relationship with my wife and daughter; but what about that which I didn't get from you...?

I looked up from the letter to find that Vrinda was not in the room. Why does this letter mention me?

12 JANUARY

I have been in Ahmedabad for so many years and yet I saw the Sabarmati Ashram only today. At eight in the morning Vrinda and I went there with a flask of masala tea for Mummy.

I saw the visuals and heard Umashankar Joshi's 'Pankhilok'. The old and wise *asopalavs* stood steadfast preserving Gandhi from harm and crowning them was a concert of birds! For a moment it felt as if it was the sound of the trees themselves, in varied tones.

We had reached very early, carried away by our excitement. Mummy's bus was scheduled to get there around nine. Vrinda and I walked about lazily and sat on the Sabarmati ghat exactly behind the ashram. How does one speak of the Sabarmati river? Its stagnant, black waters sadly mirror the pale and partial reflection of the surroundings. I was reminded of the Ganga in Banaras.

It's been four years now, but the memory of that sight remains vivid. Somewhat away from the point where the Ganga and the Varuna meet, a canal drains the city's filth into the Ganga. Farther away, towards the Aadikeshav ghat, the unmoving waters of the Ganga reflect the Aadikeshav temple, its dome, the *kalash,* the entire canopy, the steps leading to the ghat and little children on those steps as they fly kites. A white goat nosing about here and there. All this while our boat was moving towards some subterranean land. A slight gust of breeze and the king's palace seemed to sway on the waves...at times, everything got submerged and on the surface of the water were left little snakes that looked like the remains of the sinking palace. Like Ganga, this Sabarmati lies with a faded blue cover on her!

'*Eh ben,* you are not allowed to sit on the ghat.' The watchman drove us out. The sight of two girls sitting quietly by themselves must have seemed strange to him. I was about to say something to Vrinda, just then the chorus of a bhajan fell on our ears. '*Vaishnavjan to tene re...*' That must be Mummy's bus. I ran towards it. When I saw Mummy get off the bus, my ears began to resound with Vrinda's words, 'As to what it is to be an abandoned single mother, ask your own mother...'

A plain sari, light pink in colour, and a big red bindi on her forehead, a thick knot of hair tied behind her neck and a smile on her face...it seemed as if I was looking at her for the first time. The pink of her cheeks matched the pink of her sari! I found myself standing in soft, sweet sunlight...

'How's my precious Mira?' I fell into her arms. Her voice sounded different. I said to myself, 'Ma, I'll take away all unhappiness from you.' But her loneliness?

Budhiya came to my rescue. He is mummy's favourite student. He handed over a bag of berries to me and said, 'Eh Miraben, take this, my Ba asked me to give this to ben's daughter.'

On the way back Vrinda, trying to cheer me up said, 'You have just been to see your mother at Christmas.'

'Vrinda, do you also have to measure time with a calendar!!'

14 JANUARY

Vrinda went home today. I was also invited by her brother for an *undhiya* party. But I have to show my advisor the first draft of a chapter on the seventeenth. Two years are over and I have only now started to write! I have cast my net so wide, how am I ever going to finish? Hindi fiction from 1936 to 1980, how many novels can I possibly look at? If only I could work on a subject of my choice!

I have been living in a hostel for so many years but the room seems so deserted today. Within a week, I have become used to Vrinda's presence. Even this bed suddenly looks too huge for me, it's massive.

20 JANUARY

Yesterday something else was added...I think...to my relationship with Vrinda.

I waited for her the whole day. Finally I got fed up and got out of bed at four. My head was pounding. I thought of taking a shower. The geyser had been repaired in the afternoon. This bath in the evening reminded me of Ujjwala who always bathed at this time. She would then get ready and go out. Shubhangi had mentioned that these days she had become friendly with a sardar from the I.I.M. Who was I getting ready for, I asked myself as I shut the bathroom door.

When Vrinda arrived in the evening, I was sitting in a chair trying to read. Dripping long hair that fell well below the waist and my favourite silk sari—parrot green with a border of turmeric yellow—which belonged to Mummy. All an overdone affair to make one feel cheerful.

With her arrival her fragrance pervaded the entire room. It reminded me of shirish flowers. I recognized her footsteps but I refused to turn my face. She gently touched my hair. 'Look, the sun is weaving strings of gold into your hair,' she said. I did not move. She rested her chin on my shoulders, 'Do you remember, when we went on a school trip to Rajasthan? There were so many mustard fields on the way. You look exactly like that just now. A mustard field swaying in the silky light of a sinking sun...' The movement of her lips as she spoke, the tremor in her voice stirred something in my shoulders, below my ears and all the way inside my cheeks. Somebody was stoking the embers.

I got up to leave, she blocked my way. She gripped my shoulders and forced me to meet her eyes. There was a smile on her face. I found myself drowning in the dimple of her cheek. When she made me sit on the bed, or when she put her head on my lap, or covered our faces with our hair... I really don't know. My unrestrained eyes gazed at her fixed eyes in the hazy light of the evening. With her arm around my neck, she pulled me closer to her face and said, 'Do you remember Bhuvan's Abhilasha from *Nadi ke Dweep?*' I found myself saying,

The thick fragrance of whose hair does engulf me
My heart says let me call that one my own.

Involuntarily my fingers began to trace her face. Her shapely eyebrows, long eyelashes covering her large eyes, pointed nose and full lips... I bent to kiss her lips when she suddenly dodged and kissed my breasts. Her arms encircled my waist. My hands grew heavy. Something stirred and rose from the deep hollow below the waist. Eyelids drooped. Her warm breath moved away from my neck and made my entire body tremble. I fell on her. I kissed her neck, ears, breasts...and heard her say,
'I love Mira'
What about K. M. then?
Didn't he say that you are my support and anyway he is not here! Mira only in the absence of K. M. ... Rising tides began to ebb away. Did Vrinda accept me only in the absence of K. M.? But if that were so why would my body echo her own feelings?

31 JANUARY
Vrinda not around

◆

29 MARCH
The tower clock at the Agricultural Market struck eight as the S. T. bus reached the Jamalpur crossroads. After this, the river! What kind of feeling is this for the Sabarmati, when I know only too well that this river exists only in name. Yet it feels good to sit on its banks, and imagine, however momentarily, its flow...never mind if occasionally circus tents are pitched on its bed or if the Sunday market is set up there or on some days you find elephants from the Jagannath Temple bathing alongside half-naked boys in dirty puddles of water. The smoke from the *samshaan* swirling upward, its smell merging with that of rubbish burning on the

banks. Trucks leaving behind them tracks where donkeys kick up dust, or the flash of intermittent green vegetable patches.

You can hardly ever see the river itself, and yet it reminded me of the Utavali of Navanagar... In the last trip I made during Holi, the sight of a turtle basking in the sun on the causeway with its glistening back and eager, craning neck made me wonder if it was waiting for the sun to descend upon the earth. Its keen look brought thoughts of Vrinda. All through the journey, someone had been singing softly inside me. I had thought this relationship would make our individual selves complete, but now? No, I need to rethink this. After all, there's Mummy's dream. She has been calling me 'Doctor Mira' ever since I was in the fourth standard! That's all there is to her expectations of me. The rest comes later. Study I must. Am I not accountable to her for the opportunities she's given me?

1 JUNE

I feel I should go back to Navanagar. I don't want to participate in the workshop. First of all there is a constant feeling of rancour and then a deserted hostel. During the vacation the hostel looks like a tree in autumn. Girls from the two-seaters below vacate their rooms and go away, only a few research students, confined like me, are left behind! On such days none of the refectories is open.

Slow-moving and drab summer days... The hot breeze of Vaishakh loiters about in the empty corridors...doors left open at some places keep banging...the afternoon, ash-grey like the pigeons sitting on the fence—its presence makes those few green branches in the garden across look so wretched! Arid and colourless...everything has a scalding effect on me...!

—*Translated from the Gujarati by Rita Kothari*

The Parrots of Desire

A BAD CHARACTER

Deepti Kapoor

A few days later we're driving from CP around India Gate. I am holding an empty Coke can between my legs. He looks at it and says, Can I get that for you? Can I throw it away? And I say, No, it's okay. I like something between my legs.

Pointedly. A calculated phrase. He looks at me. This is all it takes.

All the marriage meetings I ever had ended in the same rejection. What they never understood was that I had rejected them long before they saw my face.

The first boy was from a middle-class family much like my own. He had a steady job as an engineer. Aspirational, shining with belief, with the ambition to go to the States himself. He had learned his role by rote. We met in the Defence Colony Barista in the March of my first Delhi year. I had no car then. Aunty escorted me, waiting in the back seat like a pimp while her driver ate chaat in the market outside. She made me wear a kurta and jeans, to be both modern and traditional at once.

He was already waiting for me inside. He had his laptop open at the low table. I recognized him from the photo in the resume that had been sent, that had just been thrust beneath my nose, and he looked up and recognized me in turn. Aunty had sent a photograph of me, taken at a studio set up at one of the wedding functions we'd attended. In a sari, a little tipsy, in the glare of the artificial light, with a posed, enforced smile, the photo stripped me of my life.

I remember very clearly the pen he kept in the top pocket of his shirt, also the new glasses he wore. They were designer, he proudly said. But his face I don't recall, his was like the million others I saw. He was simply his glasses and his pen and the starched white shirt. He talked to me from the start about the importance of family, about his mother, what his mother thought about things. My mother says, he said many times, and he listed what they looked for in a girl. I sat across from him silent, sullen, angry with myself because I had agreed to be there at all. He said he wanted a girl who was homely, respectful, but educated of course, able to have her own opinions. But she must be respectful to his mother above all else. They must get on or there'd be no point. I felt quite sick at the mechanics of it. But Aunty had told me again and again, Marriage is not about love, when will you understand this? Love is a luxury that doesn't exist in the real world.

I asked him drily if it wouldn't be better for me to meet his mother alone. Without a flicker of understanding he said no.

When it came it was one of those polite rejections, where his mother tells Aunty that he's found someone else absolutely perfect that very same day, what timing, what coincidence. What to do? Aunty smiles, What to do. But she's kicking herself. What did you say? You don't know how to talk to people, to show yourself in the best light, you don't stand up straight, you don't smile.

The next boy was from a south Delhi business family, the only son and heir, twenty-six years old. We met in another coffee shop, all around us you could spy these marriage meetings taking place. This boy was more arrogant, wealthy, dressed in a designer shirt, he wore his fat with pride, was well groomed, his pouting lips protruding from his face, his eyes heavy lidded, stirring his tea very slow. Well-manicured fingers perched on the table like exotic birds. There was something in his manner that spoke of cruelty to me. He talked at length, about his Hyundai, his plan to replace it with a Mercedes before the year was out. And all the while he eyed me with a measure of disdain. Why he ever agreed to meet me in the first place I'll never know. But Aunty was punching above her weight, saying, Nothing succeeds like success.

◆

We make love on the first of May, Labour Day. A day for the workers.

His apartment is being painted, it's full of them but he sends them home, tries to explain the concept of it as he does, this day to honour the working people of the world, but it's lost on them completely, everything about it is lost. They down tools and go anyway.

He says, Go home, get drunk, make love to your wives. They look at me as they go.

He waited until they arrived to tell them they were free, until they'd begun to work, to make it worthwhile, to see their reaction. Because theatre was important. But we'd planned this. I'd told him I wanted to know what it was like, I was ready, I wanted it to be him.

◆

We've been drinking since the workers left. Drinking to remove the awkwardness in me.

Most of the other rooms have been finished, already painted in purple, black, red or ink-blue. But in the bedroom the walls are still white.

Everything smells of paint in here. The smell catches in my nostrils, the back of my throat. The AC is on high. Outside it's approaching forty degrees. Beating the earth.

In the kitchen the fridge is well stocked: water, juice, soft drinks, a crate of beer. Several bottles of good whisky in the cupboard. There are cold cuts in the fridge, from the charcuterie in Vasant Vihar, bresaola, serrano, chorizo. He teaches me how to say these words, how to say charcuterie, from the French, obsolete: *char* for flesh, *cuite* for cooked, cooked flesh, flesh that is cooked, which we eat.

He pours a glass of whisky for me, Caol Ila. Teaches me to say that too, tapping the tip of the tongue to the roof of the mouth, mixing it with some drops of clean water, saying, This is the way. In the dhabas the whisky's dirty, you drink it with Coke, with soda, but not this. He rolls it around the glass. It coats the side and falls, like amber for fossils. Smell it, he says, close your eyes. And he raises the glass to my nose. It smells of earth and sea and salt, Bombay without the heat, in the glint of stars and mud and leaves, in woodsmoke sluiced through rain. Now taste it. I take the glass from his hands, bring it up to my lips. It burns as it touches them. He kisses it back from me and delicately, with his hands on my hips, presses himself against me. I feel the hardness of him. I bring the glass up, fill my mouth, kiss him back again. He looks up, almost surprised, like a boy.

Now wait. In the empty bedroom he smokes a cigarette, and I make up the bare mattress with a fresh white sheet. Wait. Now I'm standing before him taking off my clothes, covering myself with my arms.

Wait. He's lowering me down on to my knees, I'm breathing him in, and on my back he's looming over me, with his enormous eyes, like the statue of a dictator waiting to fall.

When it happens it hurts.

And then it doesn't hurt. Pain slips away into the distance of a blizzard, and beyond all that, with eyes closed, chest cracked open, ribcage pulled apart, my heart fills up with the driving snow.

I didn't know what to do afterwards. I lay there still as a corpse in the mortuary sheets, a vacancy of limbs, not daring to move in case it marked an end, but he was a part of me, his ugliness, his black skin. I held it all. Falling in and out of sleep with a pin drop of pain somewhere else.

He's in the bathroom now. He's come back with a cigarette and he's lying next to me. He's hard again. He puts the cigarette to my lips, holds my eyes, opens my legs, with his hand guides himself in.

◆

Seeming to wake from nowhere suddenly, from the cold. I ask for a blanket. Instead he switches off the AC.

Little by little Delhi encroaches. You can hear it. You can see the thin sliver of sunlight on the frame of the window, fading to dusk. Slowly you make out the noise of children laughing and playing in the lane behind, pans being washed there and traffic beyond.

The bathroom has retained the day's heat. The air is so thick in here you can swim in it. In the shower we stand and he washes me, his body behind mine, his hand on my belly where my heart beats, he brings it down, puts one hand around my throat, one inside. I move away, I sit at the side to watch him. There's muscle around his bones, not a shred of fat on him, and there are scars across his back that I see. We go back into the room to sleep.

◆

When I wake again it is night, the room has been filled with it, the headlights of cars shift along the fabric of the curtain, rise up the wall and are gone. The whisky bottle is half-empty. He's not here with me.

I find him in the dark of the balcony, crouching naked, one hand against the bamboo, his head tilted, listening. He turns towards me, puts his finger to his lips.

Shhh, he says. Listen.

In the dargah of Nizamuddin the qawwalis are playing. Do you hear them? Let's go before it's too late.

◆

His same sense of theatre demands we wear the right clothes. He unlocks a cupboard inside, tells me to look through it, pick out something to wear. It's full of discarded items, from family, cousins, his mother, old girlfriends maybe. His parents lived here before, left many things behind. I find a salwar-kameez, he takes out a long white kurta for himself from his own wardrobe, and in it he becomes dignified, sober, seeming older. And me, I watch myself in the mirror, covering my head with the dupatta, wrapping it around my forehead, behind my ears, around my neck, to frame my face, and I become Persian, dark-eyed, pious, transformed.

We laugh in the mirror and he holds me, touches my face, tucks my hair away.

He sits to crumble charas into a mixing bowl. I watch in fascination. Do you want to try? You'll like it, he says. He says it comes from the mountains, a deep rich scent from Parvati Valley, he'll take me there one day. Here, smell it. He holds it to my nose. Then I watch as he heats it, crumbles it in the bowl, burns the cigarette, adds the tobacco, mixes it reverently, rolls. Lights it, praises Shiva, takes a long drag and hands it over to me. He says to take it all the way in, down to the base of the lungs, hold it there as long as I can.

◆

We left the apartment that night and walked along the streets, walking without touching. Through Nizamuddin in the heat to the dargah, from the smart, clipped neighbourhood into the Muslim streets, where bearded men gathered in white and goats were tethered to butchers' shops. Left at the mosque, down the passageway, the night brighter than the day, eerie in its calligraphic pharmacy, in Urdu glowing green and gold, trimmed by the desert and the certainty of God. Men stood in their shops behind counters, beside TVs showing preachers delivering sermons, voices droning out of loudspeakers, the flutter of rose petals, a butcher's knife.

The crowds were swirling in the narrowing alleyway, the walls closing in at the sides, canopied with cloth, drawing us down lower, almost underground, as if we were being sucked downriver to a grotto. So many bodies there that we were almost lost. He grabbed my hand to keep me close. The threshold of the dargah appeared, medieval. We crossed over.

It is said that the dargah is not only a place on earth, it is also a rupture in space and time, a portal through which the saint can enter this world.

We remove the chappals from our feet, add them to the rising pile. Bump against the mass of bodies, step on the black-and-white marble that like a riverbed has been worn down, smoothed by centuries of pilgrims' feet, its corners like melted wax. Red petals fleck the ground, fluttering on to graves.

Inside, the river of people dissipates; it finds new currents, reaches up into the sky. Pilgrims slow down, scatter, form groups, they find corners for themselves, as if striking camp.

The eight players of the qawwali are sitting in the inner courtyard before the shrine, sitting in two banks of four, lining one side of a rectangle. Devotees and onlookers form the two long edges, thirty or forty of them now, their numbers increasing all the time. Everyone faces inwards to the centre they have made, a void and a well in the middle of the bodies in which the song is amplified. It has been going for an hour now.

The tabla and dholak inducing a trance.

The harmonium guiding the leader's voice.

Handclaps locking the rhythm inside.

The leader is gnomic, bold and erect, his beard hangs down his chest in a point, his eyes crinkle above it in a smile. And his voice, it undulates within the scaffold of his throat, rising to a pure note with his hand held high.

Hypnotized, forgetting ourselves, we take a place at the back of one side, enclosed in the heat, standing at the back of the crowd. We crane our necks to see. At the front they are seated, swaying, hijras among them, their painted eyes rolling around their heads.

In space, beyond the sun and moon, in the depthless universe where the stars can't be seen, there is the saint.

The music grows faster, wilder, careening towards rupture, the crowd grows so that we are pressed against one another by those around, but I can feel him, feel his body next to mine, his hand around my own. As the rhythm builds we are pushed forward until we emerge somehow at the front of the standing group. Here we remain poised on the edge.

We begin to forget ourselves, who we are, our daily lives, for half an hour we remain like this.

Then a miracle happens.

The leader in full song looks up at me, looks me in the eyes, and in the middle of his plaintive cry motions with his hand for us to sit at the front of the crowd.

The crowd parted, it did, the people smiled and moved aside, hands steadied our path, faces beamed at us, bodies rocked themselves possessed.

And now I sat at the front on my heels, fists on knees in the desert heat with the hot wind of Delhi that scours our skin, with faces etched in the rhythm and bound in the love of the saint, my entire being a percussive beat, and even he who has given me this is gone.

I am disappeared. On a plateau of rock, burst into flames.

I fall into a trance. I lose myself. How long I remain like this I can't say, but it feels like hours have passed when I open my eyes. People are looking and smiling. For as long as the music plays the world is mine.

But it wears down, it eases off, exhaustion follows, and the leader seems to avert his gaze.

Without the beat to hold us in place our hearts release themselves like birds up into the night sky. We begin to drift. Electric light falls on the land.

And walking home through the city, listening to its womb-sound, we are conquerors. We don't say another word. Hungry, bereft, slipping through the alleyways, it's only when we get back to his home that the desire returns. It comes with the force of everything we've heard. We do it again right there against the door, without undressing. He lifts me up and holds me against the wall. With sanctity, grief and passion, I bite into his flesh and he puts himself inside me and he bursts.

Aunty thinks I'm sleeping at a classmate's house. When I call her to say goodnight he takes the phone from me and he speaks as my friend's imaginary father, in an assured voice that is casual, measured, having just the right tone. He's such a convincing liar.

◆

It goes on all night, until disintegration. He drinks his whisky and worships me, and I give my body to him, feed my skin, take his dark lips and hold them to me, to the childish fat around my waist, the damp heat between my legs. I let him come to me. With such abandon, such a lack of care. And such indescribable terror too on seeing the daylight appear through the cracks, to find the room becoming visible again, to know dull shapes are real things once more. Lying down at the end of it, upheld in the empty thoughts of what we've done. I'd forgotten the night would ever end.

◆

I woke around eleven. In those few moments of unremembering, of pure animal consciousness unattached to the world, I saw him beside me, felt the pain in my hips, the tearing in me, and the dull tobacco warmth of his breath.

He stirred and rolled closer to me, opened his eyes, and for the briefest moment his face was ungoverned, appearing monstrous. But his pupils dilated, turned cunning, and when he blinked he hid the animal away. Good morning, he said. He reached to light a cigarette and smiled.

We did it again, painfully this time, all too real. In open wounds, every nerve tapped and twisted, with nothing to numb it, I cried out, I cried as a girl, lost in the fields and I held him as he poured himself into me. Like the pressing of a bruise, the pleasure of pain, I love him for this.

He held me in his arms afterwards, held me round my waist, pressed his mouth to the back of my neck, whispered in my ear, caressed me, and he asked me what it was I wanted from the world, what it was I feared. I said I feared everything, and I only wanted to be free. He kissed my forehead, my lips, my throat.

Later I showered, brushed my teeth and got changed. While he made breakfast he coached me on what to say to Aunty. Already we have slipped into a pattern, there are things we don't mention any more, movements that are unquestioned, the shorthand of lovers, things that are understood.

I drive home as if in slow motion, floating above the noise, as if the city parts for me. It's such a sudden switch inside where Aunty is dressed in a fine sari, preparing to go for a kitty party, putting on earrings in the strip-light mirror, filling an envelope with money and chatting away, trying to make me get changed to go along with her, but there's no time, she's already running late.

She leaves me alone. In the silence left behind, inside my room, I close my eyes. In the bathroom I take a shower and revel in the water's heat. I examine my body closely, look for marks and wondrous signs. Then with the ghost of his cock between my legs and Aunty far away, I fall into a deep and turbulent sleep.

THREE VIRGINS

Manjula Padmanabhan

A young cousin once asked me the meaning of the word 'virgin'. I was fourteen at the time, she was ten and we were both attending another cousin's wedding in Bombay.

'It means a lady whose son turns into God,' I said at once. 'What?' she asked, looking confused.

I didn't want to be the one to break the news to her that men did disgusting things to women in order to coax the next generation into being. Or that 'virgin' was the name given to those who had not yet experienced these horrors. As for why a term was needed to describe a condition which was defined by its loss? Well. Nine years in three different Catholic schools in three different countries had still not provided me with an answer to that puzzle.

By the time I graduated two years later, the implausibility of the virgin birth and my own attempts to find explanations obsessed me so much that the merest reference to Christmas caused lurid images to spool through my brain. Hymens made of rhino-hide; lecherous, inseminating angels; white-haired apostles poking their indecent curiosity up a young woman's private parts in order to determine whether or not she was 'pure'.

◆

I engineered my own journey past virginity as a conscious campaign. I couldn't bear to wait, passive as a dandelion seed, for a masculine wind to shake me loose and sweep me away. I wanted to choose rather than be chosen. I wanted to be the captain of my fate.

I was eighteen years old, living with my parents in Bombay. I was in Elphinstone College, with Economics as my major. A casual acquaintance whose name I have forgotten introduced me to her brother, Gai, in the canteen one day. Then she left us alone. She had no idea of my plans.

I studied him. He was an intermediate-year science student, while I was his senior, in the first year of my BA. His skin was the colour of oiled teak and his hair had a curling kink to it, parted on the right, lending an attractive asymmetry to the shape of his head. One of his two front teeth slightly overlapped the other. He wore wire-frame spectacles. He was maybe two inches taller than me and held himself very taut, like a bow tensed to receive an arrow.

There was no one else within hearing of our conversation.

I told him I was interested in finding a one-time-only sexual partner. He shrugged and said 'How about me?'

His face had interesting moulding and shadows, broad at the cheekbones with an angular jaw. His nose was sculpted with a generous hand. As he aged, it would probably become a promontory to be reckoned with, but in youth it had a pleasing earthy quality, like a shapely potato.

His surname was 'Singh' but he was an Indian Protestant, not a Sikh. So there would be no point asking him whether he believed in the Virgin Birth. Or how it came to be that two thousand years of religious doctrine depended upon the intactness of one woman's secret membrane.

We exchanged numbers. I told him I'd find us an appropriate place and time.

It was the home of another friend's aunt, an elderly Parsi lady. The aunt had gone to the hills to escape the pre-monsoon heat and her maid had gone with her, leaving the keys to an apartment filled with Belgian lace and Austrian crystal with Zarine, my friend.

I told Gai there was a time constraint as a result of which promptness was of the essence. Actually there was no time constraint: the aunt and her maid could not possibly return in time to catch us in the act because in those days there was no railway connection to Matheran, the hill station they had gone to. And Zarine had taken the precaution of speaking to her aunt on the phone that very morning in order to confirm that she and the maid were both firmly a day's journey away.

Gai rang the bell at precisely half-past two and that pleased me. I dislike the military and the violence, mayhem and destruction it stands for while nevertheless admiring its reputation for precision. I liked to think that what I was doing was sober and unromantic, conditioned by the ticking gears of well-oiled clocks rather than the unruly urgings of my hormones. I wanted to believe that I was taming the fearsome beast of uncertainty whose jaws gaped wide before me as I stood with one foot on the threshold of my future and the other foot still wearing the fuzzy slippers of my childhood.

I opened the door and led Gai through the gleaming apartment with its marble floors and the frantically barking toy Pomeranian called Shadow who was actually the reason that Zarine had been entrusted with the key to the apartment. Shadow had to be fed and watered during the two-day absence. I had done the needful, then locked him into the kitchen.

I led my visitor to the book-lined study that Zarine and I had designated as the appropriate location for my tryst. It had no windows, but the air-conditioning ducts ensured that we would not die of asphyxiation. There was a cushion-strewn divan that may have been custom-designed for late-afternoon dalliance. There was a lockable door in case of unforeseen emergencies.

I had placed a white bedsheet on the divan and beneath the sheet, a towel. All the literature supported the notion that there *would* be a spilling of bodily fluids even though I expected none.

The atmosphere was inescapably Emergency Room. Zarine had asked if I wanted music, because the aunt had speakers all over the house. I preferred silence, I said. No distractions. I had disconnected the telephone and checked for alarm clocks.

He reached into the pocket of his jeans and brought out a strip of three Government-issue condoms in their jaunty yellow-and-red packets. 'I got these at the railway station,' he said.

I glanced at them, nodding. I had asked him to get them, though I had a packet of my own, in my handbag, as extra insurance. I had been monitoring my monthly cycles and so far as I could determine, there was very little risk of pregnancy on that particular date. I sat down and began undoing the clasps on my sandals. I did not look at him.

'So. You'd like to just get down to it?' he asked.

'Of course,' I said. 'That's why we're here.'

He was wearing a tee shirt over jeans. I didn't watch him undress, but instead concentrated on getting my outer clothes off with a minimum of delay, a blouse and jeans. I had dithered a great deal over which precise blouse to wear, ultimately choosing one that opened down the front, for ease of removal. When I was in my undies, I lay down. I have long curling hair and I arranged it fan-wise across the pillow under my head. Only then did I looked up at him.

He was down to his briefs.

'I think you should lie down now,' I said.

It was, as it always is, a shock to be right up close to another person's face. Perhaps because I am shortsighted, I don't normally notice the pores on someone's skin or the precise pattern of small hairs as they rise along the edge of a temple and merge into a brow. The irises of Gai's eyes were dark and it was only at close quarters that I could see his pupils, fully dilated, like a cat's eyes in dim light. He had showered before coming over and I could smell the shampoo in his hair.

'Is this really your first time?' he asked, his voice breathy.

I had grown up in a highly sociable milieu, surrounded by my family's friends and relatives, my diplomat father's official guests and the army of domestic help, that kept our various official residences well-dusted and polished. I was trained not to let emotions out unless they served a positive function. Smiling was good whether or not it was sincere, whereas crying, screaming or indeed ever raising my voice was not acceptable under any circumstance. When I'm in an unfamiliar situation however, my face becomes an expressionless mask.

'Yes,' I said, in answer to Gai's question. He could have no idea whatsoever that just under the surface of the skin of my face, a hurricane was in progress. Winds of unimaginable speed were whipping through my brain, uprooting houses, trees, cars, trains, whole libraries of books, whole villages of thought. It was like being on several roller coasters at the same instant. An unpleasant sensation about which I could do nothing except wait for it to stop.

Gai removed his briefs with one hand.

He whispered in my ear, 'Have you seen one before?'

His breath had started to splinter into short fragments. I had heard this panting before, the sound that a man makes when he is aroused. It had alarmed me, the first time I heard it, while necking at a college picnic with a friendly but clumsy philosophy major. It was the voice of the body, not the mind and it had unnerved me. I had pushed that boy away after a few seconds, claiming ant bites as the cause.

'Only in museums,' I said.

Gai shifted his weight slightly, so that I could look down.

The sight surprised me. Pornography involving pictures of men was not easily available those days nor had it ever occurred to me to look for it. Even in museums, gods and heroes were all that I had seen, not priapic satyrs encircling Greek drinking cups, not the heaving mountainous members of Japanese sumi-e paintings. In genteel European art, men's sexual parts look soft and harmless, small pink cornets of puff pastry. Even though I knew, from textbook descriptions, that there would be a dramatic change of appearance, my imaginings had only produced smooth featureless cylinders. Surgical instruments rather than living organs with contours, bluntness and mass.

The item I could see now, even without my glasses on, looked rude and insolent, like a one-eyed eel, bouncing and wriggling according to an agenda of its own.

I took my undies off. He put on a condom. Then it was time.

All the accounts I had ever read about the act of sex suggested a vaulting up into another sphere of experience.

What I felt was the polar opposite: an absolute immersion in the here-and-nowness of the vessel of muscle and bone that is a body. There was no pain, no breaking-and-entry struggles, nor anything I would have described as pleasure. Everything I had anticipated was wrong.

That other body had its own urgency, its priorities, its heat, its weight. I was overwhelmed by the extreme otherness of its physical being—I couldn't think of it by a name, a context, or even a gender. Gai became just A Body. My own body threw aside its name and gender and history. It revealed itself as having its own existence, practically unknown to me, distinct from my mind, my thoughts, my feelings.

The tornado-atmosphere inside my brain had snapped off. My eyes were open, I was conscious and curious. It amazed me, for instance, to be pressed right up next to another being, crushed by his weight upon me, smelling the sharp raw scent of his body, hearing the moment of his orgasm, yet knowing nothing of his mind's interior. It was sublimely unavailable to me, just as mine was unavailable to him. It may seem paradoxical that I found this isolation pleasing, but I did. It told me that my mind was my absolute domain, that it could never be invaded or colonized except with my consent. It was a wonderfully liberating realization.

The rest was mundane: washing up, dressing, engaging in small talk, letting Shadow out of the kitchen. Saying goodbye. I did not meet Gai again. I don't know whether he resented the clinical nature of our connection.

I felt grateful to him even though I was disappointed by the experience. It had not answered any of my questions. Not really. What was there about this astonishingly prosaic event that deserved such attention? So far as I could tell, the abstract notion of chastity does not excite special interest in the world outside the Semitic religions. Morality is understood only in the context of society. If an act causes no social repercussions it is simply irrelevant. According to the *Kama Sutra*, a woman is considered a virgin if she has not yet been betrothed. I do not recall any reference to sexuality in discussions with my parents or larger family circle. Everything about a young person's behavior was assumed to be controlled by our social activities, the fact that we were almost never alone, the fact that we were expected to be respectful of authority, never questioning the choices made for us.

Ironically, it was my convent schools that focused my attention upon the channel between a woman's legs in a way that suggested otherworldly dimensions of sin and ecstasy, both.

◆

When I was in my mid-twenties I began a series of paintings that would bring notoriety down upon my head. I had always been able to draw realistically. Portraits of friends, of street people, of taxi-drivers and waiters. I had always enjoyed drawing people. After my BA, with the help of some friends in art school, I held a couple of exhibitions. They were so successful that I decided to leave the degree in Law I was pursuing as a preamble to sitting for the competitive exams leading to Government Service, to become an artist full-time.

It was never my intention to be blasphemous. I had just begun experimenting with oil paints when I found myself returning in painting after painting to a woman's figure, slightly elongated, with her arms parted. She wore flowing white robes and a blue shawl over her head. Of course she was the Madonna. That was obvious to me from the start. What had never struck me before was that the familiar image was an especially poetic rendering of a woman's nether corrugations. By no coincidence, since this was the late seventies, feminist art was flooding the world's media with kite-shaped images representative of vaginal folds and frills.

In my depictions, the Madonna's gentle face was the clitoris, her outstretched arms were the outer labia, her central region represented the swollen interior void that is so uniquely and problematically the source of feminine identity while her feet were the homely fundus of the human digestive tract.

The show was what might be called a catastrophic success. Riots and demonstrations were staged by different religious groups outside the Jehangir Art Gallery, across the street from what had been my college for the BA. The Christian minority believed that I, a non-Christian with a Hindu name, must surely have intended to trample on their sentiments. But conservative elements from both Hindu and Muslim groups also denounced the paintings as obscene abominations. Not only were they tainted with Christian iconography but the depiction of That Which Must Never Be Revealed, i.e., the female pudenda, made them especially vomitous.

In my interviews with the press I stammered incoherently about being areligious, about chastity and the symbol of the Perfect Woman. The elegance and beauty of her pose suggested that her female body is a portal to a higher plane of experience, I said. Her arms are spread wide in a gesture of loving invitation, generosity and hope. Her entire being deifies the female condition, with the blue of her veil representing the heavens, the white of her robes purity and the stars rimming her head the promise of eternity implied by sexual union and reproduction.

But the younger journalists gaped at me without comprehension while the older ones snickered and turned away. My preoccupations were regarded as eccentric at best and perverted at worst. My best friends encouraged me to do the city a favour and close the show before it opened. I listened to their advice. Meanwhile the paintings were sold in international auctions at ten times my original asking price even before they were removed from the gallery's walls. So it was a good time for me professionally, though I had to return to doing commissioned portraits for a while.

It was during this period that a friend called Ork asked a difficult favour of me.

We had been close friends in college, staying in touch post-graduation even as our career-paths sent us in different directions. We had never had a romantic connection though he had once sent me a note written in code expressing a carnal interest in me. He never followed up in any way however. I tried once later on to push beyond the limits of platonism by propositioning him directly.

We were both living in Bombay at the time.

'Ork,' I began. He had been coming over almost everyday, spending a couple of hours talking over increasingly tepid mugs of tea, on the balcony of my parent's spacious flat. He was no longer the long-haired, lean-cheeked youth of college, whose nickname had been a back-formation from 'stork', on account of his angularity and his height. He had the standard clean-shaven good looks of many another young North Indian man: chestnut brown eyes lavishly endowed with up-curled lashes, honey brown skin and wavy black hair. He looked up at me over the rim of his mug. 'Ork, I think we should have an affair.'

And he said, 'No.'

Just like that, without a moment's hesitation. Or even surprise.

'No. It would be a disaster,' he said.

My mind went blank with shock.

'It would lead to marriage and *that* would be awful. I mean, being married to me would be awful. For you.'

I refused to feel insulted. 'Don't be silly,' I said. 'You know very well I'm not interested in marriage.' Which was true. I was not then and had not been, from a very early age, ever willing to think of marriage as a viable future for myself.

But he shook his head resolutely. 'You don't understand. It isn't that I'm not attracted to you. It's that I don't want to *marry* you. If we had an affair, we'd end up getting married and I'd lose you as a friend. That's what I don't want.'

He was perfectly serious. I was flabbergasted. After a slight pause we continued talking, laughing and sharing anecdotes as if nothing had happened. When he went away that evening, it was just the same as on any other evening and he returned another couple of times. Then he went abroad to work in an older cousin's bank in London. We kept in touch through letters and cards. We met when we could, sharing confidences, eating dinners together. Remaining good friends.

Several years passed. I attained my minor notoriety and moved into my own apartment in Churchgate. Ork returned from his travels to live with his parents. He earned a good salary as Assistant Branch Manager at Grindlays in Worli.

One day, over lunch, he told me he was engaged to be married.

He'd never before this talked of any girlfriends. I had assumed he'd had some but that he'd chosen not to mention them to me. Out of delicacy perhaps. I didn't talk to him about my boyfriends either, even though I'd had a couple between my proposition to him and this lunch-time revelation.

He stopped me from saying that I was happy for him.

'Wait,' he said. 'it's not what you think.' He meant, it wasn't a romance.

He told me that when he'd returned to Bombay to live with his parents, it was with the realization that the scattershot approach to a private life wouldn't work for him. He'd seen too many of his contemporaries crash and burn while chasing after the Western romantic model: finding a girl, falling in love, proposing and then getting married with neither a dowry nor the collective blessings of a supportive clan. Even traditional Indian marriages were crumbling, but love-matches in particular were doomed. Starting as they did without the family's capital investment or social approval, their failure rate was hitting the 80% mark.

He had asked his parents to fix a match for him and they had gladly agreed. He said that he'd met a couple of girls before deciding upon The One. She had a childish nickname: Kiki. He liked her because of that name, which suggested that she didn't take herself too seriously. She was keen to be married, attractive without being spectacular. She worked as a receptionist at a corporate office, but expected to give up her job once they were married. He showed me a picture. A pretty little face looked out at me, with a sharp nose and careful smile.

I had always despised the notion of arranged marriages and Ork certainly knew this. But he was also an old friend. So I accepted his decision for what it was and refused to feel disappointed about his lack of idealism. I had understood by then that most Indians made choices about their personal lives based on the patterns set for them by their parents. Regardless of what they said and however they behaved in college and even for a few years after college, when it came to the big decisions about which profession to follow or whom to marry, one by one they buckled themselves into the family harness. If I was different, it was only because I had grown up away from India and lacked the protective colouration that would have allowed me to blend in.

Over the next few weeks, Ork kept me informed about the progress of his project. Kiki lived in Delhi, so he didn't often get to see her. She visited Bombay occasionally, staying with relatives while accepting invitations to meet him at his parents' apartment in Worli. He described how, on one occasion, his fiancée had worn a flowered cotton kurta which so matched the fabric with which the living room sofa was upholstered that when she sat down on it, 'she disappeared!' When describing her he used words like 'cute', 'girlish' and 'quiet'.

Late one afternoon, he called me from his office, requesting a walk on Marine Drive. That wasn't his usual style. He was not an outdoorsy person and the long drive across the whole length of Metropolitan Bombay would cost him more time and money than he was normally willing to spend. I wondered what was on his mind. The sun was low over the horizon. We walked towards the NCPA at the southern tip of the Drive, reversed direction and walked back the way we'd come. He waited until we were at the traffic light at Veer Nariman Road, five minutes from my apartment building, before saying, 'This is very difficult for me.'

The awkwardness and the time of day and maybe also the time of his life allowed me to guess what was coming. Which was a good thing, because when he did force the words out, I had already planned my response. 'You probably don't know this about me—or maybe you do—but anyway, here's the thing: I'm twenty-nine,' he said. 'I'm a virgin. And I'd like not to be. You know. Now that I'm getting married. So I wondered if...if...'

And I said, 'Of course.'

We were buddies. I would never deny him.

We set a date and he came over to my apartment, in the afternoon. His parents' flat was out of the question, obviously, but I had a live-in cook who had been installed by my parents specifically to spy on me. I had to send her away on an errand on the other side of the city in order to be assured of privacy.

I was overwhelmed by the sense of responsibility. This was going to be the end of a relationship, not the beginning of one. In a couple of months, Ork would be married and in all probability would vanish from my life. I had reached that age when socializing with married couples as a single woman was becoming uncomfortable. So I did not expect to gain anything from the event other than the satisfaction of knowing that I was doing a good friend a favour. In the back of my mind, I was also terrified that I might instead be the cause of a sexual trauma that would scar him forever.

We normally sat in the drawing room or the small kitchen-pantry but now I invited him into my bedroom, to my queen-size bed. I had set up the room for intimacy, drawing down the white Venetian blinds and peeling away the onyx-black tribal rug to reveal pristinely white sheets below. I had bought them for him, knowing that he was squeamish about bed linen.

I suggested getting in half-dressed, to save ourselves the introductory embarrassments.

He agreed without discussion.

There were no unpleasant surprises or disappointments. He was, as I expected he would be, perfectly well-equipped to perform. And he did. We were both contented at the end of it. He smoked a cigarette with the sheet wrapped around his chest and me snuggled into his side, as we talked in soft tones. If there had been a camera to record the moment, we would have presented a Hollywoodian portrait of post-coital ease.

I was impressed with myself for having been a sterling example of a true friend.

But I had misjudged the results.

Ork's marriage lasted less than six months after which he disappeared from my life for several years. When we caught up again, he told me that he had been a fool to think one episode in bed would tell him anything about being a husband to a wife. He blamed himself for having approached me for help but he blamed me even more for behaving like a professional courtesan.

'It wasn't real, what we did,' he said. He wore reading glasses now to look at the bill of the restaurant we were in. He had a slight paunch and there were tufts of hair growing out of his ears. But he had remarried and was very happy with his second wife, also a divorcee. 'The first time's about risk. About pushing past the fear. You weren't helping me to push past the fear. You just wanted me to have a nice time. At any cost.'

I stared at him, open-mouthed with dismay.

'You wanted to pat yourself on the back for a job well done. I know you too well not to know that.' He smiled, shaking his head. 'I'm not blaming you. I was an idiot for asking. You were an idiot for agreeing. We were both young and ridiculous.'

The Parrots of Desire

He was right.

The bodies in a bed are not buddies. They are combatants. Sometimes they're fighting on the same side, for the same goals. Other times not. Either way, they are alone.

Especially when one of them is a virgin.

♦

Some months ago, a friend whom I shall call Om, got back in touch with me after a lapse of many years. I had known him when I was in my final year of college, in Bombay. After Gai, that is, and long before Ork.

At the time I met him he told me categorically that he had a steady girlfriend, that he loved her and that he expected to marry her. She had gone to the US ahead of him to continue her higher studies and he was getting ready to join her. He wanted me to know that there was no romantic capital to be gained from our friendship but that didn't mean we couldn't enjoy a little friendly barter before he left.

I did not believe in either cheating on a boyfriend or being party to another woman's betrayal. Why? Because I didn't think that the emotional chaos caused was ever balanced by the pleasure gained.

Nevertheless, I was attracted to Om. Too attracted to step away. I hated to see my own rules bending and snapping in the wind yet I could not switch my attention off. I met him only every third weekend, but we talked on the phone every day. We had been a couple of times for walks at Juhu Beach, for swims at the United Services Club in Colaba and once or twice he had come home for tea. Whenever we talked, our conversations were of the kind that remained glowing and twitching in my memory for hours afterward.

Some of you reading this will recognize the symptoms: I was falling in love.

But was I ever going to admit such a thing to myself? Of course not. I had brought the case before my own internal Committee for Romantic Acquisitions and I had turned myself down. Om was, by the terms of my own Evaluation Council, unavailable to me on account of his fiancée. Being the bureaucrat's daughter that I was, I could hardly go against my own regulations.

Still. I wasn't ready to let him go. So I created a loophole. Under the heading of Research and Exploration, my internal Committee could sanction a Physical Encounter. That was how I thought of it. Any other approach would have been dishonourable and unconstitutional. The terms of my loophole specified that I could not love him, nor do anything to keep him interested in me.

I remember a particular evening when we were driving back to the southern tip of Bombay, where I lived, after spending the late afternoon at Juhu, in the north. In those days, the beach was practically deserted. Om had drawn diagrams in the sand, in the slanting amber light, to explain internal combustion engines to me.

As an Economics major, I was fascinated by the sciences and wished I knew more. He talked about a performance at his college of *Waiting for Godot* and of how, during the interval, he had walked through the crowd saying, 'Spade...spade... spade...' while holding a spade in his hands.

I was acutely aware of the outgoing tide sucking the sand away from under my bare feet as we strolled along the shoreline. My sandals were in my hands, the wind was blowing my hair into my eyes and he was just a few feet away from me. He was taller than me, and lean, his movements elastic. He wore a loose white *khadi* kurta over white pajamas. I could feel the heat of his body speaking to me across the space that separated us. I could feel a spark of electricity igniting the chamber of charged air that contained us on that open beach. I could feel an engine of desire turn over and start to hum within me.

So in the car, going home, I said, 'Would you like to sleep with me?' 'Sure,' he said.

He lived in an all-men's hostel while I was still in my parental home, where there was never any question of privacy. So I organized a place and time: my friend Bena's room, in mid-afternoon. Her own parents were out at work and the servants were off taking their siesta.

Om arrived at the appointed hour and the three of us made small talk for a few minutes.

Then Bena muttered her excuses and left.

The moment she exited, a guillotine descended between Om and me, slicing the room in half.

The spark I had felt at the beach was extinguished completely. In its place were the clean white sheets, the small sterile room on the ground floor. The sun nuzzling its way in through baby-pink curtains. The humming air-conditioner. The sounds of traffic from the street outside.

There was nothing either of us could do to improve the situation. We undressed, lay down and got the action over with quickly. It was like a medical procedure, a brief storm after which we sat up, got dressed and we went our separate ways. I remember feeling like an actor who has dropped a whole scene of dialogue from a play, causing it to end an hour earlier. We did not meet again after that day, though we talked on the phone a couple of times. The events in Bena's room were never referred to, not even obliquely.

Then his exams were upon him. Then his departure loomed. Then he flew away and we did not exchange addresses.

For a long time afterwards, the memory of him remained buzzing and stinging within me like a swarm of bees caught in a fine nylon net. He had not said or done anything out of order. He had not lied to me nor misled me. Yet I felt burgled. Even though I couldn't see what had been taken, what had been lost, I felt as if something vast had been siphoned out of me leaving me with a dense, impenetrable emptiness.

I tried to blame myself for my own inadequacies on that final afternoon—the silence, my impassivity—but I couldn't make the guilt stick. He would always have vanished westwards. The distances that had been inherent in our story would have remained obstinately in place whatever we might have said or done differently that day.

In the intervening years between then and now, we met twice, in the early eighties, while I was still in Bombay. He had divorced the girlfriend for whom he'd left India, then married twice again. I had the show that would alter the course of my professional life for the better.

Then twenty years passed.

Last month, when he got back in touch with me, the changes in both our lives were more profound than they had ever been before. We are both in stable relationships. He lives in San Francisco, working as an environmental consultant. I live in New Delhi, an established artist with the controversies of the past nacred over by my financial success.

We talked on the phone and met a couple of times for dinner. The bitterness and pain that I had felt at the time of his first departure to the West had dissipated so completely that I could smile at the dark energy of youth without feeling the least twinge. We exchanged e-messages, we Skyped, we SMSed. I did not think of these communications as especially consequential.

Then a few days ago, he called from a hotel in Cairo.

He had an unlimited supply of international minutes on his cell phone. Or maybe the UN was paying. It didn't matter. We embarked upon a light, lazy conversation which started as an exchange of anecdotes about getting through security in US airports before veering towards the past.

We talked about the visits to Juhu, about his diagrams in the sand, about calling a spade, a spade. We had always, to some extent, talked about the past. This time however, he referred with no preamble, directly to Bena's room

'I don't remember her name,' he said. 'Your friend at whose house we met. The last time. Before I went away.'

My centre of gravity shifted within me. It was true that I no longer felt resentful towards him but to talk about it was to be reminded of the tremendous waste of energy that takes place in youth. The way that we place our emphasis on the least consequential of things.

I tried changing the topic but he refused to be distracted.

He said, 'Do you remember what you were like? So stiff and so unyielding. Like you were in a hurry to get it over with.' His tone wasn't one of rebuke. It was as if we were both watching a film together, one that only he and I had ever seen, critiquing it.

I shrugged on my side of the conversation.

'Yes,' I said. 'I remember. And I *did* just want to get it over with.'

I could have mentioned the screaming vacuum I'd felt in the months that followed, the charge of anticipation that had preceded the encounter and the complete voiding of my senses during it. But I was still holding myself to the contract I had written for myself at the time, in the ink of indifference. To have claimed any passion, even a negative one, such as anger, would have been inappropriate.

'We were so young and inexperienced—' he began.

'Not you,' I said at once. The snap of accusation was audible in my voice. 'You were older than me. You had a steady girlfriend—'

'Yes, yes,' he said, cutting in. '*But you were my first.*'

His first lover. He had been a virgin.

'No,' I said. 'No.'

The boundaries of time and space dissolved around me.

I was returned to that small neat room in Bombay. I remembered the smell of his hair, his mouth. The plain bright light. The ticking of a clock.

For thirty years, that scene had remained inside the archives of my mind, irrefutable and unchangeable, showing Om as user and me as usee. But it was the early seventies and his fiancée had not considered sleeping with him before marriage. I, belonging to a different generation and indoctrination, had not even dreamt of that possibility. It had never once occurred to me that maybe he, not I, had been at the greater disadvantage. That perhaps he had been fearful and embarrassed, or awkward and clumsy, or incoherent and lacking in élan because he really did not know anything else.

Within the space of two seconds the weight of that memory shifted, trembled and vanished altogether. It was gone.

In its place was a hint of stars.

Virginity is invisible. It has no mass or atomic number. It has little to do with membranes or bloodied sheets or pain.

It means nothing to those who do not seek truth.

'I hadn't told you,' he said. 'I was too proud. I should have.'

I was literally speechless. I could not push a single word out of my mouth.

In all this time, after countless girlfriends, one-night stands, misadventures, divorces, call-girls, marriages, clandestine affairs, wives and daughters he had nevertheless maintained one tiny fragment of a distant memory intact. He knew he possessed a single electron of information that he needed to transfer to me. He wanted to confirm that however alone, apart and separate we had been then and had remained ever since, we belonged to that cohort of seekers which values truth.

It mattered to him that I should know.

Though neither of us could really say why.

ON COURTSHIP

Kama Sutra

A man having good qualities but no wealth, a man born of a low family who has mediocre qualities, a neighbour in possession of wealth[1], and one under the control of his father, mother or brothers, should not court a virgin because he will not be successful. However, if he endeavours to win the affections of a girl from childhood on, he may be successful in having her fall in love with him.[2] Thus a boy separated from his parents, and living in the house of his uncle, should try to gain over the daughter of his uncle[3], or some other girl, even though she may be betrothed to another. And this way of gaining over a girl, says Ghotakamukha, is unexceptional, because Dharma can be accomplished by means of it as well as by any other way of marriage.

When a boy has thus begun to woo the girl he loves, he should spend his time with her and amuse her with various games and diversions suitable for their age and acquaintanceship, such as picking and collecting flowers, making garlands of flowers, playing the parts of members of a fictitious family, cooking food, playing with dice, playing with cards, the game of odd and even, the game of finding the middle finger, the game of six pebbles, and other such games that may be prevalent in the country, and agreeable to her disposition. In addition to this, he should carry on various amusing games played by several persons together, such as hide and seek, playing with seeds, hiding things in several small heaps of wheat and looking for them, blindman's buff, gymnastic exercises, and other similar games, in the company of the girl, her friends and female attendants.

The man should also show great kindness to any woman whom the girl thinks fit to be trusted, and should also make new acquaintances, but above all he should attach to himself by kindness and little services the daughter of the girl's nurse, for if she be gained over, even though she comes to know of his design, she does not cause any obstruction,

---

[1]Wendy Doniger and Sudhir Kakar, *Kama Sutra*, fn. 1, p. 82: 'A man of indifferent qualities does have qualities such as good looks and a good nature, but lacks a noble birth or money and therefore lacks social status. The neighbour who lives next to the woman's house does not get her, because of all the quarrels that arise about the boundaries between the two properties and because his money makes him arrogant.'
[2]Ibid, fn. 2, p. 82: 'If she has fallen in love with him, she will marry him by herself in the love-match wedding that consists of nothing but desire.'
[3]In the South, one can marry the daughter of one's uncle, that is, the mother's brother.

but is sometimes even able to effect a union between him and the girl. And though she knows the true character of the man, she always talks of his many excellent qualities to the parents and relations of the girl, even though she may not be desired to do so by him.

In this way the man should do whatever the girl takes most delight in, and he should get for her whatever she may have a desire to possess. Thus he procures for her such playthings as may be hardly known to other girls. He may also show her a ball dyed with various colours, and other curiosities of the same sort; and should give her dolls made of cloth, wood, buffalo-horn, wax, flour, or earth; also utensils for cooking food, and figures in wood, such as a man and woman standing, a pair of rams, or goats, or sheep; also temples made of earth, bamboo, or wood, dedicated to various goddesses; and cages for parrots, cuckoos, starlings, quails, cocks, and partridges; water-vessels of different sorts and of elegant forms, machines for throwing water about, stands for putting images upon, stools, lac, red arsenic, yellow ointment, vermilion and collyrium, as well as sandalwood, saffron, betel nut and betel leaves. Such things should be given at different times whenever he gets a good opportunity of meeting her, and some of them should be given in private, and some in public, according to circumstances.[4]

---

[4]In short, he should try in every way to make her look upon him as one who would do for her everything that she wanted to be done

Anguish, Abandonment and Break Up

.... ~ ....

MY SOUL MELTS IN ANGUISH

Āntāl

My soul melts in anguish—
he cares not
if I live or die.
If I see the lord of Govardhana
that looting thief,
that plunderer,
I shall pluck
by their roots
these useless breasts,
I shall fling them
at his chest,
I shall cool
the raging fire
within me.

—Translated from the Tamil by Vidya Dehejia

YOU DO NOT COME

Amrita Pritam

Spring is waking and stretching its arms.
Flowers weave their silk threads
For the festival of colours.
You do not come.

Afternoons grow long
Red has touched the grapes
Sickles are kissing the wheat.
You do not come.

Clouds are gathering.
Earth opens its hands to drink
The bounty of the sky.
You do not come.

Trees murmur enchantment,
Airs from the woodland wander
With lips full of honey.
You do not come.

Seasons wear their beauty.
Night sets on its brow
A diadem of moon.
You do not come.

Again the stars tell me
That in my body's house
A candle of beauty still burns.
You do not come.

All the sun's rays vow
That light still wakes
From the death sleep of night.
You do not come.

—Translated from the Punjabi by Charles Brasch

WHAT SHE SAID

Ammuvanar

Friend, his seas swell and roar
making conch shells whirl on the sands.
But fishermen ply their little wooden boats
unafraid of the cold lash of the waves.

Look, my bangles
slip loose as he leaves,
grow tight as he returns,

and they give me away.

—Translated from the Tamil by A. K. Ramanujan

THE MEANS OF GETTING RID OF A LOVER

Kama Sutra

The means of getting rid of a lover are as follows:

(a) Describing the habits and vices of the lover as irritable and censurable, with a sneer of the lip, and a stamp of the foot.
(b) Speaking on a subject with which he has little knowledge.
(c) Showing no admiration for his learning, and passing a censure upon it.
(d) Puncturing his pride.
(e) Spending time with men who are superior to him in learning and wisdom.
(f) Ignoring him.
(g) Criticizing other men who possess the same faults as one's lover.
(h) Expressing dissatisfaction at the things he does when they are making love.
(i) Keeping him away from the place between her legs.
(j) Showing a dislike for the wounds made by his nails and teeth.
(k) Not pressing close up against him when he embraces her.
(l) Keeping her limbs motionless at the time of sex.
(m) Desiring him to enjoy her when he is tired.
(n) Mocking his devotion to her.
(o) Remaining unresponsive to his embraces.
(p) Turning away from him when he begins to embrace her.
(q) Pretending to be sleepy.
(r) Going out visiting to be with a crowd when she knows he wants to enjoy her during the daytime.
(s) Distorting his words and misconstruing his intentions.
(t) Laughing when he hasn't cracked a joke, or, laughing at something else when he cracks one.
(u) Stealing side glances at her attendants, and clapping her hands when he says anything.
(v) Interrupting him in the middle of his stories, and beginning to tell other stories herself.
(w) Talking in public about his faults and his vices, and declaring them to be incurable.
(x) In conversing with her female attendants, using words calculated to cut the heart of her lover to the quick.

(y) Taking care not to look at him when he comes to her.

(z) Asking him for what he cannot grant her.

And, after all, dismissing him in the end.

HE NEVER CAME

Rabindranath Tagore as Bhanusimha Thakurer Padabali

He never came to me.
In the whole long dark he never came
to tend my lacerated heart.
I'm a girl with nothing, a tree
with neither flowers nor fruit.

Go home, poor tragedy. Distract yourself
with chores, dry your eyes. Go on now,
dear tattered garland, limp with shame.

How can I bear this staggering weight?
I'm budding and blooming at once,
and dying, too, crushed by thirst
and the leaves' incessant rustling.
I need his eyes in mine, their altar's gold fire.
Don't lie to me. I'm lost in that blaze.
My heart waits, fierce and alone.
He'll leave me. If he leaves me, I'll poison myself.
...
Your flute plays the exact notes of my pain.
It toys with me.
Where did you learn such stealth,
such subtle wounding, Kan?
The arrows in my breast
burn even in rain and wind.
Wasted moments pulse around me,
wishes and desires, departing happiness—
Master, my soul scorches.
I think you can see its heat in my eyes,
its intensity and cruelty. So let me drown
in the cool and consuming Yamuna,
or slake my desire in your cool,
consoling, changing-moon face.
It's the face I'll see in death.
Here's my wish and pledge:
that the same moon will spill its white pollen
down through the roof of flowers

into the grove, where I'll consecrate my life
to it forever, and be its flute-breath,
the perfume that hangs upon the air,
making all the young girls melancholy.
That's my prayer.

Oh, the two of you, way out of earshot.
If you look back you'll see me, Bhanu,
warming herself at the weak embers of the past.

How long must I go on waiting
under the secretive awnings of the trees?
When will he call the long notes of my name
with his flute: Radha, Radha, so full of desire
that all the little cowherd-girls will start awake
and come looking for him, as I look for him.
Will he not come to me,
playing the song of Radha with his eyes and hands?
He will not, Yamuna.
I have one moon—Syama—
but a hundred Radhas yearn for moonlight at his feet.
I'll go to the grove, companion river.
Alone, I'll honor our trysting-place.
No one will make me renounce it.

Come with me into the dark trees.
You'll have your tryst,
its trembling rapture and its tears.

—*Translated from the Brajabuli by Chase Twichell and Tony K. Stewart*

WHAT SHE SAID

Kuruntokai by Paranar

Like moss on water
in the town's water tank:

the body's pallor
clears

as my lover touches
and touches,

and spreads again,
as he lets go,

as he lets go.

—*Translated from the Tamil by A. K. Ramanujan*

Anger, Punishment and Make Up

.... ~ ....

WAYS OF SLAPPING

Kama Sutra

They say that sex can be compared to a quarrel, because 'the very essence of desire is argument and its character is perverse'[1]. And so, a part of making love is slapping the body with passion, on

The shoulders
The head
The space between the breasts
The back
The middle part of the body [between the legs]
The sides

Slapping is of four kinds:

Striking with the back of the hand
Striking with the fingers a little contracted
Striking with the fist
Striking with the open palm of the hand

On account of its causing pain, slapping gives rise to moaning, which is of various kinds:

The sound Hin
The thundering sound
The cooing sound
The weeping sound
The sound Phut
The sound Phat
The sound Sut
The sound Plat[2]

Besides these, there are also words having a meaning, such as 'Mother!', and those that are expressive of prohibition, sufficiency, desire of liberation, pain or praise ['Let go!', 'Enough!'], and to which may be

---

[1]Wendy Doniger and Sudhir Kakar, *Kama Sutra* (New York: Oxford University Press), 2009, p. 56.

[2]See Ibid. p. 57. Interpreted as 'whimpering, groaning, babbling, crying, panting, shrieking, or sobbing. Whimpering is a nasal sound, rising above the throat and nose, sweetly echoing. Groaning is like the deep rumble of a cloud, coming out of the throat. Crying is well known, and should be heart-rending. Panting is another name for "sighing"'.

Anger, Punishment and Make Up   137

added sounds like those of the dove, the cuckoo, the green pigeon, the parrot, the bee, the sparrow, the flamingo, the duck, and the quail, which are all occasionally made use of.

Blows with the fist should be given on the back of the woman while she is sitting on the lap of the man, and she should give blows in return, abusing the man as if she were angry, and making the cooing and the weeping sounds. While the woman is engaged in congress the space between the breasts should be struck with the back of the hand, slowly at first, and then proportionately to the increasing excitement, until the end.

At this time she makes a whimpering sound and other sounds as well, alternately or if she wishes, with varying intensity. When the man, making the sound Phat, strikes the woman on the head, with the fingers of his hand a little contracted, it is called 'Prasritaka', which means striking with the fingers of the hand a little contracted. In this case the appropriate sounds are the cooing sound, the sound Phât and the sound Phut in the interior of the mouth, and at the end of congress the sighing and weeping sounds. The sound Phat is an imitation of the sound of a bamboo being split, while the sound Phut is like the sound made by something falling into water. Whenever the man tries to force his kisses upon her, the woman moans and does the same in return. In the excitement that ensues, when the woman is being slapped repeatedly by the man, she continually utters words like 'Stop!', 'Enough!', 'Father!' or 'Mother!', intermingled with the sighing, weeping and thundering sounds.[3] As they near the end of their passion, the man presses her breasts, the inside of her thighs, and her sides with the open palm of the hand, with some force, until she climaxes, and begins to babble like a partridge or a goose[4].

There are two verses on the subject as follows:

'A man's natural talent is
his roughness and ferocity,
a woman's is her lack of power
and her suffering, self-denial, and weakness.

---

[3]Men who are well acquainted with the art of love are well aware how often one woman differs from another in her sighs and sounds during the time of congress. Some women like to be talked to in the most loving way, others in the most lustful way, others in the most abusive way, and so on. Some women enjoy themselves with closed eyes in silence, others make a great noise, and some almost faint away. The great art is to ascertain what gives them the greatest pleasure, and what they like best.
[4]Ibid. fn. 21, p. 28: 'When he strikes her with the flat palm of his hand, she begins to babble.'

Their passion and a particular technique
may sometimes lead them even to exchange roles;
but not for very long. In the end,
the natural roles are re-established.'[5]

---

[5]Ibid. p. 58

Sighs parch my lips.
My uprooted
Heart is torn out.
Sleep doesn't come, my lover's face
won't appear.
 Night and day this husk of a
body weeps since he lay at my feet
rejected.
What were you thinking, friends—
goading me to
treat him so harshly?

◆

Hear his name
and every hair on my
body's aroused.
See his moonlike face
I get moist like a moonstone everywhere.
He steps near enough to touch
my throat
and pride is broken oh hard
diamond heart.

◆

In bed he whispers
the wrong name.
She feels her youthful enthusiasm wilt
and curls coldly away
from excuses.
He falls silent.
And she turning back softly
eyes him—
Don't go to sleep.

—Translated from the Sanskrit by Andrew Schelling

MY CONFLICTED HEART TREASURES EVEN HIS
INFIDELITIES

Gita Govinda by Jayadeva

Radha speaks

My conflicted heart
treasures even his infidelities.
Won't admit anger.
Forgives the deceptions.
Secret desires rise in my breasts.
What can I do? Krishna
hungry for lovers
slips off without me.
This torn heart grows only
more ardent.

The messenger speaks to Radha

Krishna lingers
in the thicket
where together you mastered the secrets
of lovemaking.
Fixed in meditation,
sleepless
he chants a sequence of mantras.
He has one burning desire—
to draw *amrta*
from your offered breasts.

Sighs, short repeated gasps—
he glances around helpless.
The thicket deserted.
He pushes back in, his breath
comes in a rasp.
He rebuilds the couch of blue floral branches.
Steps back and studies it.
Radha, precious Radha!
Your lover turns on a wheel,
image after

feverish image.

She ornaments her limbs
if a single leaf stirs
in the forest.
She thinks it's you, folds back
the bedclothes and stares
in rapture for hours.
Her heart conceives a hundred
amorous games on the well-prepared bed.
But without you this
wisp of a girl
will fade
to nothing tonight.

—*Translated from the Sanskrit by Andrew Schelling*

THE APPEASEMENT OF RADHIKA

Muddupalani

Hearing this and all that the embittered Radhika had to say, the slayer
of Mura addressed her respectfully, 'O lady! A slave's mistake should
be forgiven without remonstration.' Saying so, the Lord who wears
peacock feathers on his head, bowed and fell at her lotus-like feet like
a swarm of buzzing bees...

And as he fell at her feet,
She raised her left leg, anklets resounding loudly,
And with brute force
Kicked
The head adorned with peacock feathers
Revered and prayed by
Brahma, Shiva and sages wise,
As though training him
For Satyabhama's ire
In the future.

Unperturbed and yet composed he rose,
The great Yadava king,
Putting out his hands, said he gently:
'Beautiful lady, blessed am I now,
But I hope your feet don't hurt
Hitting against my solid head,
My dearest Radhe!

'Dear maiden, your thighs thundered
Your sari slipped, your breasts heaved,
And your anklets trembled,
As your foot struck my head.
But my body trembled with ecstasy,
How can I describe this euphoria?

'Your hands may shine,
But the grace of your slim waist is greater.
Your breasts may be firm,
But the allure of your buttocks is better.
Your eyebrows may be finely arched,

But the swell of your stomach is greater.
Words from your red lips are pleasant,
But the unspoken feelings speak volumes.

'Your flying sari is the sky
The liquid pouring into me is the Ganga
O beauty! The lines on your stomach are clouds
Your embrace is like rain on parched earth.

'Degrade me,
Cast piercing glances or order me away,
Whether you talk or don't,
Bathe me in milk or water
Or even throw me out!
Tell me you don't need my love,
Whatever you say or do,
I won't go away, O Radhika!'

And as he spoke thus, she wept:
'O my lotus-eyed Lord!
At last, at long last, you confess
That's enough, more than enough.
Nothing's more important than self-respect,'
She said, expressing love and anger, distrust and envy.

Slumped, holding her sari ends against her face,
As Souri looked on,
The moon-faced lady wept,
Tears streaming down her high breasts,
Like waterfalls cascading down the Meru.

As she wept, Hari bent again
And held her feet,
'My love, why do you weep?
Am I greater than you?
If you're still angry, I'm yours
To do as you wish...completely,'
He stood, clasping her tightly to his chest.

Then the maiden gave herself up
Completely to his love

He brushed her lips and stroked her cheeks
He touched her whilst she kissed him back
He caressed her stomach
And as the Love God looked on indulgently,
The lady and her lover engaged in the battle of love.

Flushed, in the rapturous afterglow of making love, they collapsed into each other's arms, delighting in each other's fragrances. Joking and laughing at each other's antics, they indulged each other, pretending and playing. She coyly prevented him from kissing her, stopping him from touching her radiant cheeks, not letting him play with her long tresses, preventing him from touching her lips. Her embroidered blouse, heavily embellished with pearls and precious stones, was unable to withstand her heaving breasts and rent apart. Struggling with each other, locked in a tight embrace, breathless, him getting on top of her, kissing her lips, gently slapping her cheeks, they continued their fierce lovemaking. The bed creaked, floral and bodily scents pervaded the room, as sparrows and swans, nightingales and parrots looked on, chirping loudly and egging them on. 'Don't leave me, don't stop, don't leave an inch between us, hold me tight, fill me...' Whispering sweet nothings, their bodies making sounds that reverberated through the house...she reciprocated, thrust for thrust, into her whole being she pressed him, body melting into body, cheek against cheek, drinking nectar from each other's lips, they made love, until exhausted, they retired.

Her tresses, covering her face
Created darkness.
Bruised jaji flowers pressed against her face
Looked like tired, collapsed stars
The glistening sweat on her delicate forehead
Brilliant smiles radiant like moonbeams.

Her celebrated beauty arousing desires,
Loving smiles emanating like moonlight
Like Krishna paksha,
The dark-haired lovely
Fell on Krishna, indulging in intercourse.

Like flower petals dropping,
She fell on him.
Like breeze circulating,

She spun him around.
Like a mechanized ball,
She bounced around.
Like the spinning top,
Giddily she played him with gusto.
She posed and preened
Slapping his cheeks
Chiding him lovingly
Kissing him incessantly
Touching his organ
Caressing him slowly
They made love,
Bala Hari and his Radhika.

As the lotus-bodied beauty embraced Hari, the pearl necklaces and ruby jewels fell off one by one, like the flower-tipped arrows of Manmatha, dropping to the floor. Then the father of the Love God, looking at his lady awash with desire, said teasingly:

'What are those marks on your breasts, Radha?'
'As if you don't know O lotus-eyed one!'
'Why the bruised lips, Radha?'
'As if you don't know, O Lord of the gods!'
'And the smudged kajal, Radha?'
'As if you don't know, O God of gods!'
'And where's all the gold gone, Radha?
'As if you don't know, O father of the Love God!'

—*Translated from the Telugu by Sandhya Mulchandani*

AT MIDNIGHT RESURRECT OUR LOVE

Pritish Nandy

At midnight
I move in on strangers, for the caress
or the kill. I have come to terms with shadows,
I have been assaulted by gentler lovetimes: once
in a long while a face comes near, our eyes meet
in challenge, or is it love? Our bodies come alive
in secret oneness: one spring ago, terrified to be
touched, you draw me tonight, at last, deep within
your frantic countryside.

Tonight I draw your body to my lips: your hand, your
mouth, your breasts, the small of your back. I draw
blood to every secret nerve and gently kiss their tips, as
you move under me, anchored to a rough sea. I cling to
you, your music and your knees. I touch the secret vibes
of your body, I fill my hands with the darkness of
your hair. This passion alone can
resurrect our love.

WHEN MY FACE TURNED TOWARD HIS

Amaruśataka

When my face turned toward his,
I averted it
and looked at my feet.

When my ears clamored
to hear his talk,
I stopped them.

When my cheeks broke out
in sweat and goosebumps,
I covered them with my hands.

But Friends,

when the seams of my bodice
burst in a hundred places,

what could I do?

Men's Wish to be Women

[WHO HAS BETTER SEX?] MEN OR WOMEN?

from the Mahabharata, Anushasana Parva, 12.11-53

Yudhishthira said, 'When men and women have sexual intercourse, which one of them experience greater pleasure? It would be appropriate for you to clear my doubts about this, sire.'

Bhishma said, 'An example from long ago about the enmity between Bhangashvana and Indra will suffice to explain the matter. In the old days, there was a royal sage named Bhangashvana who was exceedingly righteous. He had no sons and so, tiger among men, he decided to perform a sacrifice for the birth of a son. The sacrifice he performed is called the Agnishtuma and men do it either as repentance for some misdeed in the past, or to obtain sons. But this ritual displeases Indra. When Indra, the king of the gods, heard about the sacrifice, he could find no weakness in that great king although he tried his best to do so.

After some time, the king went on a hunt. Indra took this as an opportunity and stupefied the king. Thus confused, along with his horse, the king wandered around, directionless, and soon he was oppressed by hunger, thirst and fatigue. Then, the king saw a pleasant lake, filled with clear water. He got off his horse and led him to the shore.

After the animal had finished drinking, the king tied him to a tree and entered the waters of the lake to bathe. To his great consternation, he found that the waters had turned him into a woman. When he saw himself transformed, he was deeply embarrassed and that most excellent king grew extremely agitated in his mind and heart. 'How will I mount my horse, how will I go to my city? The Agnisthum ritual gave me one hundred sons, born from my loins. They are strong—what will I say to them? And to my wives, my retainers, my people from the towns and the countryside? Great sages who are learned in matters of duty and religion say that softness, gentleness and a tendency towards confusion are the qualities of women whereas physical energy, hardness and virility are the qualities of men. My manliness has been destroyed and this femaleness has come over me. How will I mount my horse again?' Deeply depressed, the king returned to his city in the form of a woman.

His sons and wives and relatives and his people from the towns and the countryside were amazed at what had happened and said, 'What is this!' That royal sage, who, now had the form of a woman, said to all of them, 'I was on a hunt, surrounded by my army. As fate would have it, I got lost and entered a huge forest that was thick and dense.

In that dense forest, I was overcome by hunger and thirst and almost fainted. Then, I saw a beautiful lake that was visited by birds of all kinds. As I bathed in it, fates transformed me into a woman.' Calling his sons and wives and relations together, each by name, that best of kings who had been transformed into a woman, said to them, 'My dear sons, enjoy this kingdom happily. I am going to the forest.' The king bade his one hundred sons farewell and went into the forest.

There, she came upon an ascetic's hermitage and with him, she had one hundred sons in the hermitage. She took her hundred sons and went to her previous sons and said to them, 'You sons were born when I was a man. These one hundred sons were born to me when I am a woman. Have fraternal feelings for each other, enjoy the kingdom together, like brothers, dear sons!' And the brothers did so, immediately.

When Indra, the king of the gods, saw the sons sharing the kingdom happily, he fell into deep thought. 'I seem to have the done that royal sage a favour instead of harming him.' Then, Indra, he of one hundred sacrifices, took on the form of a brahmin and went to the king's city where he managed to sow dissension amongst the princes. 'Even brothers who are sons of the same father do not live happily together. Look at the gods and the demons, both sons of Kashyapa. They got into a dispute about kingship. You are the sons of Bhangashvana and these are the sons of some ascetic. The gods and demons were both sons of Kashyapa. These fellows, the ascetic's sons, are enjoying your father's kingdom!'

Separated thus by Indra, they began to fight each other. When the ascetic woman heard about this, she burned with grief and began to wail. Indra came to her disguised as a brahmin and asked, 'Lady with the lovely face, what is the sorrow that burns you up? Why are you crying?' The woman saw the brahmin and said pathetically, 'I had two hundred sons, brahmin, but they were taken away by Death. I was a king, once, and I had a hundred sons. They were brave and strong and looked like me, best among the twice-born. I went hunting and I got lost in the dense forest. I was transformed into a woman after I bathed in a lake and so I established my sons in my kingdom and came back to the forest. As a woman, I had another hundred sons with a great-souled ascetic. They were born in the hermitage and so I took them to the city. Time created disunity among them, brahmin, and that is why I am crying, afflicted by fate.'

Indra looked at that grieving woman and spoke harshly to her. 'Long ago, my dear woman, your actions caused me great pain. You performed a sacrifice that is despised by Indra and you, creature of perverted wisdom, you did not include me in the honours. I am Indra!

And you have willfully sought hostilities with me.' The royal sage saw Indra and touched his feet with his head. 'Show me your grace, lord of the thirty three gods! That sacrifice was performed for the sake of obtaining sons. Tiger among the gods, you should forgive me!' Indra was pleased with the prostrate monarch and wanted to give him a boon. 'Which of your sons should I revive, king—the ones born when you were a woman or those born when you were a man?'

The ascetic woman joined her palms and bowed her head and said to Indra, 'Let the ones born when I was a woman live, Indra!' Indra was surprised and pleased and he questioned the woman ascetic again. 'Why are you not fond of the sons that were born to you when you were a man? Why are you more fond of those born to you when you were a woman? I am eager to hear the reason for this, you should tell me.'

The woman said, 'A woman is capable of more affection than a man. That is why I asked for the sons born to me when I was a woman to be brought back to life, Indra!'

Bhishma said, 'When she said that, Indra was pleased and said to her, 'You speak the truth, dear lady! All your sons shall be restored to life! Choose another boon, best of kings, man of good vows. Ask for anything you wish! What do you want from me—to be a man or to be a woman?'

The woman said, 'I choose to stay a woman, Indra, if it pleases you!' Spoken to thus, Indra said to the woman, 'How is it that you want to renounce manliness and enjoy the state of being a woman?' The best of kings who had been transformed into a woman said, 'Women always experience greater pleasure than men during sexual intercourse. It is for this reason, Indra, that I choose to remain in a state of womanhood. I tell you truly, I have far greater pleasure as a woman. And so, I am happy to remain a woman. You can leave me now, lord of the thirty three gods!'

'So be it,' he said and went back to heaven.

And so it is, great king, that women experience more pleasure.

—Translated from the Sanskrit by Arshia Sattar

CHAPTINAMAS

Jur'at

1.

Yesterday Sukkho and Mukkho started a strange litany:
These wretched husbands have made our lives a mess and misery.
How can the heart's bud blossom until one wanders the garden?
How can the glance but stray till one roams from alley to alley?
Come, let's play at doubled clinging, come Dogana, let's play chapti
why sit around, better labour free.

Let's invite all the women in town who are given to clinging,
Welcome them to our house with flowers and betel, embracing,
Perfuming each other; when of their husbands they start to complain,
That's when you and I begin our chant, teach them our refrain:
Come, let's play at doubled clinging, why sit around, better labour
free.

This play, my love, is better than all others in the universe,
It's worth staking your life on, in thoughts of it yourself immerse—
When some old woman comes and starts doling out her thoughts
adverse,
Laughing, we'll say between ourselves each moment through
gestures:
Come, let's play at doubled clinging, why sit around, better labour
free.

To the enjoyment of this clinging what other pleasure can compare?
This rubbing above, below, is intercourse wondrously rare,
Making love with one's own likeness is a strange, delightful thing,
Even if you get entrapped, being so consumed is comforting:
Come, let's play at doubled clinging, why sit around, better labour
free.

Sometimes you'll be on top of me, sometimes I, your slave, will
be on top,
When the body's rubbed all over, the heart's delight is multiplied,
When passion overflowing swells the womb's mouth, how can I stop?
Let the whole family be my foe, enough to say this to me:
Come, let's play at doubled clinging, why sit around, better labour free.

To let the rains pass, sitting idle, is to brew a storm within,
Drink this hidden wine, get drunk, the time will fly happily.
If anyone's opposed to you, who cares, to hell with them,
Exchange a glance between yourselves that says this intimately:
Come, let's play at doubled clinging, why sit around, better labour
free.

When the heart is sorrowful, all space, all time, appear empty.
To live with unfulfilled desire—such a life is burdensome.
All are absorbed in their own pursuits throughout the city—
Waves arise in hearts that enjoy the river of beauty:
Come, let's play at doubled clinging, why sit around, better labour
free.

We've been betrayed to the Mirza by that wretch of a Chameli—
The saying has turned out true—Ravan's own brother destroyed
his city—
Now he will confine us strictly, he's entered the house looking
very angry.
Tell me, my dear, what else is there to do besides this remedy:
Come, let's play at doubled clinging, why sit around, better labour
free.

What else can I write about Sukkho and Mukkho's daring acts?
When their husbands forbade them to do what they were doing,
They said, We are now famous everywhere as clinging women—
Why not act upon it then—when going out to dance, why wear
a veil?
Come let's play at doubled clinging, why sit around, better labour
free?

2.
There's no love lost between women and men these days—
New ways of being intimate are seen all around.
Everyone knows about women who love women—
At night these words are always to be heard:
The way you rub me, ah! it drives my heart wild—
Stroke me a little more, my sweet Dogana.

I'd sacrifice all men for your sake, my life,
I'd sacrifice a hundred lives for your embraces

How delightful it is when two vulvas meet—
This is the tale they tell each other all the time:

The way you rub me, ah!...

When you join your lips to my lips,
It feels as if new life pours into my being,
When breast meets breast, the pleasure is such
That from sheer joy the words rise to my lips:

The way you rub me, ah!...
How can I be happy with a man—as soon as he sits by me
He starts showing me a small thing like a mongoose—
I'd much rather have a big dildo
And I know you know all that I know

The way you rub me, ah!...

When I take your tongue in my mouth and suck on it—
With what tongue shall I describe the state I am in?
Long are the hours I wait for you, deprived of love—
Why then, my life, should I not lose myself and say:

The way you rub me, ah!...

What other companion or confidante do I have but you?
The truth is no one can match you in what you do,
All the other Chaptis should become your pupils—
Instead of coyness why shouldn't these words rise to my lips:

The way you rub me, ah!...

You are the best of all—to whom can I compare you?
Whoever I tell about your skills, starts desiring you.
Oh, oh, what kinds of pleasure your strokes give me—
To tell the truth, there is no delight greater than this:

The way you rub me, ah!...

Let my shoe go close to that wretched man.
Let her go to men who want stakes hammered into her—

Can she ever get these hours and hours of pleasure?
How can I persuade myself to find pleasure with men?

The way you rub me, ah!...

I'd give up anything for that moment when you come in,
Dressed pretty as a picture, and put your arms around my neck!
For that pleasure when our nipples touch and meet,
And when we caress each other any way we please!

The way you rub me, ah!...

I'm taken with your manner, your style is entrancing,
I from above, you from below, let's put in more energy,
When our bodies come together, we will lose ourselves—
Oh how much I enjoy this, why shouldn't I tell you:

The way you rub me, ah!...

Who can find words for the pleasure of this act?
For hours when we're together, I'm deaf to other voices.
How to describe the taste of sweets eaten in secret?
There's no pleasure in the world like clinging to a woman.

The way you rub me, ah!...

When you run your tongue over my lips,
My heart and being experience a myriad pleasures.
I think of men, young and old, as one thinks of a holy man—
I have forsaken the whole world for you:

The way you rub me, ah!...

What fools they are who run after men,
It's absurd to burn oneself up like a candle for men!
When one woman clings to another, such is the happiness
They never want to part or let their desire decrease:

The way you rub me, ah!...

That wretched man should feel ashamed of coming so soon—

It's sheer humiliation to be in that useless fellow's company.
Why in this garden of the world do women lovers not have pricks?
In any case, I would much rather have your fruit than that banana!

The way you rub me, ah!...

However much daring a man may have,
However much energy and lustful desire,
I'd rather see a face that gives me pleasure—
I'd give anything for this intimacy which I much prefer.

The way you rub me, ah! it drives my heart wild—
Stroke me a little more, my sweet Dogana.

—*Translated from the Urdu by Saleem Kidwai, versified by Ruth Vanita*

WHY SHOULD YOU GO WANDERING INTO THE GARDEN, MY LOVE

Raskhan

Why should you go wandering into the garden, my love,
For let me show you a garden right here.
My heels have the luster of little pomegranates
My arms sway towards you like boughs of the champa.
On my chest you'll find two lemons full of juice,
I'll lift my veil to have you taste my lips like grapes.
Between my legs is a chalice of joy
And I'll let you loot my flower of love.

—Translated from the Hindi by Harish Trivedi

A MILKMAID TO KRISHNA

Raskhan

She was sleeping nicely in her bed when he came in
And wrapped his arms tightly round her.
She started and stretched and got up scared
And, quivering, struggled to break free of his hold.
In the skirmish was torn her scarf and her blouse
And pearls sewn on it came undone and rolled off.
'Rasakhan:' she could barely speak, as in anger:
'Get off, dear Krishna, for my waist-knot throbs.'

—Translated from the Hindi by Harish Trivedi

Women On Their Own

NASREEN

Krishna Baldev Vaid

Whenever I am alone and sad and a little high I sit down to replay my first night with you and can never decide where to begin and find myself beginning at a new point each time—sometimes at the Kala Bhavan, sometimes with the first drink we had together or with our first kiss or with the first spark ignited by our gazes meeting or with some antic of yours at Reva's party or something you said there. I then try to bring back moment-by-moment the entire duration from the Kala Bhavan up to that very last moment that night. Without forgetting a single thing that was said or done or thought or even the silences. But the attempt always fails and like some greedy little girl I go running ahead flying to the moment when on returning from Reva's house my gaze had promptly, shamelessly and lustfully settled on that stately and youthful bulge in your trousers and you were brought up short by the nakedness of my gaze and then follows a blackout after which I sight again the sapling growing from your loins and the wave that ripples through my still clad body thrills me to my heels and at that very moment the chilling question resounds through me whether you too would thrill or not when you see me naked, and I then find that you are advancing towards me step by step with the unseeing carefulness of some sleepwalker and I lose all control when I see your scales swaying and in a dreamy drunken voice you ask me why I'm laughing and at this question that simple and straightforward part of you too straightens as if asking me the same question and my breasts are jumping around with laughter and your gaze is fixed on them as if a killer's and you have now come so close that the tip of your dagger is touching my sari with a droplet of moisture on its tip looking like dew and I immediately stop laughing and as my lips part and quiver I hear your voice again asking so tell me why did you laugh and with the air of an innocent yet sprightly girl I gesture to your groin and you reproach me with a stern face saying no heedless woman dolt make fun of this poor orphan and I start laughing again and you too are laughing now and it is swaying like some loose bough and I realize that I have never before felt so silly and casual with any other man and my eyes drop down to your softening spear and as I compare it with others before I'm puzzled by my own shamelessness and begin wondering how you opened up suddenly after keeping primly to yourself all evening and then you begin like an expert magic-worker to undress me and my body sways to each touch of yours and now we are face to face naked as we were born and it makes me wonder now how we could stand silently like that for so long but maybe the silence wasn't that long and I recall that I looked at you in those moments more deeply than ever after and then you push up my breasts from below as we sometimes do to other people's unweaned babies by pushing their chins up with our fingers to make them gurgle and I feel the desire to tuck up those apricots of yours but I stay my hand thinking of what you may say but the very next moment without any hesitation I bend down and kiss that Blinded Mughal of yours on its mouth and it is so pleased it stands to attention as if ready and all set to obey each command and when I look up I find you've closed your eyes as if you are about to die but then with your eyes still closed you lower your mouth to my right breast as if some tired and thirsty tourist were bending to drink from a tap at some museum or some sybaritic king bending over some blossoming bud in his garden and now you are sucking one breast of mine and with your other hand fondling the other one and my body is turning to wine and as I kiss your bent down and greying head I feel as if I am rewarding some exceptionally courageous courtier of mine standing in my Diwan-e Khas and then by some special skill you somehow tweak my two little plums with your teeth and fingers at the same time that my whole firmament is lit up with twinkling stars and my heels come off the ground and one of your hands now is wreaking havoc in my world below and your other hand seems determined to reduce all distance between my two breasts while my hand has grabbed tight your jumping owl as if holding it back from flying off while also stirring it to go fly and my knees have now turned to water and the floor is slipping away from my feet and between my legs is brewing up some mire and I sway and come cling to you like some village woman tired out of her mind clings to a tree and we then lurch and stumble towards the bed and as we stand there you stop like some non-initiate at the edge of a wrestling pit or some shy guest on seeing for the first time his host's lovely wife and I smile enjoying your timidity and then you suddenly go down on your knees before me and as you nuzzle with your nose the dark grass spread out below my navel you coo and gurgle like a baby or puppy as it laps up milk and my thighs come together and at the touch of your tongue I feel that ants are crawling all over my body and now you are tracing such tender and pretty arabesques between my waist and my ankles that I can no longer keep hold of my blooming body and I pull you up by your hair and obeying your silent but insistent order go down on bended knees and you begin tousling my hair and you are emitting now a moaning sound like that of a woman dying and looking up from below I see your lips withdrawn over your teeth and your brow wrinkled and your eyes in a dazzle and my lips and my tongue get even more madly fidgety and after an age you step back suddenly and pull me up by my breasts and make me stand in front of you and I don't know why I think of a joke and make a face and say if I knew this is what you intended to do I'd have thought of getting some protection for the last thing I want at this age is to be an unwed mother and when you hear this you begin prancing around like a child and your fat little clown is dancing too and when I see it cavorting like a silly fool I begin to laugh and now we are both stamping our feet and laughing away and the jiggling load on my chest seems to me so good and so strange for this is the first time for me to be laughing and dancing like this with a smart naked man and we now fall on the bed and after a dark while I find that your head is caught between the scissors of my thighs and your tongue in a pool of mine and your be-all and my end-all is in my mouth and I have no other wish left in the world for I am whole and all my desires have been fulfilled and I am heaving like a sea and also calm and as for you you are writhing like a fish and now we are lying side by side with our mouths a little bruised and I can taste myself on your tongue and you can taste yourself on mine and now we lie in a soft embrace and are gently stroking and rubbing each other and in a while another round of wild frenzy begins and as we try to emulate the untramelled statues of Khajuraho and the paintings of Picasso we forget that we have not as much command over our bodies as those nameless sculptors had over stone or that master Picasso over colour and line....

—*Translated from the Hindi by Harish Trivedi*

BRAIDS SCATTERED

Gāthā Saptaśatī

Braids scattered,
earrings and necklaces tossing about,
a half-flying
half-divine creature
she mounts her
beloved

—*Translated from the Maharashtrian Prakrit by Andrew Schelling*

I HAD A DREAM

Mahadeviyakka

Listen, sister, listen.
I had a dream

I saw rice, betel, palmleaf
and coconut.
I saw an ascetic
come to beg,
white teeth and small matted curls.

I followed on his heels
and held his hand,
he who goes breaking
all bounds and beyond.

I saw the lord, white as jasmine,
and woke wide open.

He bartered my heart,
looted my flesh,
claimed as tribute
my pleasure,
took over
all of me.

The Parrots of Desire

I'm the woman of love
for my lord, white as jasmine.

Other men are thorn
under the smooth leaf.
I cannot touch them,
go near them, nor trust them,
nor speak to them confidences.

Mother,
because they all have thorns
in their chests,
I cannot take
any man in my arms but my lord

white as jasmine.

—Translated from the Kannada by A. K. Ramanujan

THE KNOT GAVE WAY

Amaruśataka

The knot gave way, and the skirt clung to my hips
fastened somehow by only the cords
of the unsteady girdle
as my lover approached the bed.
That's all I know, dear friend.
Who he was, or who I was, or how we did it
I don't remember even for a moment
once he took me in his arms.

—Translated from the Sanskrit by Andrew Schelling

Mridula Garg

Mahesh drained his cup of tea, lit a cigarette and said gaily, 'I have resigned.'

'You've left your job!' I was astounded.

'Yes.'

'But, why?'

'Just like that. Felt like it. Had enough of Jamshedpur.'

'Have you something else lined up?'

'No.'

'You haven't applied anywhere?'

'No. I don't intend to do a job any more.'

'Then?'

'Something of my own.'

'A factory?'

'Perhaps.'

'You will need money.'

'Yes.'

'Where will it come from?'

'The Government gives loans...there is also my provident fund. I can arrange something, I guess. If not,' he laughed softly, 'we will sell your jewellery.'

I laughed with him.

'Where do you propose to stay?'

'Don't know. I want a holiday first.'

'And I?'

'Go to Delhi.'

'What! You will wander around the world and I'll sit in Delhi looking after your kids,' I retaliated.

Mahesh gave a startled look and then said, 'If you wish, you can roam around the world, I'll look after the kids.'

'What do you know about children?'

'Nothing. That does not mean you have to know everything.'

'I am a woman.'

'So?'

'It's my job.'

'Who says so?'

'Why else did I have children?'

'You did not have them because of that.'

'Why then?'

Mahesh took a while to reply. 'When we got married,' he said, 'You were in love with me and wanted to do all that you thought an Indian wife should do to make her husband happy.'

Now it was my turn to be taken aback.

He was, of course, dead serious. He never laughed without reason, without a deep meaning behind his laughter.

I was reminded of the day I had introduced him to Richard.

'Richard Hutchison,' I had said, 'My husband, Mahesh Goyal.' Mahesh had burst out laughing.

I had been dumbfounded.

'Why laugh?' I had mumbled.

He had given his hand to Richard and said, 'I am Mahesh, Mr. Hutchison. Husband's not a title of mine.' Richard had laughed too.

'Please call me Richard,' he had said and looked at me with envy. He had told me later, 'Mahesh is the only person I sympathise with in this whole affair.'

...'And you?' I asked Mahesh now, 'What did you want?'

'But I did not love you,' he replied.

How strange that I accepted as a statement of fact, something that would have devastated me ten years ago. I had always known it. I knew when we got married that it was nothing more than a marriage of convenience for Mahesh. All the love was from my side. I had never asked him if he loved me because I was afraid he might say no. I had quietly committed myself to giving him all that I believed an average husband wanted from his wife. A well-appointed house. Healthy and well behaved children. An attractive, attentive and properly groomed wife. A hospitable hostess attuned to the needs of our social circle. We were soon accepted as made-for-each-other in the small town of Gorakhpur, where he was posted then.

For eight years, I had not looked at myself or Mahesh, for that matter, with my own eyes. Whichever town we went to, big or small, my vision was determined by what the average man thought to be the average view of society. Even when I looked at myself in the mirror, I saw not my face but the image of the average woman acceptable to society. That was the role I played through the day but...

When Mahesh returned home in the evening, my eyes fixed themselves on his face and the unasked question gnawed at me. Did he love me the way I loved him? All right, not as much but he did love me...or did he not...not at all?

'...So you know?' I said.

'Yes.'

'Did you...then too?'

'Yes.'

'Why did you marry me?'

He was quiet for a while then asked, 'How old was I when we got married?'

'Thirty-two.'

He gave a short laugh.

'Not everyone finds love,' he said.

'But if one does?' I sounded desperate.

He looked surprised. 'Then one will,' he said.

'Suppose you had been in love with someone?'

'I would have married her.'

'What if you fall in love now?'

'With you, here?'

'Yes.'

'What if I fall in love with you?' he laughed again.

'Please answer me. If you fall in love while married to me, what then?'

'If I...really do...?'

I knew he was trying hard to lie but he could not. In the last ten years, he had not lied about anything important. After a long tussle with himself, he said gently but firmly, 'I don't consider the ties of marriage binding, Manu.' He avoided looking at me.

'What if I fall in love?'

He did not say anything.

'Tell me, what if I am in love?'

He was silent for so long that I thought he had forgotten my question and was preoccupied with something else. After all, he had just resigned from his job. There was so much to occupy him. I grew anxious. A man who could give up a prestigious and lucrative position at a moment's notice could do anything.

At last he broke his silence. 'If you do,' he said, 'Try not to tell me.'

Richard had said once, 'Confession is cowardly.'

'But you people believe in confessions,' I had objected.

'Catholics do.'

'You are a Protestant?'

'Yes.'

'You don't have to confess?'

'No.'

'What would you say to Jenny?'

'Nothing.'

'Won't that be lying?'

'Maybe. But confession would be worse. It might lighten my burden by making me feel self-righteous, that's why one confesses. But imagine, what it would do to the one wronged. Torn by jealousy and insecurity, would she not lose her peace of mind forever?'

'Do you feel you have sinned? Is there guilt in your heart?'

'No.'

'Why not?'

'Maybe because you have become part of God, no, God himself for me. I am incomplete without you.'

'Is that not a sin against God?'

'No.'

'What then is sin?'

'That which makes one feel like a sinner.'

'This is not a sin because you are not a sinner?'

'Yes.'

'That means, one sins against oneself, not against God?'

'Yes.'

'You are not a sinner because you chose me of your own free will. Chose, as a conscious act, something that could have been a sin?'

'Yes.'

'But society considers it a sin.'

'Society is not God.'

'Nor are you.'

'I am cast in the image of God.'

'So is society. You are a part of it.'

'God created man, not society in his image.'

'You mean man created God in his image.'

'You can say that, not I. All I know is that God determines our birth and death but not our will. The Testament says, thou mayest.'

'You mean we act according to our will.'

'Yes.'

'You chose me of your own free will?'

'Yes.'

'There's no guilt in you.'

'No.'

'Then you will be with me forever, Richard.'

Mahesh got up and came to me. He stood by me with his hand on my head so that I could not see his face.

He laughed, sadly, but without malice.

'Manu, something strange has happened to me,' he said, 'I...when you stopped loving me, about that time, I went and fell in love with you.'

What was Mahesh saying?

Was it the truth...perhaps it was...I had not looked at him for so long. I had regained my personal vision after I met Richard but I had not turned it towards Mahesh. I would have known otherwise that he spoke nothing but the truth.

But I...Richard... I loved him...only him.

I felt like falling in Mahesh's lap, clasping him to my breast and crying...what am I to do, Mahesh, I love Richard...only him. He is not here...there's no way I can go to him. Still I love him...only him.

Others may not understand this, but Mahesh will. Had he not known, even then, at the time of our marriage and soon after, that he did not love me but I loved him? He will understand. Most definitely, he will, and that is exactly why he cannot be told.

Tears fell from my eyes into my lap as I sat erect and unmoved. I used all my will power not to double up but I could not stop the tears from falling. I pressed my lips with my palms and hoped that he could not see my face just as I did not see his. His hand continued to rest on my head.

'Don't be sad,' he said. 'Perhaps two people can never love each other at the same time. When one does, the other does not and when the other does...It is my fault. I was late.'

My tears turned into a flood.

'The important thing is to love, not to be loved,' he whispered more to himself than to me but the utterance reached my ears.

I sat straight and silent with clenched teeth, trying unsuccessfully to dam my tears.

He removed his hand from my head and sat down beside me. He did not take the chair facing me. I knew he wanted me to pretend that he had not seen my tears. I was not to look at him until my eyes were dry.

'Tell me one thing,' he said, 'won't society find it difficult to function if all husbands and wives were madly in love with each other?'

He laughed freely now.

'If everyone was to get engrossed in the business of love, who would take care of the mundane but important matters. Children would be neglected. The old and the infirm would die. Business would come to a standstill. No one would go into politics. Men and women would lie drunk with each other and the country would go to the dogs. One can't think of all that when in love, can one?'

I did not say anything. My tears had stopped but I could not trust my voice.

'Our society is so mature. It has found a foolproof safeguard. Arranged marriage. Right?'

'Right,' I said. My voice did falter a bit but I managed to control it. Soon, I could speak normally. 'What kind of factory do you want to have?'

'We'll see. At the moment, all I want is a hot cup of tea.' I got up and brought in fresh tea.

I gave him his cup and said brightly, 'Really, we have been in Jamshedpur for too long. It'll be good to go somewhere else now.'

'Yes. We have never lived at one place for four full years before.'

'Nor have we left it so suddenly.'

'A deep-rooted pole has to be pulled out quickly.'

'You mean we are free to go wherever we like now?'

'Yes, where would you like to live?'

'Anywhere,' the words sprang to my lips but I pushed them back. I knew that he knew, it was all the same to me where I lived, but it could not be said.

It did not matter to me whether I lived in Jamshedpur, Gorakhpur, Kanpur, Mumbai, Chennai or Modinagar. We had been to all those places in turn. Mahesh took and left jobs just as he picked up cards and threw down his hand in a game. So far, he had been lucky...the game had been his...at least the game of cards. A new place, perhaps, this time...Calcutta...Hyderabad...Bangalore...

'Bangalore,' I said. 'That's a nice place.'

'What's nice about it?'

'Well...open spaces...lots of flowers...good weather...the same throughout the year, neither hot nor cold.'

'It's no fun living in a place where even the weather does not change.'

'Hyderabad then?'

'Hyderabad!' he sounded contemptuous. 'What about Delhi? The weather would change all the time.'

'Yes...it...would...' I had begun to lose interest.

'How about another cup of tea?' he said.

'Tea. I'll get it,' I jumped up.

'Shall we go to Ooty?'

'Let's,' I concurred promptly.

'Where shall we go?'

'Where did you say?'

'Ooty.'

'Ooty...yes, it'll be nice to live there.'

'Not to live, for a vacation.'

'When do we go?'

'Why are you not saying no to anything,' he said so quietly, it shook me.

'Of course, I am,' I took hold of myself, 'I mean...there is nothing to say...no to. Now, if we go to Ooty...'

'Forget it,' he said. 'Get the tea.'

◆

Mahesh came home for lunch today.

I grew alert. I watched him carefully as I served him food. Engrossed in his thoughts, he ate slowly, chewing each morsel unhurriedly as he always did. He never spoke while eating. He was not a great talker in any case, but he grew absolutely silent when engaged in anything physical.

I watched him eat but could not fathom what exactly he intended to do afterwards.

I served him but I did not eat myself. He did not notice. It was all a matter of habit. I left my food uneaten so often that it escaped notice whether I ate or not. I could not eat when my senses were on the alert. That is why my body was in a stupor most of the time. But we do not live by the body alone. We have a heart and a mind too. Both ordered it about. The poor body stands by and waits silently as the heart and mind fight to gain suzerainty over it. There is an uneasy truce after each fight as one emerges the winner. The body knows whom it will have to obey that day.

My body had grown so lethargic those days, it was always in a state of somnolence. Yet, it managed to carry out the dictates of the heart.

I sat in my room writing letters. I did not know how many I had written in the last five years.

One day someone had mistaken my poems for letters and had torn them up. My letters might now be mistaken for poems...if someone cared to read them.

My right hand was the energetic one. It took hold of the pen and ran fast on the paper as directed by the heart. The rest of the creature continued to sleep. I was aware of only one part of my body, the right hand.

My body had got fragmented into parts and I became one or the other as the occasion demanded.

Mahesh finished eating. I waited. Would he rest now or would he... it was for him to decide...

Mahesh washed his hands and face. He was ready to go...he looked alert, not tired at all.

I went to the door to see him off.

He stretched his arm to open the door, then turned round to look at me, to feel my physical closeness. He pulled me to him and turned back to the door. I was thrown against his chest. His hands were free to come to my breasts. He squeezed them hard with the possessive fondness of he who knew himself to be the owner. I knew he would make love to me that night.

I started turning into an object from that moment. Mahesh did not say anything nor did he look at me again. The pressure of his hands on my breasts lessened. He pushed me away from him, opened the door and went out.

I always knew beforehand when Mahesh planned to make love to me...long experience had taught me. As soon as I came to know of it, I began to turn into a creature of the flesh.

◆

I decided to take a bath that afternoon.

I had all the time at my disposal. I did not plan to write letters that day.

I took off all my clothes and scrutinized my naked body. It was still young...perhaps beautiful too...it was beautiful. The beauty of the body lay in its youth.

I began to wash it carefully. No unconscious pouring of mugs of water on the shoulders. No pause in the process to reflect on the contents of the letter to be written that clay. My mind was fully involved in the cleansing of my flesh. I washed my body with the same attention to detail with which Mahesh washed his car every Sunday. It had to last him a whole week. I was more ruthless than he. More like a nurse getting a patient ready for surgery.

I took his razor and shaved off all the hair on my body.

I rubbed my feet clean with a pumice stone. The heel, sole and each of the toes. They went white then grew pink with the scrubbing. They looked like a pair of tiny robins.

I fell in love with my feet. Shyly I touched their pink heels, the dimpled soles, the baby soft toes one by one.

It tickled me. I kept stroking them tenderly...the dull ache turned into undulating waves of pain that rose to a peak, then flowed out.

I wanted someone to smother them with his hands, then to kiss them. No, I did not lose sight of my goal. I knew my body was not just my feet. There were other parts of it and each had its use. I left my feet to their fate.

I took each part into my hands, rubbed it mercilessly with soap then washed it...not one could escape from the attack...my mind stood resolutely on guard. Ruthless in the execution of its duty till the time came, when I was reduced to nothing more than a living mound of flesh.

◆

Mahesh's hands were kneading my breasts.

He had powerful and beautiful hands. Square fleshy palms. The long tapering fingers of an artist. He was an industrialist, not an artist. But he could have been an artist. Definitely. Passionate would have been the music that would have flowed from the sitar, had his fingers run on its strings like this.

I was the instrument his fingers used for his musical practice. Not I...my breasts.

Suppose the whole of my body had been a breast, an enormous, gigantic palpable boob. Round like a globe. Mahesh could have lain sprawled on it. His lips and hands and feet could have played with it, sucked and mauled it and trampled upon it at the same time. He would have squeezed the nipple with his lips and at the same time pummelled the rest of the breast with his powerful hands. It could have borne his cruelest blow, its increased dimensions would have lent it the power. It would have throbbed like a piano under his fingers. Violent tumultuous music would have filled the room...if only I had been a massive boob! Mahesh's lips would have left mine to latch onto the breast, helping his fingers to bruise it. My senses would have exploded within me. I would have moaned with passion. My passion would have touched him. His lips would have mauled the nipple, his fingers grown savage in their flagellation and...he would have entered my body long before now...

Now his lips were on mine. He had pushed my mouth open with his tongue and taken possession of mine. The tissues of my tongue were tingling...I was only a tongue.

But...his hands were on my breasts. Two fingers formed a noose, tightened round the nipple, twisted and pulled it and thrust it away. I understood he wanted his lips to molest it now. He must be yearning for three pairs of lips. He could then keep one pair on my lips and one each on my boobs. Or he could have pulled them close to bring the nipples together and captured both with one pair of lips. He could then put the third pair on the lips within my legs that panted even then in expectation of his imminent penetration. But he had only one pair of lips and they were busy helping his tongue. Had my body been an enormous boob he would not have been put to so much inconvenience. His lips and fingers could have assaulted me at the same time. My eyes were closed but my body lay awake. It totted up every touch of his. I could not see anything, the room was in darkness. I was grateful for that. But my body was familiar with each stroke and shot of the game being played on it.

To make love was a game, an art, a need, a demand of the body. To love was...stupid?

My body was a sentient being. It perused well the elaborate engraving carved on it. Many of the flowers had been etched with its active participation. It was the fountainhead of desire...this my body...it was I...

I did not know exactly when I clasped Mahesh in my arms and carved flowers of red, blue and purple on his neck and arms with my lips and tongue.

My eyes were closed...I could clearly hear, right there in my room... the tinkle of ankle bells...the beat of the tabla...an exquisite rhythm. Not for a moment did the beat falter. Whenever I was with Mahesh that sound held me in thrall...those women who sold their bodies for money, they who were nothing but flesh. They immersed themselves in the worship of the flesh once they had the money in hand. But they worshipped music and dance too.

...The body is the music and the dance too is the body. The body is the Lord and the invocation too is the body. The body is the spirit and its ecstasy too is the body. As long as the body is pledged, the heart and the mind are irrelevant. But it is not greedy. As soon as it extracts its due, it lets go.

Once the body pays back all its debts, every bit that was due, it will be set free. It can then go to sleep if it so wishes...till the next instalment falls due.

Every part of mine was in contact with some part of Mahesh's body. My body was still torn into fragments but the cohesive touch of his body on mine had, for the moment, integrated it into a single whole.

What was I but a body and that too not mine but Mahesh's, his touch and his flesh...

There was no one in the room except Mahesh's body and mine, not even light. Even if we had opened our eyes, we would have seen nothing, it was so dark in the room. But we kept them closed, afraid that the facility to see might dam the rising tide of passion.

Mahesh entered my body. It was nothing, this intercourse between man and woman, nothing but an inherited, intense longing in every man to fill a hole.

Our bodies merged and lay as one on the bed, writhing, moaning, sweating for the currents of ecstasy to sweep over us till the final shock left us insensible with a last shuddering cry.

Mahesh could then go to sleep and I could open my eyes after casting aside my half-asleep body.

The darkness of the room was peaceful...what of the body...it went to sleep eventually...always did.

But let me first go to the bathroom and wash it all away. The blue marks are of no consequence, they would go of their own in a day or two.

◆

I was standing outside.

The postman came and tossed the letters before me. He did not put them in the letterbox. After all, I was standing right there. The blue envelope fluttered its wings and took off, falling on the ground a little distance away from the other letters. I knew the flutter well. It was exactly the way a caged bird, eager to reach the sky, quivered if it sensed that the cage had opened. I took a deep breath. The tangy scent of salty seawater filled my nostrils. A piquant smell. Strange but not a stranger. This had to be his letter.

I know, I know, it was the strong breeze blowing outside which had lifted the envelope to me.

The sour smell, neither fragrance nor odour, of seaweeds and saline water that I longed for months, existed only in my imagination. That too I knew. A special smell could hardly permeate an envelope just because it had travelled across the sea. I know the greatest asset of a human being is his rationality and this reasoning faculty tells us that nothing ever happens without cause and effect. Great. We should be proud of our rationality. As for me, I was prouder of the fact that I could instantly recognize his letter by its sound and smell. Not proud really. It was more a sense of reprieve. As if someone had massaged my body gently to relieve it of all tension and pushed it into a state of sweet somnolence.

The blue envelope lay quivering on the floor waiting for me to pick it up. I knew it would not attempt to fly any more. It would lie there flapping its wings and hoping for my caress. Poor little captive, how it strained to break free of the prison of the envelope and come to me. Why did I not run and pick it up, you wonder, why did I not tear the outer cover and shower kisses on the letter with my eyes? You can wonder because, obviously, you have never waited for anyone.

I had waited for it for four months, throbbing with longing every minute. How could I squander the precious life-giving moments by tearing through them in a hurry.

I will go forward slowly. Pick up the envelope in slow motion. I will first kiss it with my eyes, then caress it with my fingers. Then... after quite a while...I will ever so carefully tear the edge, stuck with gum. Be patient...wait a while...I have waited for four months...do not tremble so...I will read...in a while all that you have written...

The envelope came open. The letter was before me. Lines in blue ink lay scrawled across a fine, crisp, blue paper. Really Richard, what horrible handwriting. I have got used to it, otherwise I don't know how often I would have had to go through it to decipher anything. It would have been fun.

My eyes went from the top to the bottom tasting each word.

Only one word was clear to me... Richard.

My eyes perused the contents again and this time I read. Manu. 'Manu-Manu-Manu!'

That was how he addressed me in each of his letters. Never dear or dearest or beloved. Only Manu-Manu-Manu...my name exploding from his throat.

Signed Richard. Just Richard. Not even yours.

Richard-Richard-Richard! The music bursting forth in the final moment of ecstasy...its cry and...its fulfilment.

Now the contents. Once...twice...thrice...again and again. I am waiting for the day when I will come to India...to Delhi and see you...I will take a lot of pictures this time...I am waiting...impatiently...a few days more.

Now the envelope. That too had to be read. Where was it from this time? Lebanon. It came once in three or four months. It could be from any corner of the earth. Greece...Istanbul...Dhaka...Jerusalem...Korea... Vietnam...or...anywhere.

This time it was from Lebanon. So that's where the war was. That was what he had said, wherever the army was, there was the church. Wherever man is engaged in torturing and killing other men, I am there... cast in the image of God. Yes Richard, we need someone to replace God and remind men that they alone are responsible for what they do.

When you are there Richard, I have no need of myself.

The contents once more...I wait...when will I come to Delhi...
When Richard? When?

My wait was over...my wait began.

I'll come every year, he had said before he left.

He had kept his word for five years. Twenty-five days of happiness.
I was rich indeed.

You know how to live three-hundred-and-sixty-five days in five days?
You don't. I did not either. I learnt it slowly. It is an art. You want to
learn it. Fine, fall in love with a gypsy. It will come to you of its own.
It will be painful. Three hundred and sixty days of pain. Five days of
joy. The account will balance.

I had only one complaint. My five days were full of fear. What if
they were the last five days? What if he were never to come again?

It was easy for someone constantly on the move to wait. What
about the one who was fixed at one place?

Could one know the agony of the other? One who had never stood
still. Never needed patience. Who went through the moments of waiting
at a run?

How could one make him understand that the sun rose in front
of the same window every morning. That every day the little rabbit
of sunshine hid in the corner of the same verandah, running back in
fear of certain death to its cave, much before the sun sank. That the
approaching darkness painted the corners of the same room black every
night. And the same bed saw sobs strangle in the throat before they
were born every day.

He did not know how long three-hundred-and sixty-five days could
be in that room, he whom the sun awakened at a different time and
from a different direction each day.

I know, the sun rises from the east every day, but what of a man
whose window opens into a different country each time?

East-west-north-south, it was not around me that the wheel turned.
He had a family. A wife. Three children. It came to rest next to them
at the end of each journey. Five days for me and a hundred for them.

That left only two hundred and sixty days for travel. Negligible for
him. The days ran close on each other's heels. But for me...everything
stayed put.

One wait ended...another began. Yet, there was a difference between
the two. There was the wait, inert like an old rag that was mine before
the letter came, when I did not know if I was alive or not. The other wait
began now, like a bird fluttering its wings, after the arrival of the letter.

Richard-Richard-Richard! Manu is alive. Manu knows she is alive.

Manu can see...the cushion on the chair is yellow in colour. The tablecloth has a peacock embroidered on it. The aroma of cumin seed and asafoetida sautéed in ghee wafts from the kitchen. Someone sings in the house next door. The sun is shining outside. The edge of her sari is torn. People are running on the road. Bells are ringing in the church nearby. Birds have broken into song in the solitary neem tree outside her house. A stray dog barks on the road. A sunbeam has crept into the verandah. The chrysanthemum in the earthen pot looks taller than yesterday...and all these are proof of her being alive.

She sees a film of dust on her doorstep and knows that this dust too is not meaningless but a manifestation of life. She is alive and will be alive every moment till he comes.

No...she is lying.

She will start dying again after a few days of living...as the crisp fine blue paper splits into four parts with repeated perusal. Despite all her care, it will begin to crack at the edges. She will begin to wait all over again...for the letter to arrive. Dying through the days yet forced to live because his letter will come...one day. It was sheer hell for someone fixed in space to wait in tune with the time of a man constantly on the move...patiently...impatiently...living in the past.

DARK ONE

Mirabai

Sister, the Dark One won't speak to me.
Why does this useless body keep breathing?
Another night gone
and no one's lifted my gown.
He won't speak to me.
Years pass, not a gesture.
They told me
he'd come when the rains came,
but lightning pierces the clouds,
the clock ticks until daybreak
and I feel the old dread.
Slave to the Dark One,
Mira's whole life is a long
night of craving.

—*Translated from the Brajbhasha by Andrew Schelling*

The Parrots of Desire

LIHAAF

Ismat Chughtai

In winter when I put a quilt over myself its shadows on the wall seem to sway like an elephant. That sets my mind racing into the labyrinth of times past. Memories come crowding in.

Sorry. I'm not going to regale you with any romantic tale about my own quilt. It's hardly a subject for romance. It seems to me that the blanket, though less comfortable, does not cast shadows as terrifying as the quilt, dancing on the wall.

I was then a small girl and fought all day with my brothers and their friends. Often I wondered why the hell I was so aggressive. At my age my other sisters were busy drawing admirers while I fought with any boy or girl I ran into!

This was why when my mother went to Agra she left me with an adopted sister of hers for about a week. She knew well that there was no one in that house, not even a mouse, with which I could get into a fight. It was severe punishment for me! So Amma left me with Begum Jaan, the same lady whose quilt is etched in my memory like the scar left by a blacksmith's brand. Her poor parents agreed to marry her off to the Nawab who was of 'ripe years' because he was very virtuous. No one had ever seen a nautch girl or prostitute in his house. He had performed Haj and helped several others to do it.

He, however, had a strange hobby. Some people are crazy enough to cultivate interests like breeding pigeons and watching cockfights. Nawab Saheb had contempt for such disgusting sports. He kept an open house for students—young, fair and slender-waisted boys whose expenses were borne by him.

Having married Begum Jaan he tucked her away in the house with his other possessions and promptly forgot her. The frail, beautiful Begum wasted away in anguished loneliness.

One did not know when Begum Jaan's life began—whether it was when she committed the mistake of being born or when she came to the Nawab's house as his bride, climbed the four-poster bed and started counting her days. Or was it when she watched through the drawing room door the increasing number of firm-calved, supple-waisted boys and delicacies begin to come for them from the kitchen! Begum Jaan would have glimpses of them in their perfumed, flimsy shirts and feel as though she was being raked over burning embers!

Or did it start when she gave up on amulets, talismans, black magic and other ways of retaining the love of her straying husband? She arranged for night long readings of the scripture but in vain. One cannot draw blood from a stone. The Nawab didn't budge an inch. Begum Jaan was heartbroken and turned to books. But she didn't get relief. Romantic novels and sentimental verse depressed her even more. She began to pass sleepless nights yearning for a love that had never been.

She felt like throwing all her clothes into the oven. One dresses up to impress people. Now, the Nawab didn't have a moment to spare. He was too busy chasing the gossamer shirts, nor did he allow her to go out. Relatives, however, would come for visits and would stay for months while she remained a prisoner in the house. These relatives, freeloaders all, made her blood boil. They helped themselves to rich food and got warm stuff made for themselves while she stiffened with cold despite the new cotton in her quilt. As she tossed and turned, her quilt made newer shapes on the wall but none of them held promise of life for her. Then why must one live...such a life as Begum Jaan was destined to live. But then she started living and lived her life to the full.

It was Rabbu who rescued her from the fall.

Soon her thin body began to fill out. Her cheeks began to glow and she blossomed in beauty. It was a special oil massage that brought life back to the half-dead Begum Jaan. Sorry, you won't find the recipe for this oil even in the most exclusive magazines.

When I first saw Begum Jaan she was around forty. She looked a picture of grandeur, reclining on the couch. Rabbu sat against her back, massaging her waist. A purple shawl covered her feet as she sat in regal splendour, a veritable Maharani. I was fascinated by her looks and felt like sitting by her for hours, just adoring her. Her complexion was marble white without a speck of ruddiness. Her hair was black and always bathed in oil. I had never seen the parting of her hair crooked, nor a single hair out of place. Her eyes were black and the elegantly-plucked eyebrows seemed like two bows spreading over the demure eyes. Her eyelids were heavy and eyelashes dense. However, the most fascinating part of her face were her lips—usually dyed in lipstick and with a mere trace of down on her upper lip. Long hair covered her temples. Sometimes her face seemed to change shape under my gaze and looked as though it were the face of a young boy...

Her skin was also white and smooth and seemed as though someone had stitched it tightly over her body. When she stretched her legs for the massage I stole a glance at their sheen, enraptured. She was very tall and the ample flesh on her body made her look stately and magnificent. Her hands were large and smooth, her waist exquisitely formed. Rabbu used to massage her back for hours together. It was as though getting the massage was one of the basic necessities of life. Rather—more important than life's necessities.

Rabbu had no other household duties. Perched on the couch she was always massaging some part of her body or the other. At times I could hardly bear it—the sight of Rabbu massaging or rubbing at all hours. Speaking for myself, if anyone were to touch my body so often I would certainly rot to death.

Even this daily massaging was not enough. On the days she took a bath, she would massage the Begum's body with a variety of oils and pastes for two hours. And she would massage with such vigour that even imagining it made me sick. The doors would be closed, the braziers would be lit and then the session began. Usually Rabbu was the only person allowed to remain inside on such occasions. Other maids handed over the necessary things at the door, muttering disapproval.

In fact—Begum Jaan was afflicted with a persistent itch. Despite using all the oils and balms the itch remained stubbornly there. Doctors and *hakims* pronounced that nothing was wrong, the skin was unblemished. It could be an infection under the skin. 'These doctors are crazy... There's nothing wrong with you. It's just the heat of the body,' Rabbu would say, smiling while she gazed at Begum Jaan dreamily.

Rabbu! She was as dark as Begum Jaan was fair, as purple as the other one was white. She seemed to glow like heated iron. Her face was scarred by smallpox. She was short, stocky and had a small paunch. Her hands were small but agile, her large, swollen lips were always wet. A strange, sickening stench exuded from her body. And her tiny, puffy hands moved dexterously over Begum Jaan's body—now at her waist, now at her hips, then sliding down her thighs and dashing to her ankles. Whenever I sat by Begum Jaan my eyes would remain glued to those roving hands.

All through the year Begum Jaan would wear Hyderbadi *jaali karga* kurtas, white and billowing, and brightly coloured pyjamas. And even if it was warm and the fan was on, she would cover herself with a light shawl. She loved winter. I, too, liked to be at her house in that season. She rarely moved out. Lying on the carpet she would munch dry fruits as Rabbu rubbed her back. The other maids were jealous of Rabbu. The witch! She ate, sat and even slept with Begum Jaan! Rabbu and Begum Jaan were the subject of their gossip during leisure hours. Someone would mention their name and the whole group would burst into loud guffaws. What juicy stories they made up about them! Begum Jaan was oblivious to all this, cut off as she was from the world outside.

Her existence was centred on herself and her itch.

I have already mentioned that I was very young at that time and was in love with Begum Jaan. She, too, was fond of me. When Amma decided to go to Agra, she left me with Begum Jaan for a week. She knew that left alone in the house I would fight with my brothers or roam around. The arrangement pleased both Begum Jaan and me. After all she was Amma's adopted sister! Now the question was—where would I sleep? In Begum Jaan's room, naturally. A small bed was placed alongside hers. Till ten or eleven at night we chatted and played 'Chance'. Then I went to bed. Rabbu was still rubbing her back as I fell asleep. 'Ugly woman!' I thought. I woke up at night and was scared. It was pitch dark and Begum Jaan's quilt was shaking vigorously as though an elephant was struggling inside.

'Begum Jaan...,' I could barely form the words out of fear. The elephant stopped shaking and the quilt came down.

'What's it? Get back to sleep.' Begum Jaan's voice seemed to come from somewhere.

'I'm scared,' I whimpered.

'Get back to sleep. What's there to be scared of? Recite the *Ayatul kursi*.'

'All right...' I began to recite the prayer but each time I reached *ya lamu ma bain...* I forgot the lines though I knew the entire *ayat* by heart.

'May I come to you, Begum Jaan?'

'No, child... Get back to sleep.' Her tone was rather abrupt. Then I heard two people whispering. Oh God, who was this other person? I was really afraid.

'Begum Jaan... I think there's a thief in the room.'

'Go to sleep, child... There's no thief,' this was Rabbu's voice. I drew the quilt over my face and fell asleep.

By morning I had totally forgotten the terrifying scene enacted at night. I have always been superstitious—night fears, sleepwalking and sleep-talking were daily occurrences in my childhood. Everyone used to say that I was possessed by evil spirits. So the incident slipped from my memory. The quilt looked perfectly innocent in the morning.

But the following night I woke up again and heard Begum Jaan and Rabbu arguing in a subdued tone. I could not hear what they were saying and what was the upshot of the tiff but I heard Rabbu crying. Then came the slurping sound of a cat licking a plate... I was scared and got back to sleep.

The next day Rabbu went to see her son, an irascible young man. Begum Jaan had done a lot to help him out—bought him a shop, got him a job in the village. But nothing really pleased him. He stayed with Nawab Saheb for some time, who got him new clothes and other gifts; but he ran away for no good reason and never came back, even to see Rabbu...

Rabbu had gone to a relative's house to see him. Begum Jaan was reluctant to let her go but realised that Rabbu was helpless. So she didn't prevent her from going.

All through the day Begum Jaan was out of her element. Her body ached at every joint, but she couldn't bear anyone's touch. She didn't eat anything and kept moping in the bed the whole day.

'Shall I rub your back, Begum Jaan...?' I asked zestfully as I shuffled the deck of cards. She began to peer at me.

'Shall I, really?' I put away the cards and began to rub her back while Begum Jaan lay there quietly. Rabbu was due to return the next day... but she didn't. Begum Jaan grew more and more irritable. She drank cup after cup of tea and her head began to ache.

I again began rubbing her back which was smooth as the top of a table. I rubbed gently and was happy to be of some use to her.

'A little harder... open the straps,' Begum Jaan said.

'Here...a little below the shoulder...that's right... Ah! what pleasure...' She expressed her satisfaction between sensuous breaths. 'A little further...' Begum Jaan instructed though her hands could easily reach that spot. But she wanted me to stroke it. How proud I felt! 'Here...oh, oh, you're tickling me... Ah!' She smiled. I chatted away as I continued to massage her.

'I'll send you to the market tomorrow... What do you want?... A doll that sleeps or wakes up as you want?'

'No, Begum Jaan... I don't want dolls... Do you think I'm still a child?'

'So you're an old woman then,' she laughed. 'If not a doll I'll get you a *babua*... Dress it up yourself. I'll give you a lot of rags. Okay?'

'Okay,' I answered.

'Here,' she would take my hand and place it where it itched and I, lost in the thought of the *babua* kept on scratching her listlessly while she talked.

'Listen...you need some more frocks. I'll send for the tailor tomorrow and ask him to make new ones for you. Your mother has left some dress material.'

'I don't want that red material... It looks so cheap,' I was chattering, oblivious of where my hands travelled. Begum Jaan lay still... Oh God! I jerked my hand away.

'Hey girl, watch where your hands are... You hurt my ribs.' Begum

Jaan smiled mischievously. I was embarrassed.

'Come here and lie down beside me...' She made me lie down with my head on her arm 'How skinny you are...your ribs are coming out.' She began counting my ribs.

I tried to protest.

'Come on, I'm not going to eat you up. How tight this sweater is! And you don't have a warm vest on.' I felt very uncomfortable.

'How many ribs does one have?' She changed the topic.

'Nine on one side, ten on the other,' I blurted out my school hygiene, rather incoherently.

'Take away your hand... Let's see...one, two, three...'

I wanted to run away, but she held me tightly. I tried to wriggle out and Begum Jaan began to laugh loudly. To this day whenever I am reminded of her face at that moment I feel jittery. Her eyelids had drooped, her upper lip showed a black shadow and tiny beads of sweat sparkled on her lips and nose despite the cold. Her hands were cold like ice but clammy as though the skin had been stripped off. She had put away the shawl and in the fine *karga* kurta her body shone like a ball of dough. The heavy gold buttons of the kurta were open and swinging to one side.

It was evening and the room was getting enveloped in darkness. A strange fright overwhelmed me. Begum Jaan's deep-set eyes focused on me and I felt like crying. She was pressing me as though I were a clay doll and the odour of her warm body made me almost throw up. But she was like one possessed. I could neither scream nor cry.

After some time she stopped and lay back exhausted. She was breathing heavily and her face looked pale and dull. I thought she was going to die and rushed out of the room...

Thank God Rabbu returned that night. Scared, I went to bed rather early and pulled the quilt over me. But sleep evaded me for hours.

Amma was taking so long to return from Agra! I had got so terrified of Begum Jaan that I spent the whole day in the company of maids. I felt too nervous to step into her room. What could I have said to anyone? That I was afraid of Begum Jaan? Begum Jaan who was so attached to me?

That day Rabbu and Begum Jaan had a tiff again. This did not augur well for me because Begum Jaan's thoughts were immediately directed towards me. She realised that I was wandering outdoors in the cold and might die of pneumonia! 'Child, do you want to put me to shame in public? If something should happen to you, it'll be a disaster,' She made me sit beside her as she washed her face and hands in the water basin. Tea was set on a tripod next to her.

'Make tea, please...and give me a cup,' she said as she wiped her face with a towel. 'I'll change in the meanwhile.'

I took tea while she dressed. During her body massage she sent for me repeatedly. I went in, keeping my face turned away and ran out after doing the errand. When she changed her dress I began to feel jittery. Turning my face away from her I sipped my tea.

My heart yearned in anguish for Amma. This punishment was much more severe than I deserved for fighting with my brothers. Amma always disliked my playing with boys. Now tell me, are they man-eaters that they would eat up her darling? And who are the boys? My own brothers and their puny, little friends! She was a believer in strict segregation for women. And Begum Jaan here was more terrifying than all the loafers of the world. Left to myself, I would have run out to the street—even further away! But I was helpless and had to stay there much against my wish.

Begum Jaan had decked herself up elaborately and perfumed herself with the warm scent of *attars*. Then she began to shower me with affection. 'I want to go home,' was my answer to all her suggestions. Then I started crying.

'There, there...come near me... I'll take you to the market today. Okay?'

But I kept up the refrain of going home. All the toys and sweets of the world had no interest for me.

'Your brothers will bash you up, you witch,' she tapped me affectionately on my cheek.

'Let them.'

'Raw mangoes are sour to taste, Begum Jaan,' hissed Rabbu, burning with jealousy.

Then Begum Jaan had a fit. The gold necklace she had offered me moments ago flew into pieces. The muslin net dupatta was torn to shreds. And her hair-parting which was never crooked was a tangled mess.

'Oh! Oh! Oh!' She screamed between spasms. I ran out.

Begum Jaan regained her senses after much fuss and ministrations. When I peered into the room on tiptoe, I saw Rabbu rubbing her body, nestling against her waist.

'Take off your shoes,' Rabbu said while stroking Begum Jaan's ribs. Mouse-like, I snuggled into my quilt.

There was a peculiar noise again. In the dark Begum Jaan's quilt was once again swaying like an elephant. 'Allah! Ah!...' I moaned in a feeble voice. The elephant inside the quilt heaved up and then sat down. I was mute. The elephant started to sway again. I was scared stiff. However, I had resolved to switch on the light that night, come what may. The elephant started fluttering once again and it seemed as though it was trying to squat. There was the sound of someone smacking her lips, as though savouring a tasty pickle. Now I understood! Begum Jaan had not eaten anything the whole day. And Rabbu, the witch, was a notorious glutton. She must be polishing off some goodies. Flaring my nostrils I smelled the air. There was only the smell of *attar*, sandalwood and henna, nothing else.

Once again the quilt started swinging. I tried to lie down still but the quilt began to assume such grotesque shapes that I was thoroughly shaken. It seemed as though a large frog was inflating itself noisily and was about to leap on me.

'Aa... Ammi...' I whimpered courageously. No one paid any heed. The quilt crept into my brain and began to grow larger. I stretched my leg nervously to the other side of the bed to grope for the switch and turned it on. The elephant somersaulted inside the quilt which deflated immediately. During the somersault the corner of the quilt rose by almost a foot...

Good God! I gasped and plunged into my bed.

—*Translated from the Urdu by M. Asaduddin*

Nostalgia
On missing the sex we had

.... ~ ....

SMELL[*]

Saadat Hasan Manto

It was a day during the rainy season—a day just like today. Outside the window, the leaves of the peepal tree stood drenched in the rain. A young woman from the hills, a ghatan, was lying curled up against Randheer on the spring mattress of this very same teak bed, which had now been moved away from the window a bit.

Beyond the window, the leaves washed by the rain quivered like earrings in the milky darkness of the night, very much like the shivers the girl clinging to him sent coursing through his body.

Randheer had been reading an English-language newspaper the whole day and had been through not just every news item but practically all the ads as well. Toward evening he stepped out onto the balcony to amuse himself a bit and spotted the girl under a tamarind tree shielding herself from the downpour. She probably worked in the neighboring rope factory. He cleared his throat and coughed a couple of times to draw her attention and, after a while, he motioned to her to come up.

He'd been feeling quite despondent for the past several days. With the war going on, nearly all the Christian girls of Bombay, who could be had at a bargain price, had enlisted in the Auxiliary Force. Some had moved to the Fort area and set up dancing schools, which only gora soldiers were allowed to enter. Randheer was feeling quite miserable. One reason was that the Christian girls were no longer readily available. Another was the colour of his skin: although enviably suave and well-mannered, educated, in good health, and quite a bit more handsome than most young men, he was barred from practically all the brothels of the Fort area. After all, he was not a gora.

Before the war came along he had physical relationships with umpteen Christian girls around the Nagpara and Taj Hotel areas. He was far more adept in matters of the flesh than any of the Christian boys with whom those girls conducted fleeting affairs just to appear chic until eventually settling down with some dumbo or other.

He had called the ghatan over to get even with Hazel who had recently acquired this air of mannered haughtiness. Hazel lived in the flat below his. Every morning, outfitted in her army uniform, her khaki cap set at a rakish angle over her short-trimmed hair, she marched out

---

*'Bu,' from the author's collection *Manto-Nama* (Lahore: Sang-e-Meel Publications, 1990), 641–48.

of her place with such a swagger, as if everyone should roll themselves out as a carpet for her to walk on.

Why in the world did he feel so drawn to Christian girls?—he'd often wondered. Well, yes, they did show off all the seductive assets of their bodies to good effect, spoke unabashedly of their irregular periods and even their former love affairs, and swayed their legs the minute some dance tune or other drifted into their ears—but any woman could just as easily boast of these qualities, couldn't she?

When Randheer gestured to the ghatan to come up he had no thought whatsoever of getting her into bed with him. Noticing how thoroughly soaked she was, he feared the poor thing might catch pneumonia so he said, 'Take off those wet clothes! You'll catch a cold.'

She thought she understood what was implied and blushed. When Randheer took out a fresh white dhoti and handed it to her, she hesitated for a moment and then undid her kashta, its grime made more visible by the rain. She pushed it aside and quickly threw the white dhoti around her hips and started to undo her tight-fitting choli, the two ends of which she had secured with a tight knot that had disappeared in the faint but grimy cleavage of her shapely breasts.

With her worn down nails she struggled with the knot for quite a while but couldn't manage to loosen what the rainwater had tightened so firmly. Eventually she gave up and muttered something to Randheer in Marathi which meant, 'What shall I do? It just won't open.'

Randheer sat down beside her to give it a try but he couldn't make the knot budge either. In exasperation he grabbed the two ends and tugged at them so vigorously that the knot came undone. His hands lurched from the force of the pull, baring two trembling breasts. For a moment he felt as though, with the dexterity of a master potter, his own hands had shaped a lump of soft, moist clay into a pair of exquisite cups on the girl's breast.

Her youthful breasts had the same rawness and allure, the same moist freshness and cooling warmth that oozes from vessels just fashioned by a potter. A strange glow was implicit in the earth colour of those pristine young breasts. A diaphanous layer of a sort of muted luminescence beneath their darkish complexion was giving off that strange glow, which was almost not a glow. The two swellings on her chest looked more like a pair of earthen lamps set afloat on the muddy waters of a pond.

Yes, it was a day during the rains—a day just like this one. The leaves of the peepal were trembling outside the window. The ghatan's dripping-wet, two-piece dress was lying on the floor in a messy heap, while she herself was wrapped around Randheer. The warmth of her naked, unwashed body produced the same sensation in his own that he felt in the hot, filthy hammams of the barbers during blustery winters.

She had clung to his body all night long, as if their two bodies had melded together. They hadn't exchanged more than a couple of words. They had no need to. Their breath, their lips and hands conveyed all that needed to be communicated. With the tenderness of the gentlest breeze, his hands caressed her breasts all through the night—and however light the touch, her tiny nipples, in the middle of their large, dark, coarse areolae, responded, sending a wave of tremulous pleasure through her body that never failed to produce the same in his own.

Such tremors were not something Randheer hadn't experienced before. He had, many times, and he was familiar with the pleasure they gave. Hadn't he, after all, spent many nights with his chest pressed against the soft or firm breasts of some girl or other? And even spent time with such capricious girls that they had no qualms about sharing the kind of intimate stories about their families that are usually kept from strangers? He'd had sexual relations with women who took the initiative and did all the work themselves without encumbering him in any way. But this girl from the hills whom he'd beckoned to come up—she was something else again. So unbelievably different!

A strange smell wafting from her body flooded his senses all night—a smell at once pleasant and nauseating. It flowed from every part of her body: under her arms, around her breasts, her hair, her belly, and it permeated every breath he took. All night long he wondered about this smell: without it creeping into every crevice of his mind, crowding out all his thoughts, new and old, could he have felt as close to this ghatan as he did now? Absolutely not!

This smell had fused them together for the night. They had taken possession of each other so totally, plunged into each other's depths so fully that they were carried away into pure human ecstasy—fleeting yet somehow immutable, in motion yet frozen, like a bird soaring so high in the sky's limitless azure that it appears perfectly still.

Even though he was familiar with the smell radiating from every pore of the girl's body, he couldn't quite describe what it was. It was like the smell of fresh earth just sprinkled with water. But not exactly. It was different somehow. And it didn't have the artificial aura of lavender or attar. It was something primal and timeless—like the relationship between man and woman.

Amazingly, though Randheer detested the odour of perspiration and routinely dusted his body with talcum powder and daubed his underarms with deodorant after every bath, he found himself madly kissing the ghatan's hairy armpits over and over—yes, over and over—and felt no revulsion; instead he found it strangely pleasurable. Damp with sweat, her soft, underarm hair was releasing a scent that was very conspicuous and yet completely unfathomable. He felt that he knew it, was familiar with it, and even understood what it signified, but couldn't explain it to anyone.

It was a day during the rains—just like today.... He was looking out the same window. The peepal leaves were trembling in the pouring rain, their rustling sound blending into the atmosphere. It was dark outside, but the darkness was suffused with a soft fluorescence, as though a little light had escaped from the stars and descended to the earth with the raindrops....

Yes, it was a day during the rains. His room had a single teak bed then, now it had two—the new arrival next to its mate—and a brand new dressing table stood in one corner. It was the same season, the same weather, and a barely discernible light was coming down from the stars along with the raindrops, but now the atmosphere was filled with the overpowering scent of henna.

One bed was empty. On the other, Randheer lay with his head down watching raindrops dancing on the fluttering leaves outside the window, and lying next to him was a fair-coloured girl who seemed to have fallen asleep after her futile attempts to cover her nakedness. Her red silk shalwar lay bunched up on the empty bed, the tasseled end of its dark red waist-cord dangling. Her other clothes were also on that bed. Her shirt with a golden floral pattern, her bra, underpants and dupatta were all of a deep red colour—a garish, dark red—and saturated with the strong scent of henna.

Flecks of glitter were scattered in her dark black hair like specks of dust, and together with a heavy layer of powder and rouge, gave an unbelievably strange colour to her face—pallid, as though all the life had been squeezed out. The dye from her bra had bled, leaving reddish stains on her fair chest.

Her breasts were milky white with just a hint of blue and her underarms were shaved clean, leaving behind a grey shadow. Randheer glanced at her several times, and each time he would find himself thinking that he'd just pried open some crate and taken her out—as if she were a consignment of books or china. Her body had marks in several spots just like the marks and scratches left on books and china from packing and shipping.

When he undid the strings of her tight-fitting bra Randheer noticed that it had creased her back and the soft flesh of her bosom. And the cord of her shalwar had been done up so tightly it left a mark around her waist. The sharp edges of her heavy, jewel-studded necklace had apparently grazed the delicate skin of her bosom in many places, as if unforgiving nails had scraped it.

Indeed, it was just like that other day. The rain was producing the same sound as it pelted down on the tender leaves of the peepal—the same pitter-patter that had filled his ears that other night long ago. The weather was divine. A cool breeze was blowing softly...but it was laden with the pungent scent of henna.

Of course his hands had roved over the girl's milky-white bosom for a long time, like the breath of a gentle breeze; he'd felt her body quiver in intermittent waves under his touch, and even felt the suppressed passions stirring within her. When he pressed his breast to hers every pore of his body heard the notes rising from her body—but where was that call: the call he had sensed in the strong odour emitted by the ghatan's body, more compelling than the cry of an infant thirsting for milk, the call that had gone beyond the limits of sound and needed no words to convey it.

Randheer was looking out through the grillwork of the window, somewhere far beyond the trembling leaves of the peepal, farther into the distance where he could make out an unusual subdued glow enmeshed in the dark grey of the clouds, the same glow he had seen radiate from the breasts of the ghatan, hidden like a secret, but discernible all the same.

The girl was stretched out beside him. He looked at her inert body, as soft and white as flour kneaded with milk and butter, the scent of henna leaping from it now faded a bit. He found it immensely revolting—this exhausted smell in the throes of death, somewhat tangy, oddly tangy, like the sour belches of indigestion. A pathetic, sickly smell!

He again looked at the girl lying next to him. The femininity in her being seemed strangely compressed...the way white globs float listlessly in colorless liquid when the milk has gone bad. Actually, the smell that flowed from the ghatan so naturally, unbidden and without effort, still pervaded his senses. It was a smell infinitely more subtle and far-reaching than the perfume of henna, not at all anxious to be inhaled. It had flowed into him quietly and settled into place.

In one last attempt, Randheer ran his hand over the girl's milky white body but felt no tremor. His new bride, the daughter of a distinguished magistrate, with a bachelor's degree, the heartthrob of countless boys at her college, failed to rouse her husband's passion.

From the dying scent of henna he desperately tried to retrieve the smell that had wafted from the ghatan's unwashed body and flooded his

senses on just such a rainy day when the leaves of the peepal outside
the window were bathed in a downpour.

—*Translated from the Urdu by Muhammad Umar Memon*

The Parrots of Desire

THEN AND NOW

Silabhattrika

I lost my virginity to the man
who is now my husband.
These are the same moonlit nights,
and this is the same breeze that floats
down from the Vindhya mountains,
laden with the scent of flowering jasmines.
I too am the same woman.

Yet, how I long with all my heart
for the riverside, overgrown with rushes,
that once knew our wild, joyous lovemaking!

—*Translated from the Sanskrit by R. Parthasarathy*

KAILASAM

Ambai

The moment she began to watch a ghost serial on the TV, Kailasam began to judder violently. Accompanied by a loud sound that went 'diku-diku-dak diku-diku-dak'. Annoyed, she stood up, put on a pair of rubber chappals, went up to Kailasam and touched it. Stroked it. Kailasam showed no signs of subsiding. In the serial, the ghost pushed open the lid of its coffin, sat up and stared. The actor must have fancied himself as another Christopher Lee. The ghost glared. It was bald; its eyes gave out a yellow light. Kailasam shuddered incessantly. She put her arms around it and hugged it. 'Kailasam, Kailasam,' she said in a gentle voice. Kailasam only juddered the more, as if in a religious frenzy. She laid her cheek against it. 'Enough now, Kailasam', she said, 'pull yourself together.' It began to wind down, its 'dak dak' sounding more and more slowly. She gave it a fond pat and went back to her chair, continuing to watch her serial. The ugly ghost was wandering about now, looking for young girls, whose blood it wanted to suck.

She watched the serial without much interest. Why couldn't the ghost have been a bit younger? What sort of ghost was this, with a bald pate and paunch? Only female ghosts tended to be young and pretty, dressed in thin cotton saris, their undergarments showing through; they walked delicately, anklets tinkling; they even sang songs.

Kailasam had fallen silent. Kailasam was her refrigerator, bought in 1985. In the early years, there were no problems with it. At that time, it had no name either. But in the past ten years, the freezer compartment began to get iced up as if the Himalayan mountains had planted themselves inside it. She had never travelled to those parts. Yet in Mumbai, in the third storey of a building, which looked as if it were falling down, her refrigerator seemed to fill with ice peaks reminiscent of the holy places of pilgrimage which lay all along the Himalayas. Sometimes a single piece of ice, tightly frozen, stood upright at its centre, exactly like a Siva lingam. However many times the defrost button was pressed, it simply would not melt. Sometimes it had to be broken down and removed. But even after it was thrown into the sink, it would take a long time to melt. A lingam which refused to melt. After that the name 'Kailasam' was conferred ceremoniously on the refrigerator.

All their household goods had been given names. The cactus plant given to her by Dhananjayan was Dhanush. The creeper with tiny flat leaves was Megha.

The plant that mistook itself for a tree and had shot up so high—it was the first thing she set eyes on when she woke up—was Usha. The plant that was attempting to grow awkwardly, with crooked branches, was Vakkiran. Jayan teased her one day, 'Why have you given men's names only to the plants with thorns or awkward shapes?'

This giving of names wasn't entirely at random, it struck her. Was there a connection between Kailasam, her refrigerator, and another Kailasam, perhaps? When she was a university research student, the students' hostel was in two sections. The rooms adjacent to the warden's house belonged to the women. The men students had the building opposite. Between the two were the dining hall, a common room with a TV, and a grassy lawn. It was by way of a diversion from the boredom of their constant research work that she and her friends started giving nicknames to the men students. At first these remained straightforward names such as 'Broomstick' and 'Matchbox'. Gradually they changed into names which held complex and hidden meanings. It was Professor Gulati who started them off on a long chapter of conferring names with thousands of insinuations. Gulati had just been married. Gunwant Kaur brought the news that his wife was deeply unsatisfied. He finished his business in a great hurry, before she could feel any pleasure, apparently. The doctor whom the Professor consulted was a distant relative of Gunwant's uncle. That evening they named Professor Gulati, 'Waterfall'.

Dipika's boyfriend, Sikander, had a room on the first floor of the building opposite the women's hostel. He would often send signals to Dipika, who was on the second floor. The windows of the women's rooms were curtained most of the time, or their shutters were closed. One morning Sudha banged on her door, urgently. When she opened it, Sudha said excitedly, 'Open your window.' Even before she could do so, Sudha herself flung open the shutters and called out, 'Look!' Beneath them on the first floor, Sikander's window was wide open. Sikander lay on his bed naked, his sheet at his feet. His long male member fell to one side. The first penis she had ever seen. It had been circumcised. Sudha said it was a first time for her, too, and ran to fetch her binoculars. The two of them gave the penis their serious attention. When they focused on just that part of his anatomy, it seemed like a small snake, detached from the rest of his body; a gentle snake which fell away from him this way and that as he moved in his sleep.

One by one the rest—excepting Dipika—came in, took a hurried look, and left. Quite unaware that he had become an object worthy of darshan, Sikander lay there, fast asleep. They named Sikander, 'Snake'. Sudha could sing beautifully. If ever Sikander came within sight, she would begin to murmur, 'Oh Cobra, coiled above Siva's hair.' She'd repeat the refrain, 'Dance Snake! Play and dance Snake!' Sikander would applaud her. 'A very good song, Sudha. One day you must sing me the entire song.' 'Of course, of course,' she'd agree.

It was during this nicknaming period that they came up with the name, 'Kailasam'. Kailasam's real name was 'Sivagnanam'. His trousers, apparently, had been made by their family tailor. This tailor had made all his clothes since he was a child. Perhaps this man had never thought fit to change the pattern he had always used. At any rate, always when Kailasam leaned back or stretched his legs out when he sat down, his trousers would stick out at the crotch. Gunwant Kaur gave him the name 'Kailas Parbat', the Hindi version of 'Mount Kailasam'. She and Sudha shortened it to 'Kailasam'.

The nicknaming went on for several days. Then, suddenly, the craze left them just as speedily as it first came upon them. They discussed often whether the nicknames they gave the men were just a way of expressing their sexual feelings. The body, at that time, was beginning to be of huge importance to them. Its every cavity, every mound, every fold and every curve was a secret revealed. It was a time when the body took manifold forms and became a whole world. Kailasam was a small link in that world.

◆

Kailasam was a little older than the rest of them. He had been a lecturer at a college for five years before he took up his research. He was not a lively man. He was not prone to sudden laughter. Somewhat stern features. Closely cropped hair. Well-shaven chin. Spectacles with a black frame. It was his opinion that the rest of them were immature. When they giggled at every little thing, he would reprimand them sometimes, saying, 'Be serious'. The reason why they hung about him was that they hankered after the ghee, the chutney powder, pickles, sweet and savoury snacks, the fruit which arrived for him in a constant flow from his family. They thought he was well aware of this.

One day Kailasam walked in while she was in the common room eating with relish one of the special bananas that had come for him from his home. There was no one else in the common room at the time. She could smell the string of jasmine flowers in the leaf-parcel he held in his hand.

He sat down next to her, suddenly, and gave her the jasmine flowers. 'Why do you never wear flowers in your hair? Take these,' he said.

She was a little taken aback. 'What's this for?' she asked.

'You have lovely long hair. You haven't cut it all off like the others. It would look so beautiful if you wore the flowers.'

He was not one who said such things, usually. She was quite startled. She didn't refuse the flowers. When she tucked them into her hair casually, he said, 'Gently, gently. So that it doesn't hurt.'

He began to speak, as if reciting a lesson he had learnt by heart. 'Kamalam, I have fallen in love with you. I want to come close to you and touch you. I don't know anything about women. But I want to take you to myself entirely. I feel my body burning, night and day. Would you please marry me?'

'What's all this, Sivam?' she said, absolutely shocked now.

'Why, is it wrong of me to ask? Sometimes when you walk along with me, your hand falls on me. Sometimes your breast grazes against me, like fire. Even if its touch is as soft as a flower, it is fire, Kamalam.' Having blurted out all this, he made as if to kiss her.

'Sivam, please. This is awful. I don't like it,' she said, pushing him away.

He was trembling all over. His eyes had filled. 'Forgive me,' he said, and left the room.

He distanced himself from her after that. Before he left for England on fieldwork, he returned home. He came back, married. His wife, they were told, was a doctor. She too arrived, before his trip to London. There was no room in the university guest house at the time, so when the warden asked her whether she would accommodate Kailasam's wife in her own large room at the end of the corridor, she could not refuse. It did strike her, however, that the couple could well have taken a room in a hotel, and stayed together.

Doctor Thenmozhi was a lively companion. She had an important position in a hospital and had the poise, dignity and smartness that went with it.

One evening, when Sudha and she were chatting together and lounging on her bed, Thenmozhi came in, unwound her sari, and put on her night-clothes.

'Doctor, where did you have dinner?' Sudha asked.

'At a restaurant in Connaught Place,' came the casual reply.

'At Nirula's?'

'Madras Cafe; meals. Today's special was sago payasam.' Thenmozhi sat down on her bed.

Sudha looked at her friend. She rose and made as if to leave.

Thenmozhi took hold of her hands and made her sit down again, saying, 'Stay awhile.' Then she asked, 'Have you two eaten?' She smiled at them both. And so the conversation began.

Thenmozhi was distantly related to Sivam. Plans for her marriage had been postponed for quite a while, as she had waited for a highly educated bridegroom who would respect her work. A family friend had told them about Sivam. And Sivam's father had carried out all the marriage negotiations. He had no mother; his aunt, his father's sister, was the one who brought him up. He had no siblings either. Thenmozhi very much approved of the fact that he was also a well-educated man. She saw him face-to-face only at their wedding; until then she was only acquainted with his photograph.

'What sort of man is Sivam?'

'You are the one married to him. Surely you know?' asked Sudha.

'No, Sudha. I have no idea who he is. He is certainly well behaved. He never loses his temper or anything like that. But he hasn't yet touched me. Even when we walk together, he never lays his hand on me. He never puts an arm around my shoulder to embrace me. I am saying all this to you two who are not even married yet, but please don't misunderstand me. He seems like a mere puppet without any passion, or strong feelings or desires of the body. He is a good man, of course. He hasn't spoken a single harsh word to me. I tried to convince him we should stay in a hotel, but he wouldn't listen. Now I'm putting you to such inconvenience, staying in your room... It seems to me that at some time in his life he became frozen inside. Who knows when he will melt...?'

Thenmozhi sat there, her head bowed, kneading her hands.

◆

What are the secrets of a woman's body? What is the shape of her pubis? When you touch her pubic hair, will it be like silk, or coarse, like a blanket? An ancient poem likens it to a cobra rearing its head. What might Kamalam's pubis look like?

Is passion like an intoxicant? Subramania Bharati says, 'I am made dizzy', and adds, 'as if I had drunk a pot of mature toddy.' How can one come upon a pot of mature toddy in these parts? I talked the watchman into fetching me the local brew. But that intoxication was different; it shook up the body. What I feel is of a different nature. Once, when Kamalam bent over and reached across to pick something up, her breast touched me. I had a sudden sensation, as if I were floating gently. At the same time it was as if all the world's weight had fallen on my male member. On the one hand, a gathering heaviness; on the other, a weightlessness. Uncertainty. Dizziness. I gasped for breath.

Is this passion? I don't know the rules of desire.

◆

I am overwhelmed by passion.

◆

I want Kamalam to spin upon me like a ball of iron. I want her to press down on me. I want to flow over her like a ball made of flowers. Without hurting her, without crushing her.

◆

When I tighten my arms around her, I want her breasts to be squeezed against my chest. I want her nipples to stiffen and stand erect. I want to freeze forever inside her.

◆

In spite of so great a passion, her body never strikes me as a mere collection of limbs and organs. In my imagination, her body takes several forms: a river swirling as it flows; a lake that is the refuge of many birds; the turbulent sea. I want to sink into her.

◆

One evening she was sitting in the common room, having slipped off her chappals. She sat on the sofa, with her knees drawn up, her face down on her knees, her eyes closed. She looked like a small hill, in her green sari. Her hair ran down her back like a black stream. Her feet were like newly open leaves.

◆

They describe women's features as edible things: eyes like grapes, apple cheeks, lips like ripe fruit. I think of myself as a rough piece of earth, full of stones, and thorny. I want Kamalam to plough me. I want her to turn me into arable land. Kamalam, though, is like marshy land. A mysterious region where you could be drawn within the mire at any step. I want to put my feet there, and daub myself with the wet earth. I want to sink into its bubbles. I want to make it fertile land.

◆

I want Kamalam to possess me.

◆

Will my member ever touch the entrance to her body? How will that touch be? Will it be like the cool thrill of the first drop of rain falling, after many thousands and many millions of years of waiting? Or will it be the sweet caress of fire?

◆

The telephone rang during the course of the morning. A woman's voice came on at the other end.

'Is Kamalam there, please?'

'This is Kamalam speaking.'

'I'm Dr Thenmozhi, Kamalam. Do you remember me?'

'Aren't you Sivam's wife?'

'So you still remember me? That's pretty good!'

'How come you're contacting me after all these years? And how did you find my telephone number?'

'I'll tell you when I come. I'm standing at the gate of your building, with my husband and children. May I come up now?'

'How can you ask? Yes, do come up, Thenmozhi.'

The doorbell rang. There were four of them. The person entering with Thenmozhi was not Sivam.

'Kamalam, this is my husband, Dr Kumarasamy. This is my son, Arun. He is a doctor, practising in the United States. This is my daughter, Arulmozhi. She too is a doctor. She wants to build a hospital of her own. At the moment, she works in Bangalore.'

They all sat down together and conversed generally, as they drank tea. After a while, Thenmozhi began to speak.

'Kamalam, Sivam and I separated within a year. There was no quarrel whatsoever. He was like a corpse, though. He himself said I should leave him. I met Kumarasamy in London, where I had gone for further studies. But I didn't cut myself off from Sivam totally. These children used to call him Periappa. After his father died, we were his only family. Kumarasamy and he became good friends. He became a professor locally, in Coimbatore. He lived alone like that, writing his research papers. He never married again. During the holidays he came to us; he'd stayed with us. Time went by in that way...'

It was as if what she said was a long prologue. It struck Kamalam that she spoke of Sivam in the past tense.

Thenmozhi continued, 'He had gone to Bangalore in order to make arrangements for building Arulmozhi's hospital. He went out for his walk in the morning, but never returned. It was winter weather. He could never endure the cold. As he was just leaving, Arulmozhi actually said to him, "Don't go, Periappa. It's very cold this morning." He didn't listen. He just wrapped his muffler round his head and went. Sometime later, his body was found in the Sankey Tank. We couldn't understand what happened, nor why. Perhaps, after he retired, he was yearning after something, we don't know. When we cleared his house of his belongings, this notebook came to light. On top, he had written all your addresses, ending with your latest one, and your phone number. I brought it away without opening it. Did he ever speak to you?'

'No, never. I still keep in touch with many of those friends. Sudha telephoned just last week. But I lost contact with him entirely.'

There was silence for a while. Then Thenmozhi took out a notebook from her bag. It had been placed inside a plastic folder. She held it out to Kamalam.

'You keep this now. He has written your name on top. Let him be at peace, somehow. Please don't take it amiss. We've given away all his books to the library. There wasn't much else. He had willed all his property to my children. He lived like a sannyasi, and now he's gone. What can we say? Because your name is written here...'

Kamalam accepted the notebook. She felt herself shaking as her fingers touched the plastic cover. She put it away on a table to one side.

Her visitors stayed a little longer, and then left.

The notebook lay on the table, within its plastic folder.

◆

Gently she set aside the plastic folder. Inside, the hard cover was handmade. There were a few entries dated 1974, 1975. The rest of the notebook was empty.

◆

A body at the bottom of the lake. A body which never gave anything away. A body which held all its secrets frozen within.

◆

She sat down on a stool next to the refrigerator and leaned against it.

Kailasam, I never realized how much yearning you kept locked inside yourself. At that time, for me my body was a mystery, a riddle from which I had to free myself. I can only say I was just coping with my body. It was only later that I faced up to the hugeness of it. It was only gradually I learnt of its valleys, depths, scales, extensions, petals. I didn't dive into it and rise up fighting for breath, straightaway. It began very gently, and happened like the breaking of monsoons, accompanied by thunder. Like a song which begins softly, and reaches a peak with heightened rhythm.

When you approached me, I wasn't there. I was immersed in so many anxieties. About my research, about my future. It wasn't that I lacked any interest or curiosity about the male body, but it came and went like swiftly moving clouds. I didn't feel it with any depth.

You wrote about my pubis. At that time I wasn't aware of it myself. I never thought about the pubic hair upon it. Sometimes, during my periods, there was blood on it. Even when I washed it, it was done with indifference. People like me carried our bodies as if they were sinful burdens. The body was a cross one had to bear. That is what we were taught. The body could tip you into a deep and dangerous hole. You must stamp on the body, crush it, control it.

There was a young woman who worked in our house. She did the cooking. There were a couple of peons from my father's office who used to come and go on errands, Raman Nair and Venkatappa. The other woman who worked for us, Narasamma complained to my mother that as she did the washing, Thangam kept exchanging glances with Raman Nair who waited under a tree. Soon after this, Amma reported that she too had caught them at it, 'red-handed'. After that, Raman Nair wasn't seen again. Thangam too was sacked. When I asked my mother why, she said that otherwise, a disaster could happen.

Sometime later, I chanced to meet Thangam at a music concert and asked her, Thangam what was the disaster that was going to happen because you looked at Raman Nair?'

'Who told you all this?' she asked.

'Amma.'

'No disaster happened. I just looked at him, that was all,' she said, smiling. She stroked my hair.

But the anxiety that my body possessed a capacity for bringing about disaster never left me. That truth about my body only began to reveal itself after I left home and went outside.

It was Narain Singh, a Trinidadian, who taught me to have a true vision of my body. He was an artist. When I was with him, my body shone like a natural landscape. Its mounds were transformed into mountains, its depths became valleys, its hidden parts were running streams. His body, too became other aspects of the same landscape. It too looped and curved and gave, like a creeper, like earth. It grew as dense as unploughed land. It tightened. It pulled like quicksands.

I thought it was love. It hurt when he started to go out with an American girl. Later, I became immersed in my other concerns. When I met him, two years later, he looked weary. He said he was very much alone. Some of us went to his house that day. When he approached me that night, I allowed him. The next morning I set off early, while the others were still asleep. Narain accompanied me to the bus station.

'When shall we meet again?' he asked.

'Never, Narain. Yesterday I saw you and felt sorry for you. That's why I agreed...' I said.

He was as shocked as if he had trodden on fire. 'You felt sorry for me?'

'What other reason could there be, Narain?'

'You've changed,' he said.

The bus arrived. I climbed in. I waved to him through the window. 'Life is a good teacher,' I said.

It became possible for me to give my body and take it back. It became possible to make it my own.

It was only with Dhananjayan that I learnt to accept my body with all its faults and its merits, neither overrating nor undervaluing it. He allowed my body to fly. He returned it to my safe-keeping. He said I had taken his body to unknown regions, and established a path for its return. He said I redressed and balanced out the arrogance regarding the male body he had once held to. How wrong he had been to assume that the truth about a male body was its erect penis. When I pointed out the beauty of his penis as it lay prone, when we were not making love, he marvelled at the many meanings of the body.

It is now twenty five years since we got married. I still don't understand love, Kailasam. It is easy to understand passion. Love is not like that. The relationship between a man and a woman is extremely complicated. How much closeness there is in it, how much distance. How much that is hidden, how much that is open. How much violence, how much gentleness. How much rigidity, how much giving. How much tenderness, how much frenzy. There are times when you are angry enough to poison and kill the loved one. Then the anger ebbs away. It binds you in the closest of kinships. It comforts, like a nest. It burns. It cools.

When I consider my body as if it were a text, it isn't a stable text, Kailasam. It changes. Its appearances and meanings keep changing. My breasts have slackened and droop slightly. Green veins run along my thighs. And on my arms and legs too. My pubis is like a withered leaf. My pubic hair isn't thick and dense as before. Nor is it black. It has gone grey. It has lost its freshness, and looks dry.

Jayan's body too, shows many changes. His once-tightly-knit body is at times like clothes left soaking, ready to wash. When he comes out of his bath, his genitals, not yet dry, look curled up like a snail. The hair on his head is completely grey. Mine too. Even today I lean my breasts against his back and kiss his neck. He tells me he thrills then. When he strokes me, it is comforting. My hair stands on end.

So the body goes through many stages.

Why did you never contact me, Kailasam? You made Thenmozhi your friend, couldn't you have considered me as a friend, too? Had you asked me at another time in my life what you asked then, I don't know whether I would have agreed. But I don't think I would have shunned you.

Your body, which lay at the bottom of the lake, has now been cremated. Its ashes have been scattered on river waters. May that water, in which your ashes are dissolved, flow over a dry land. May grass grow upon the land, made fertile. May some cow or goat feast on that grass. May its udders fill with milk. May that milk sweeten some child's mouth.

Then may the river swell again, into a great flood that breaks its banks. May it flow over sand and stone and mud, bringing to life all that is parched. May it grow in richness. May a speck of those ashes become a seed, a plant, grow into a tree hung with fruit. May its branches look up to the skies.

◆

The doorbell rang. When Kamalam woke from her reverie, the fridge had defrosted, and ran at her feet like a small rivulet flowing away from a great river.

—*Translated from the Tamil by Lakshmi Holmström*

Suspicion and Confusion
Who are we having sex with, really?

.... ~ ....

WHO WAS I?

Govindasvami

Holy sixth day
in the woods they worship the
trees then
then my heart beat hard
at how far I was going into
the woods
a snake appeared in front of me
and I fell down
I started writing and rolling
this way and that way
my dress fell off
my hair burned along
my back
thorns scratched me
everywhere
suddenly who am I
who was I
how I
love those celebrations

—*Translated from the Sanskrit*
by W. S. Merwin and J. Moussaieff Masson

WITH THE LAST OF MY GARMENTS

Vidyapati

With the last of my garments
shame dropped from me, fluttered
to earth and lay discarded at my feet.
My lover's body became
the only covering I needed.
With bent head he gazed at the lamp
like a bee who desires the honey of a closed lotus.
The Mind-stealing One, like the *chataka* bird,
is wanton, he misses no chance
to gratify his thirst; I was to him
a pool of raindrops.
                    Now shame returns
as I remember. My heart trembles,
recalling his treachery.

So Vidyapati says.

—Translated from the Sanskrit
by Denise Levertov and Edward C. Dimock Jr.

The Parrots of Desire

SUSPICIOUS

Gāthā Saptaśatī

What can I do?
we make love in the common position
he calls it sedate
but invent
something new
he asks where I
learnt it

◆

I made love
To you in that particular way
For a taste
Of your nectar
Don't think me shameless
Love is an art of
Refinement
No one has trained me

—Translated from the Maharashtrian Prakrit by Andrew Schelling

ONE PART WOMAN

Perumal Murugan

At that moment, someone came and sat rubbing against her. In her head, she tried to classify the nature of that graze. But she couldn't. Was this her god? She glanced slowly at the man who was rubbing and pressing down on her right shoulder. She saw an eager face with a thin moustache. His eyes looked directly into hers. She felt she had seen those eyes somewhere, but she could not remember where and when. She closed her eyes and searched her mind. By then he had sat down comfortably, huddling against her, and was trying to rest his face on her shoulder. She could not decide whether to allow it or not, but she knew she had to make up her mind before it proceeded any further. She shifted her body gently and suggested her disapproval. But she did it in a way that did not mean rejection either. It made her wonder when she had become so clever. Perhaps she had always been so. Perhaps it was finding expression only now.

Kali was adept at reading the nuances of her movements. Even if he sensed a slight rejection, he would move away immediately. At those times, it would become very hard for her to get him interested again. She jerked her head to get Kali off her mind, and his image receded and vanished. She turned and looked. The eyes and the face she saw nudged a memory—it was as though a bolt of lightning flashed across her face, and for a moment she thought she recognized him. But it was not him; only a likeness. Ponna came of age when she was fourteen. And the face that had been in her mind then was Sakthi's. He had been a goatherd in their farm for many years, and she had grown up playing with him. Later, when she was a young woman, his had been the face of her dreams and her imagination. When it was decided that Kali would marry her, she had struggled a lot to replace Sakthi in her mind with Kali.

Whatever she started imagining with Kali in her mind would end up with Sakthi's face being part of the fantasy. For some time, she even vacillated between the two faces. But after the wedding, Sakthi's face slowly faded away and over time she even forgot him completely. But here it was again, and so close to her. Suddenly, she decided she did not want him. She moved away a little and avoided the intimacy. But his heavy sigh wafted in the air and bothered her. When she turned around, his eyes were pleading with her, and his arms were stretched out towards her. She felt like laughing, but she showed him an angry

The Parrots of Desire

face, shook her head in refusal, and turned her back to him. How easily he asked for what he wanted even in the middle of such a crowd! It amazed her that she could conduct an entire conversation with him without anyone noticing. It was only then that she grew conscious of her surroundings. She looked around and dropped her head shyly.

On stage, Siruthondar had entered in a dance movement and was introducing himself. It looked like the dance performance might actually be good. She looked towards the man through the corner of her eye. He wasn't there. She thought she would leave too. But that might give him the idea that she had come out looking for him. It might be good to leave after a while. The things this god did! He dug out a forgotten face from the depths of her heart and placed it in front of her. Was it her punishment to remember that face forever? 'Please appear with a new face, one I am not familiar with,' she prayed. Had she earned his wrath after having rejected two of the gods? Is this a crowd of gods too? Is he watching me?

It looked like there was a way leading out in every direction; there were gods wandering everywhere. 'Come to me with a form I like,' she kept praying. She went past the Omkali temple and reached the west chariot street. There was a wide space at the intersection with the north chariot street. Hearing some loud whistling from there, she walked in that direction. She was thirsty. Was it her mind's thirst that was peeping out through her tongue? On the west street, there were four or five unmanned water pandals. Anyone could help themselves to the water. She drank some and splashed some cold water on her face. She felt refreshed.

She glanced at the temple down the slope. In the moonlight, its tower looked taller. When she reached the crowded street corner, all the while praying in her mind, she saw a team of Oyilattam dancers performing there. There were over twenty of them; they all wore yellow headbands and held long red streams of cloth in their hands and danced in rhythm to the drums. She looked in amazement at how, when they took four steps in unison and turned around suddenly, the several pieces of coloured cloth that waved in the air flared and settled like snakes flying in the air with their tongues out. She was familiar with the dance. This was the same dance that was performed on all nine days of the Mariamman temple festival. Youngsters trained in summer with a teacher. Also, because it was done in the temple, it was called Koyilattam. It started with a slow movement of the hands and feet, but it gradually gained speed and reached a crescendo. And as the dance grew faster, the whistles grew louder. Sometimes, the performance opened with a song and every dance was alternated with a song. But this dance looked different, perhaps because of the colours that had been added to it.

Whenever she heard the whistles, she was beside herself, clapping and jumping in joyful laughter. It looked like she might even join the dancers. The beauty of it, when they moved to the front and turned around, was so intense that it wrapped itself around everything in the vicinity. Looking at the dancers, she wondered if men were really such beautiful creatures. She felt a wild urge to run and embrace them. She jumped and almost fell on the girl standing next to her. But the girl didn't take it amiss; she just laughed. 'I don't see women performing anywhere,' she said in a gossipy tone. It looked like she too would have liked to join them. Ponna gave her a friendly smile.

When she felt something touching her earlobes, she reached back and wiped herself. It felt as though someone was blowing gently on her nape. She turned around and saw a pair of eyes to her side. She knew it was the touch of these eyes that had bothered her. Those eyes pierced the glow of the burning torches, and touched and teased her. The folded dhoti and the towel that was around his neck and fell over his chest made him look like no one she knew. His hair had been combed carelessly, and it looked like he had not even started shaving. It occurred to her that this was her god. His eyes smiled. His lips too were parted in a permanent grin. In a delightful, repetitive game, his eyes moved towards the dance only to turn back to her suddenly. She looked fondly at that desire-filled face. Then she closed her eyes and tried holding it in her mind. But it slipped away. She could recollect the eyes, the lips and the head separately, but she could not put them together. Why wouldn't it stay in her mind?

It was unlike any other face that had stayed on in her mind. It was never easy for a new face to make its place in a shelf of faces. 'This is how I expected you to be, god,' she thought. Then his eyelashes lowered and eyebrows slanted. She understood that he wanted her to walk out with him. She was overcome with shyness. When she remembered that Kali too often spoke this way—in signs—her mind closed up. She was never able to keep Kali aside. In twelve years, he had gradually etched himself on every fold of her heart. No one could do anything to him. She would find him in any man. She could recognize him in anyone. She felt like screaming at this image, pleading with him not to remind her of Kali. If she spoke to him in signs, he would respond like Kali too. She knew she had to leave from there and get to a place where they could talk in words.

When she emerged, parting her way through the crowd gathered around the Oyilattam troupe, he too came and joined hands with her. She was surprised that he read her mind so quickly. She felt that just a small shift of the body was enough for a man to understand a woman. The grip of his hand was comforting. He walked with her along the north chariot street. She decided to let him lead. Along the way were shops selling puttu laid out on baskets layered with white cloth. There were small crowds here and there. His lips grazed her ears when they said, 'Shall we eat puttu?' A male voice dripping desire and intoxication. She didn't even think. She nodded. He peeped into every store, but didn't stop at any.

Finally, he stopped at a shop that was halfway down the street and got hot puttu on a leaf plate covered with dry leaves stitched together. There were four portions of puttu with gravy on the side. Though she thought she might not be able to eat so much, she did not refuse. He brought his plate and ate standing next to her. She liked the way he carefully chose the puttu after considering several shops. It made her happy to think that he would have chosen her the same way. She took some puttu and put it on his plate, but she was too shy to look up at this face. 'Why? Enough already?' he said.

'Please speak some more,' she pleaded in her mind. With a man, that was how she always felt—like he did not speak enough. You want your dear one to talk to you non-stop.

She was eating, her head bent low, when he said, 'Selvi, look here.' When she looked up in shock, wondering who Selvi was, he brought a handful of puttu close to her lips. She let him feed her. 'He has given me a new name so that no one around here gets suspicious.' She found this cleverness very attractive. He continued to feed her without any hesitation. But her diffidence came in the way of her desire to reciprocate. As if he sensed that, he said, 'Hmmm,' and, bending close to her, held her hand and brought it to his lips. She fed him without looking up.

When they started walking again, she literally stuck to him. She did not know the way, and she had no sense of the people around her. 'He is my god. My job is to go where he takes me,' was all she could think. Like a rain-soaked chicken, she huddled in his warmth. It appeared that he was taking her far away from the crowds and the noise.

—Translated from the Tamil by Aniruddhan Vasudevan

ANGER JUST CAN'T KEEP ITS GRIP

Amaruśataka

Scowling, I knot up
my forehead
but this traitorous eye shamelessly lifts.
I refuse words but
my rebellious face softens.
Make a stone of my heart
and on its own
this aroused body tingles.
Anger just
can't keep its grip
when that boy
comes into view.

—Translated from the Sanskrit by Andrew Schelling

CUCKOLD

Kiran Nagarkar

Ah yes, the truth. What a to-do we make of this word when we all know we would be so much better off without it.

The wedding party returned home. Her favourite uncle Rao Viramdev accompanied her to Chittor. She was allowed to bring a friend or servant along with her who would stay with her all her life. She brought her childhood friend and maid, Kumkum Kanwar. They had never been outside Merta and Kumkum was full of wonder and alarm at the sights, scenes and smells of Chittor. Merta was a small town compared to Chittor. Chittor was wealthy and worldly. It was filthy, spacious, corrupt, crowded and self-assured. Kumkum Kanwar could not keep a lid on her excitement. She tugged at her friend's sleeve, pointed breathlessly at the Victory Tower, she screamed with delight at the size of the custard apples, she was horrified at the boldness and number of the beggars, her eyes enlarged in disbelief at the variety of precious stones, pearls and jewellery exhibited so casually in the market-place. Her mouth remained agape that whole day.

Her young mistress was quiet. But she was neither snobbish nor supercilious from a sense of inferiority. She was as eager, impressionable and excited as her maid. Since the time she reached her teens, she had always been shy and quiet. Her new status as bride to the Maharaj Kumar of Chittor had added an edge of reserve to her temperament because she did not understand the implications and nuances of entering such a large and alien household. She was at the epicentre when she would rather not even have been on the outermost periphery.

Her husband did not speak to her the first six days of her stay. He looked pale and anaemic and hurt beyond mortal help. She tried to do things for him, get his slippers, fetch his saafa, button his kurta, dry his wet hair after a bath. He turned away. If he needed something he asked Kausalya. Kausalya, she learnt, was his dai, the one who had breast-fed and looked after him. Kausalya was silent and aloof though never insolent or disrespectful to her.

On the seventh day she went back to Merta with her uncle. Her husband came to see her off. He did not speak to her nor did he wave goodbye. How lonely, how desolate he looked despite that deliberately impassive face. She felt his pain but did not know how to reach out to him. She was happy to be going back. She could stay two or three months with her family in Merta. If she set her mind to it, she could charm her uncle Viramdev, and extend her stay by another month. This was the last indulgence she would be permitted. It was meant to soften the severing of all connections with her maika. Whoever designed and wrought the fabric of tradition understood that you cannot be a girl one day and a wife the next; that the distance between your parents' home and that of your husband is farther than infinity; that if you try to bridge it overnight, the effects may be traumatic.

She knew what she had to do on this visit. She must brand in her memory the images of her village, of her house, of her horse, of her favourite people, of the well, of her father and grandfather and aunts, of the god in the temple, of the sands and the trees and the kumatiya, khajri and kair of the desert. And the sound of the school bell and the sound of a sandstorm and of rain hissing into the sand, her aunt beating the water out of her hair with a thin towel, the bucket at the well hitting the water some hundred feet below. And the smell of the sun burning the sand, of dry kachra frying in oil and spices, the powdery, bleached smell of her father's armpit when he came back from a long day of surveying their lands, the fierce smell of the kevda leaves in their garden. All these she must etch on her memory. They would have to last her a lifetime. Of course they would permit her to come back and visit. But this was definitely goodbye, her last long stay at the home of her grandfather and father.

She did not have to coax and cajole her uncle into allowing her to stay an extra month. He could not bear the thought of her leaving home. He had never prospect of her as his niece. She was his daughter, not her father's. Which is why her father and her uncle were at loggerheads when the subject was the daughter one had fathered and the other one was father to. But the month was soon over and neither father nor uncle had the heart to argue.

'Who is it?' his voice was low.

She did not answer. She had been back for seven weeks now. Every night he asked the same question. He looked more haunted than before she had left. There was a tightness to his mouth and his eyes were the water at the bottom of the hundred foot well in her home. He no longer tried to sleep at night. He held himself erect, it was something his body could not unlearn after so many years of military training. But it was an empty shell that managed to be at work at six; conducted the affairs of the ministries under him, talked business, assisted his father in formulating strategy, attended official functions, presided at the small causes court on Thursdays, played cards on new year's night. But there was no person there, only the pain of not knowing and the fear of discovering the truth.

'Who are you betrothed to? I have a right to know.'

He did, he did, he had every right to know. Would to God she could clutch him to her breast and cool his searing brow and soothe that racked body. But didn't he know that you cannot take the name of the beloved?

He came home late in the evenings. As soon as he got in, he told the maids and the eunuchs and even Kausalya to leave. They giggled and smirked. They thought the Prince was besotted with his wife. She brought his food in a silver thali. He kicked it away.

'Why did you get married? I didn't force you to.'

No, he hadn't. She had tried to tell her aunt but she had looked puzzled at first and then laughed it off. When she had broached the subject again, her aunt had lost patience. 'Enough of this childishness. He is a fine young man, a prince. Not just a prince, the Maharaj Kumar. Don't be an ingrate. It's not just you who's getting married. The betrothal will bond the two houses.'

Then he stopped kicking the plate. His body shook with rage. He turned away.

Kausalya came into her room one afternoon as she sat writing by the altar when everybody in the palace was asleep.

'What are you doing to the Maharaj Kumar, Princess? What wasting disease have you visited upon him? Speak woman.'

She put aside the quill and closed her papers.

'What spell have you cast upon him? You are going to kill him with lovemaking. I've watched you for weeks now. He comes home from work in the evening, throws everybody out, and locks the door. There's never any talk between the two of you, is there? What insatiable appetites you must have, woman, that you keep him up all night long, night after night? And what strange witchery do you practise upon him that he shuns all those who love him, even me, who would give my life for him?'

◆

She was back a couple of months later.

'How is it that you are always writing when he is not here?'

She raised her head slowly and put her writing materials away. Kausalya looked uneasy. She was silent for a long time. It was as if she had something on her mind but didn't know how to find the right words to unburden herself.

'Why do you deny him?' Kausalya couldn't hold it back any longer and didn't care how she phrased it.

The Princess didn't know how to react. This was a completely different tack from the one Kausalya had taken the previous time. She was thrown off her guard. How did she know? Was it a shot in the dark? Or had he spoken to her? He was so proud, that didn't seem likely. What was the point of answering her? No amount of explaining was going to make anyone understand.

'Are you frigid? Do you not like your body? Why do you make him suffer so? What ails you, woman?'

Kausalya stretched out her hand and touched her cheek gently. 'Are you lonely, child? Do you miss home? Look at you. There's not a line or blemish on your face. I'll wager your life is as flawless and untouched as your complexion. You've led such a sheltered life, you don't know what cruelty or hatred is. There is no pride in you but innocence, which maybe is a pride of sorts, I do not know. Has anybody been mean or nasty to you? Have we said something to hurt you?'

She shook her head but did not speak.

'You are killing him, you realize that, don't you? Oh, I know he'll live but more dead than alive.' Kausalya held her by the shoulders and shook her hard. 'If something should happen to the Maharaj Kumar, I'll kill you.' Kausalya let go of her. There was no resistance in the Princess, just the despair of the cornered animal. 'Is it me? Do you loathe my presence? Would it help if I went away? Forever. For if it is so and however difficult it may be for me, I will leave. I will never again show my face to him or to you. Tell me, just tell me, woman, put an end to the Prince's agony.'

Kausalya gave up. She walked out. She was back the next minute.

'I won't leave. I don't know what black magic you have worked upon him. Beware Princess, I'll keep a watch on you. You are bound to slip up some time. Whatever your devious designs, and however subtle, I'll get you. Then God help you.'

Kausalya was as good as her word. She was not in the Princess's hair all the time nor did she watch her like a comic spy in a high drama of intrigue and discovery from a bhavai. She was around, if anything, even less than she was before.

Kausalya wasn't quite sure whether it was something about the Princess's writing or the way she put it away that struck her as odd. She knew that her mind was working overtime these days imagining clues and omens in everything and everywhere. But you had to admit that it was a little unusual for a Princess, even a literate one, to be always writing. The Maharani, for instance, or even the favourite, Queen Karmavati, never wrote, they got some scribe to do it.

It was a mystery where she hid all her writing material. Kausalya had gone through almost everything in her rooms. It had taken a long while. The only time you could search the place was when she was having a bath and when nobody was around. It was a little disconcerting to find that she did not keep anything under lock and key, not even her jewellery. She was a trusting fool, she was. But after you had said that, the question still remained: where had all those months of writing gone?

Kausalya made friends with Kumkum Kanwar. It was not difficult one day to casually broach the subject of her mistress's constant scribbling. 'Who knows? To her father perhaps. Or her uncle and aunt. But how would I know anyway? I can't write or read.' There was no prevarication or guile in Kumkum Kanwar's face.

Neither can I, thought Kausalya.

Kausalya found the material in the last place she would have imagined. In the Princess's prayer room. Her gods and goddesses sat on a yellow pitambar which covered a raised platform. There was a black stone Shivlinga, an exquisite Saraswati in bell metal, a foot high marble Shri Krishna, a copper Eklingji, the triumvirate of Ram, Laxman and Sita, a gold Surya and a jade Vishnu and a fierce Chamundi made from black marble. The pages were wrapped in muslin and, along with an ink-pot and quills, were stowed away in a drawer under the platform and the holy silk.

There must have been at least four or five hundred pages then of which more than a half were full of written matter. The individual letters were beautifully formed like black studs carved with infinite care and often an entire sentence stood out like a necklace of black pearls. But if you took in all the lines together, the total filigree work on the page looked a confused and convoluted mess. There were long stretches which seemed to have been written in a scrawl that was trying to catch up with her frenzied thoughts. Kausalya could not relate the writing to its mistress. She was so neat, tidy and unruffled. She had to have things just so and no other way. And to make sure that she got what she wanted, she almost always did everything herself. If you looked at the writing, what you saw was a person of extremes, of violent swings of mood, confused and chaotic.

Kausalya laughed. For someone who could not read, and the letters, for all she knew, may have been in some foreign tongue, she wasn't doing badly at all as a quack character-reader. She might as well set up shop interpreting the lines on the palm of a hand, or the signs of the zodiac in a horoscope. She didn't want the Princess to find out that some of the pages were missing. She chose a wad of fifty from somewhere in the middle and stuck them inside her choli which came down all the way below the navel. She put the pile of writing papers back in the drawer and covered the platform with the silk pitambar. Then she carefully placed the gods back in their original positions. As far as she knew, it was impossible to tell that someone had tampered either with the idols or what lay under.

Now that she had the papers, she was at a loss to understand why she had gone to such lengths to find and steal them. What was she going to do with them? She could show them to her son Mangal. He knew how to read. He had attended classes with the Maharaj Kumar. But there was a grey and grim distance that had come between the mother and son over the years. Nothing had been said, there was no single cause but Kausalya suspected that her son hated her. They had one thing and only one thing in common: the Maharaj Kumar. There was not much else they lived for. Kausalya didn't find it improbable that one of these days the two of them might kill each other because of him.

She kept the papers with her for a week. Then she stood outside the entrance to the Prince's palace. He was late. She had to wait over two and a half hours. He saw her and turned his head away as he had been doing since his marriage. He was about to disappear behind the doors when she called out to him softly, 'Maharaj Kumar, I have something to show you.'

'I'm not interested.'

'How would you know till you see what it is?'

'Leave me alone.'

She grabbed his hand. He tried to shake it off. She held on to it. 'Let me go Kausalya, for if you don't...' he had raised his hand.

'If I don't, you'll slap me, right?'

He took a deep breath. He would not look at her. 'No, I would not.'

She shook her head. 'I don't know whether I would mind it so much if you did. It would be some kind of conversation at least, something which you and I seem incapable of having nowadays.'

'May I go now?'

'You don't want to see what she writes?'

It was as if she had stuck a dagger in his heart. He stood motionless. His shoulders drooped. He closed his eyes.

'Who are you talking about?'

'You know who.'

'Is there something exceptional in that? People who know how to write, an illiterate like you might find that a little difficult to understand, may want to communicate with their relatives and friends at home.'

What had happened to him? Why this wanton and superfluous cruelty which was so alien to his nature?

'Write every afternoon and not send these communications to anybody but hide them from all eyes?' She took the papers out from under her choli and handed them over to him.

'I am not interested. I am not.' He clutched the papers in his hand and walked in.

◆

He did not pretend to lie down that night. He told the eunuch on duty not to let anyone enter his room, not even the Princess, and sat down at his low desk. He went through the pages, ten, fifteen, a hundred times. There were places where he couldn't link the zigzag of her writing. It rose from the middle of the page, went to the next one, came back to the margin of the previous page, gave up the sentence, started another, abandoned that, and tried to revive the earlier one. But disconnected and disjointed though the writing was, it was all addressed to one person. It was a delirious raving, a mad outpouring of passion and plaint, the most abject grovelling and fits of temper and tantrums. Haughty rejections, passages of fierce and naked eroticism, begging and pleading with him to come and visit her, take her away once and for all from the rest of mankind, hold her in his arms tightly, giddily, till every bone in her body was broken. Why did he not come, wherefore this arrogance, this playing hard to get, she could do without him, she had no need of him whatsoever, she was sufficient unto herself, she would commit suicide, plunge the Maharaj Kumar's sword into her heart, free the Maharaj Kumar once and for all, the poor dear man, how she had made him suffer. Enough is enough. She was going on a fast unto death, today was her fifth day, she was so thirsty, she had a little water to drink, then the maid brought some cold fresh lime juice with honey, it was like amrut, oh forget it, why should she starve herself for someone who didn't have the courtesy to reply to her letters, answer her urgent calls, admittedly there were at least a dozen of them every day but was this any way to treat your beloved? Sometimes she thought love was just a blind alley. She gave her all and he didn't say yes or no, he didn't accept it, neither did he reject it. What was she to make of him and of her unrequited love? What was the point of being betrothed if your beloved never thought of you, never called out your name, never remembered your birthday, didn't remember the first song she had sung to him? And then suddenly, out of the blue, the skies darkened, and the thunder was a python crushing and grinding mountains, and the lightning was a scorpion that flashed and flared and stung her and the rain pierced and raked her flesh and there he was, the love of her life, the undertow of the sea, the spirit of the drifting sands, the tongue of the wind in her ears, the caress of the peacock feather and the hardness of the flute was against her.

There were quatrains and broken verses and entire poems. There were padas that she had started and scratched out. The lyrics were the only text that he didn't read. Poetry left him cold. His curiosity was intense but try as he might, he couldn't overcome his resistance to verse. And anyway there was so much prose, he decided to look at the poems later. There were invocations and laments and requiems and hymns and soliloquies and excruciatingly detailed descriptions of her life at Chittor, her aloneness, her conversations with Kumkum, brilliant pen portraits of the Rana, an insightful assessment of Queen Karnavati, aching and unflinching introspections about the magnitude of the pain and suffering she was causing the Maharaj Kumar and her inability to reach out to him or bring him peace; sharp memories of her uncle, her grandfather and her father's guilt that her mother had died and the child deprived of her love and also his own guilt because he didn't know how to talk to her. She told her lover everything, about the tiny, almost invisible tentacle that a seed was tentatively sending out as a feeler into the universe and why did the woodpecker's beak not wear out or lose its sharpness although it had been boring a hole for its nest for the past seventeen days and did the phases of the moon have anything to do with the state of her moods and whether her love for him was flooding the plains and making the rivers change their courses. She couldn't stop talking about the greenery and woods and forests of Chittor. She wondered if there were two earths, one for Merta and one for Chittor. She had never seen so much green. She tried to take it all in with her five senses. Her greed was insatiable. She described trees and branches and leaves and flowers as if they were creatures with whom she could talk. Each branch was an arm and a tree was a thousand-armed goddess and the leaves were her brood of children. She could look at a leaf for hours, dilate upon its network of arteries and veins, draw it and distinguish hundreds of kinds of greens. The wind was a flute at times and a shameless intruder at others. Its lambent touch gave a tree goose pimples and it talked dirty and roused the tree and became frisky and felt it up and down till the tree told the wind to leave if alone, but that only made it bolder and it was all over the tree and then there was no stopping it and the tree didn't want it to stop either.

The eunuch was dozing. He woke him up and asked him to fetch Kausalya.

'Where's the rest?'

'I thought you weren't interested.'

'I asked you where's the rest. Please, Kausalya.'

Oh God, what had she gone and done. What was this arrow stuck in his soul? Where was this wound that bled day and night and yet had no mouth? What had those scribbled pages told him that there was now a hot fever on his brow and his breathing was shallow and his eyes blind with hurt?

'My Prince, my precious one,' she touched his hand, 'is there anything I can do to relieve your agony?'

He did not push her away when he disengaged himself.

'Yes, you can. You can tell me where the rest of the papers are.' She showed him.

There was more of the same. It went on. Dogfights and torrid reconciliations.

At three o'clock he dismissed the eunuch and went into the Princess' bedroom. She lay on her side. You couldn't have known that she was alive unless you placed your ears against her breast. The faces of human beings are lies. She lay quiet and dreamless as a child. Who would have guessed what tumultuous upheavals took place beneath that calm? He shook her awake. She was awake instantly without the disorientation that gives you time to adjust from one consciousness to another.

'I am going to kill him,' he said. 'Whoever he is, I am going to kill him.'

She smiled.

YOU COME TO ME

Adivaraha Sattasai

You come to me
in secret
and I taste unimaginable pleasures
What transports do they know
who you
visit without the
deceit?

—Translated from the Maharashtrian Prakrit by Andrew Schelling

SANATAN CHOUDHURI'S WIFE

Kamala Das

His marriage was six years old when Gopi Menon began to have a suspicion that his wife was deceiving him. One morning, two hours after midnight he woke up and drowsily moved closer to his wife. Still half asleep and without opening her eyes at all she embraced him and whispered: 'Sanatan, my love....'

Sanatan. Whose name was it? Menon could get no sleep afterwards. Even when the brilliance of the sun entered through their window he was lying awake and afraid in the snuggery of her arms. But he was too proud to rouse her from her slumber to ask her about the mysterious Sanatan.

When she was making breakfast in the kitchen, he opened her wardrobe to have a look at her clothes. How did she manage to buy for herself all those silk sarees? He had given her one during last Diwali. But there were more than fifty silk sarees in the cupboard, swinging shimmeringly from their hangers. She carried the tray to the bedroom asking, what are you searching for in my cupboard?

How did you get so many expensive sarees, he asked her. Aren't these genuine Kanjivarams?

Kanjivarams? She laughed aloud. The canine tooth that protruded a little made her mouth prettier. He had always thought that her smile resembled Audrey Hepburn's. These are sarees one can pick up for ten rupees. They are art-silks brought here by a man from Matunga who sells them to all the ladies in this building, she said, still laughing in mirth.

When he was standing on the platform waiting for the fast train to Bandra, he suddenly decided to put her to a test, to clear his own mind of suspicions. He returned home immediately.

When he reached the end of their street, he stopped in surprise. His wife was coming out of their house swinging a handbag, and wearing a blue saree. He hid behind a lamp-post. She was walking fast to the taxi stand. He caught a taxi and followed her. At Ridge Road in front of a huge house surrounded by a garden, she stopped her cab. She opened the gate and disappeared into the house. He dismissed his taxi and loitered near the gate. He could see the heavy door of the portico open and a servant greet her with a salute. Then the door closed again.

Menon walked around the house and reached the open window of a large room at the back which he recognised as the dining room. He peered in through the panes. His wife was seated opposite an elderly man at a large dining table, and was busy eating her breakfast. The man was in a silk dressing gown. After she had finished eating, she rose to kiss the man gently on his forehead. He fondled her for a minute. When she left the room, the man lit a cigarette and began to read the newspapers. Menon was shocked. Was she capable of such deception? This girl born and brought up in a Kerala village? How could she enter another man's house, eat a Western-style breakfast with him and allow him to fondle her? Oh God, let this be nothing but a nightmare, prayed Menon.

With a new-found courage, he walked up to the portico and rang the doorbell. Open the door, he roared out to the inmates of the house. A servant opened the door and scrutinised his shabby work-clothes with disdain.

I must see your master immediately, said Menon.

The Saheb and the Mem Saheb are having their breakfast. You will have to wait for a short while, said the servant. What is your name?

My name is Gopi Menon, said the aggrieved husband.

In a few minutes, the host came to the door. He extended his well-manicured hand to Menon. I am Sanatan Choudhuri, he said. What can I do for you?

I heard from somewhere that you wish to let out a portion of this house, said Menon. I have come to find out if it is true...

Somebody has been playing a practical joke on you, said Choudhuri. This was built ten years ago according to a plan drawn by my wife herself. All four of my children were born in this house. So neither my wife nor I will ever dream of letting out any part of this house to strangers.

At that moment, she entered the portico. When she saw Menon, she quickly covered her head with the edge of her saree and tried to return to the interior of the house.

Wait for a second, Mrinalini, said Choudhuri. This poor gentleman was led to believe that we were letting out a portion of our house. Somebody was obviously trying to tease him.

She smiled pleasantly, revealing the prominent canine which made her smile so special, so Audrey Hepburnish. Somebody has been trying to fool you, she said.

I am sorry to have bothered you in the morning, said Menon.

That does not matter, said Choudhuri.

ON SUBJUGATING THE HEARTS OF OTHERS

Kama Sutra

(a) If a man, after applying a mixture of the powders of the white thorn-apple, the long pepper, and the black pepper, and honey on his penis, engages in sexual union with a woman, he puts his subject in his power.

(b) If you make a powder by pulverizing the leaf of the plant vatodbhranta, the flower garlands thrown on a human corpse when carried out to be burnt, and of the bones of the peacock, and of the jiwanjiva bird, it produces the same effect.

(c) The remains of a kite which has died a natural death, ground into powder, and mixed with cowhage and honey, has also the same effect.

(e) Anointing oneself with an ointment made of the gooseberry [amla] plant has the power of subjecting women to one's will.

(e) If a man cuts into small pieces the knotty roots of the milkwort and milk-hedge plants and dips them into a mixture of red arsenic and sulphur, and then dries the mixture seven times and applies it mixed with honey to his penis, he can put his sexual partner in his power. Or, if he burns this powder at night and he sees a golden moon through the smoke, he will then be successful with any woman. If he mixes the powder with the excrement of a monkey and scatters it upon a maiden, she will not be given in marriage to another man.

(f) If pieces of the orris root are dressed with the oil of the mango, and placed for six months in a hole made in the trunk of the rosewood tree, and are then taken out and made up into an ointment and applied on the penis, it can put someone in your power.

(g) If the bone of a camel is dipped into the juice of bhringaraj, and then burnt, and the black pigment produced from its ashes is placed in a box also made of the bones of the camel, and applied together with antimony to the eyes with a pencil also made of camel bone, then that pigment is said to be very pure, and wholesome for the eyes, and puts someone in your power. The same effect can be produced by black pigment made of the bones of hawks, vultures and peacocks.

Thus end the ways of subjugating others to one's own will.

Coda

OUT FOR ANY SHAME

Paranar

One is desperate
to ride a palm-stem horse,
to wear a wreath of
milkweed buds
and be a laughing stock
of the marketplace.
One is out for any shame
when the blinding passion of love
overwhelms the heart.

(what the lover told the girl's friend)

—Translated from the Tamil by M. L. Thangappa

◆

PLEASE MOTHER GET THE CAGE OUT

Sattasai

Please mother
get the cage
out of our wedding hut
this parrot has taught the whole village
to mimic our
love cries

—Translated from the Maharashtrian Prakrit by Andrew Schelling

I LEFT SHAME BEHIND

Manikkavacakar

He grabbed me
lest I go astray.

Wax before an unspent fire,
mind melted,
body trembled.

I bowed, I wept,
danced, and cried aloud,
I sang, and I praised him.

Unyielding, as they say,
as an elephant's jaw
or a woman's grasp,
was love's unrelenting
seizure.

Love pierced me
like a nail
driven into a green tree.

Overflowing, I tossed
like a sea,

heart growing tender,
body shivering,
while the world called me Demon!
and laughed at me,

I left shame behind,

took as an ornament
the mockery of local folk.
Unswerving, I lost my cleverness
in the bewilderment of ecstasy.

—Translated from the Kannada by A. K. Ramanujan

LOVE'S FONDNESS

Tamil Sangam Poetry

If it be strength
to shake off love and kindness
and depart in pursuit of wealth
leaving us to languish,
let him be strong.
And let us womenfolk be
fools in our fondness.

(what the girl told her friend on her husband's departure)

—*Translated from the Tamil by M. L. Thangappa*

EIGHT POEMS FOR SHAKUNTALA

When God is a Traveller by Arundhathi Subramaniam

1
So here you are,
just another mixed-up kid,
daughter of a sage
and celestial sex worker,
clueless
like the rest of us
about your address—
hermitage or castle,
earth or sky,
here or hereafter.

What did you expect?

What could you be
but halfway,
forever interim?

What else

but goddamn
human?

2
The trick, Shakuntala,
is not to see it
as betrayal

when the sky collapses
and closes in
as four windowless walls

with a chipped Mickey Mouse magnet
on the refrigerator door

or as eviction

when the ceiling crumbles
and you walk
into a night of stars.

3
Yes, there's the grizzled sage Kanva
his clarity
that creeps into your bones
like warmth on a winter evening
as you watch
the milky jade
of the river Malini flow by,
serene, annotated
by cloud

and there's a home
that will live evergreen
in the folklore of tourist brochures,
detonating
with butterflies.

But what of those nights
when all you want

is a lover's breath,

regular,
regular,

starlight through a diaphanous curtain,
and a respite
from too much wisdom?

4
Besides, who hasn't known Dushyanta's charms?

The smell of perspiration,
the sour sharp beginnings
of decay

that never leave a man
who's breathed the air
of courtrooms and battlefields.

A man with winedark eyes who knows
of the velvet liquors and hushed laughter
in curtained recesses.

A man whose smile is abstraction
and crowsfeet, whose gaze
is just a little shopsoiled,

whose hair, mussed
by summer winds, still crackles
with the verbal joust of distant worlds.

Who hasn't known
a man cinnamon-tongued,
stubbled
with desire

and just the right smear
of history?
The same hackneyed script.
The same old cast.

Springtime
and the endless dress rehearsal—

a woman lustrous eyed,
a deer, two friends,
the lotus, the bee,
the inevitable man,
the heart's sudden anapest.

Nothing original
but the hope

of something new
between parted lips.

A kiss—
jasmine lapis moonshock.

And around the corner
with the old refrain,
this chorus,
(Sanskrit, Greek, whatever):

It's never close enough
It's never long enough
It's never enough
It's never

6
As for his amnesia,
be fair.

He recognized the moment
when lie saw it—

sun springtime woman—

and all around
thick, warm, motiveless
green.

Can we blame him
for later erasing the snapshot
forgetting his lines
losing the plot?

We who still wander along alien shorelines
hoping one day to be stilled

by the tidal gasp
of recollection?

We whose fingers still trail the waters,
restless as seaweed,
hoping to snag
the ring in the belly of a deep river fish—

round starlit uncompromised?

7
What you might say to the sage:

It only makes sense
if you're looking for me too—

wild-eyed
but never despairing,

certain
I'll get through eventually

through palace and marketplace,
the smoky minarets of half-dreamed cities,

and even if you know
how it all ends

I need to know you're wandering the forest
repeating the lines you cannot forget—

my conversations with the wind and the deer,
my songs to the creeper,

our endless arguments
about beginnings and endings.

Let's hear it from you, big daddy
old man, keeper of the gates.

I need to know wise men
weep like little boys.

I need to hear your words,
hoarse,
parched,
echoing

through the thickening air
and curdled fog
of this endless city—

'Come back, Shakuntala.'

8
And what you might say of the ending:

Yes, it's cosy—
family album in place,
a kid with a name
to bequeath to a country,

perhaps even a chipped magnet
on the refrigerator door.

I'm in favour of happy endings too
but not those born of bad bargains.

Next time
let there be a hermitage
in coconut green light,
the sage and I in conversation,

two friends at the door, weaving
garlands of fragrant dream

through days long and riverine

and gazing at a waterfront
stunned by sun,
my mother, on an indefinite sabbatical
from the skies.

And let me never take for granted
this green into which I was born,

this green without ache,
this green without guile,

stippled with birdcall,
bruised with sun,

this clotted green,
this unpremeditated green.

And as wild jasmine blooms in courtrooms
and lotuses in battlefields

let warriors with winedark eyes
and hair rinsed in summer wind

gambol forever with knobble-kneed fawns
in the ancient forests of memory.

MIFFED WITH THE PATRON

*He is Honey, Salt and the Most Perfect Grammar
by Kala Krishnan Ramesh*

What's
in your wares-basket today?
(Is there anything
there at all?)

If
it doesn't grab my attention,

I swear I'm going to go
to that other trader across the
rivers, on
that other hill the libertine,
in whose stock are jars
full of intoxicants,

and
he

will undo everything
you've had me learn;
he will strip me
bare
of
language, script, grammar
and
enter into me
a rogue programme that
recognizes neither patron
nor slave.

Then
I will be no one,
and
you will be

lonely,

Guha,
who longs to company with his poets.

THE START AND END OF SEX

Kama Sutra

In the pleasure-room, decorated with flowers and fragrant with perfumes, attended by his friends and servants, the citizen should receive the woman, who will come bathed and dressed, and will invite her to take refreshment and to drink freely. He should then seat her on his left side, and holding her hair, and touching also the knot of her garment, he should gently embrace her with his right arm. They should then begin an engaging conversation on various subjects, and may also talk suggestively of things which would be considered as coarse, or on things not mentioned generally in society. They may then sing, either with or without gesticulations, and play on musical instruments, talk about the arts, and persuade each other to drink more. At last when the woman is overcome with love and desire, the citizen should dismiss the people that are with him, giving them flowers, ointments and betel leaves, and then when the two are left alone, they should proceed as has been already described in the previous chapters.

Such is the beginning of sex. At the end of lovemaking, the lovers, embarrassed and not looking at each other, should go separately to the washing-room. When they return, they sit at their own places, eat some betel leaves, and the man applies some pure sandalwood ointment, or ointment of some other kind, on the body of the woman. He should then embrace her with his left arm, and with gentle words should urge her to drink from a cup held in his own hand, or he may give her water to drink. They can eat sweetmeats, or anything else, according to their liking and may drink fresh juice, soup, gruel, extracts of meat, sherbet, the juice of mango fruits, sweet lemonade, or anything that may be liked in different countries, and known to be sweet, soft and pure. The lovers may also sit on the terrace of the palace or house, and enjoy the moonlight, and carry on an enjoyable conversation. At this time, too, while the woman lies in his lap, with her face towards the moon, the citizen should show her the different planets, the morning star, the pole star, and the seven Rishis, or Great Bear.

This is the end of sex.

ACKNOWLEDGEMENTS

My partner and daughters for putting up with my brooding and constant disappearances into books.

My parents, my first links to the life of reading, who encouraged me to read widely, hungrily, thoughtfully, and when necessary, rapidly.

The Homi Bhabha Foundation in Mumbai whose generous support allowed me the reflective time and space that I needed to write the introductory essay.

Harish Trivedi, for translating more than I asked.

Simar Puneet of Aleph Book Company whose insistence made this anthology happen.

NOTES

The extracts in this volume have been taken from dozens of different books and the way in which they spell proper nouns and use hyphens, italics and so on is often different. The extracts are reproduced exactly as they appear in the original sources.

WHY BOTHER WITH SEX?

'You Are Your Desire' from the Brihadaranyaka Upanishad in *The Upanishads*, introduced and translated by Eknath Easwaran. First published in California by the Blue Mountain Center of Meditation/Nilgiri Press in 1998.

'Why Does Sex Exist?' from *Ka: Stories of the Mind and Gods of India* by Roberto Calasso. Copyright © Adelphi Edizioni, S. P. A Milano, 1996. Reprinted by permission of The Wylie Agency (UK) Limited.

'The Garden of Kama: Kama the Indian Eros' from *The Garden of Kama: And Other Love Lyrics from India* by Laurence Hope. First published in London by William Hieneman in 1901.

'The Girl and the Woman' by Vidyapati, translated by Edward C. Dimock Jr. First appeared in *The East-West Review* in 1966.

'Girl With Bright Thighs' from *Amaruśataka* in *Erotic Love Poems from India: A Translation of the Amarushataka* by Andrew Schelling. First published by Shambhala Press in 2004. Reprinted by permission of the translator.

'The Firesticks of Love' from the Shvetashvara Upanishad, in *The Upanishads*, introduced and translated by Eknath Easwaran. First published in California by the Blue Mountain Center of Meditation/Nilgiri Press in 1998.

'Delightful' by Bhartrihari, translated by Kala Krishnan Ramesh, in *The Devil Take Love* by Sudhir Kakar. First published in India by Penguin in 2015. Reprinted by permission of the author.

THE ART OF SEDUCTION

'Lifestyle of the Man About Town', adapted from *The Kama Sutra of Vatsyayana*. First published in Benares by The Hindoo Kama Shastra Society in 1925.

'Sixteen Daily Stations in the Body of your Gazelle-eyed Lady' from the Koka Shastra, translated by Alex Comfort, in *The Koka Shastra: Being the Ratirahasya of Kokkoka and Other Medieval Indian Writings on Love*. First published by Stein and Day in 1964.

'Who Are You Having Sex with?' from 'Of The Physical Types and Their Seasons'. Ibid.

'Re-kindling Exhausted Passion' from the *Kama Sutra*, adapted from *The Kama Sutra of Vatsyayana*. First published in Benares by The Hindoo Kama Shastra Society in 1925.

An excerpt from *The Ascetic of Desire* by Sudhir Kakar (pp. 58–71). First published by Penguin India in 1998. Reprinted by permission of the author.

ENNUI IN MARRIAGE

'How Our Bodies Were One Before' from the *Subhasitaratnakosa* by Bhavakadevi, translated by R. Parthasarathy in 'Women's Wisdom Through the Ages', *Manushi* Volume 149, October 2005.

An excerpt from *Ek Pati Ke Notes* by Mahendra Bhalla. First published by Rajkamal Prakashan in 1967. This translation copyright Harish Trivedi.

'A Little Kitten' by Kamala Das, in *Padmavati, the Harlot and Other Stories*. First published by Sterling Publishers in 1994. Reprinted by permission of The Estate of Kamala Das. Unauthorized copying is strictly prohibited.

Two on Marriage from the *Gāthā Saptaśatī*, translated by Andrew Schelling, in *The Cane Groves of the Narmada River: Erotic Poems from Old India*. First published by City Light Books in 1998. Reprinted by permission of the publisher. Reprinted with the permission of the Permissions Company on behalf of City Lights Books.

'The Wife Unlucky in Love' from the *Kama Sutra*, adapted from *The Kama Sutra of Vatsyayana*. First published in Benares by The Hindoo Kama Shastra Society in 1925.

RAPTURE AND LONGING

'The Seasons' from *Ṛtusaṃāram* by Kalidasa translated by Mani Rao in *Kalidasa for the 21st Century Reader*. First published by Aleph Book Company in 2014.

'My Bare Legs' from the *Gāthā Saptaśatī*, translated by Andrew Schelling, in *The Cane Groves of the Narmada River: Erotic Poems from Old India*. First published by City Light Books in 1998. Reprinted by permission of the publisher. Reprinted with the permission of the Permissions Company on behalf of City Lights Books.

'Soil My Bed with Indigo Footprints' from the *Gita Govinda* of Jayadeva, translated by Andrew Schelling, in *Love and the Turning Seasons: India's Poetry of Spiritual and Erotic Longing* edited by Andrew Schelling. First published by Counterpoint Press in 2014. Reprinted by permission of the publisher. 'Morning Chill' from *The Alchemy of Desire* by Tarun Tejpal. First published by Picador UK in 2005. Reprinted by permission of the author. 'Infinite' by K. Satchidanandan. Used by permission of the author.

THE FIRST TIME

'The Cure' from *Junglee Girl* by Ginu Kamani. First published by Aunt Lute Books in 1995. Reprinted by permission of the author.

'Winning a Virgin's Trust' from the *Kama Sutra*, adapted from *The Kama Sutra of Vatsyayana*. First published in Benares by The Hindoo Kama Shastra Society in 1925.

An excerpt from *Mira Yagnik Ni Diary* by Bindu Bhatt, translated by Rita Kothari, in *Speech and Silence: Literary Journeys by Gujarati Women*. First published in 2006 by Zubaan. Reprinted by permission of the translator.

An excerpt from *A Bad Character* by Deepti Kapoor. First published by Penguin India in 2015. Reprinted by permission of the publisher.

'Three Virgins' by Manjula Padmanabhan from *Three Virgins and Other Stories*. First published by Zubaan in 2013. Reprinted by permission of the author.

'Making Advances to a Young Girl' from the *Kama Sutra*, adapted from *The Kama Sutra of Vatsyayana*. First published in Benares by The Hindoo Kama Shastra Society in 1925.

ANGUISH, ABANDONMENT AND BREAK UP

'My Soul Melts in Anguish' by Antal, translated by Vidya Dehejia, in *Āntāl and Her Path of Love*. First published by SUNY Press in 1990. Reprinted by permission of the State University of New York.

'You Do Not Come' by Amrita Pritam, translated by Charles Barusch, in *Black Rose*. First published in Delhi by Nagmani in 1967.

'What She Said' by Ammuvanar translated by A. K. Ramanujan, in *Poems of Love and War*. First published by Columbia University Press in 1985. Reprinted by permission of The Estate of A. K. Ramanujan.

'The Means of Getting Rid of a Lover' from the *Kama Sutra*, adapted from *The Kama Sutra of Vatsyayana*. First published in Benares by The Hindoo Kama Shastra Society in 1925.

'He Never Came' by Rabindranath Tagore, translated by Chase Twichell and Tony K. Stewart, in *Love and the Turning Seasons: India's Poetry of Spiritual and Erotic Longing* edited by Andrew Schelling. First published by

Counterpoint Press in 2014. Reprinted by permission of the publisher. This poem originally appears in *Bhanusimha Thakurer Padabali* (The Songs of Bhanushingho Thakur), 1884. Bhanu Simha (Sun Lion) was the pen name Tagore wrote under when he was sixteen.

'What She Said' from *Kuruntokai* by Paranar, translated by A. K. Ramanujan, in *Poems of Love and War*. First published by Columbia University Press in 1985. Reprinted by permission of The Estate of A. K. Ramanujan.

ANGER, PUNISHMENT AND MAKE UP

'Ways of Slapping' from the *Kama Sutra*, adapted from *The Kama Sutra of Vatsyayana*. First published in Benares by The Hindoo Kama Shastra Society in 1925.

'Three on Forgiveness' from the *Amaruśataka* in *Erotic Love Poems from India: A Translation of the Amarushataka* by Andrew Schelling. First published by Shambhala Press in 2004. Reprinted by permission of the author.

'My Conflicted Heart Treasures Even His Infidelities' from the *Gita Govinda* by Jayadeva, translated by Andrew Schelling, in *Love and the Turning Seasons: India's Poetry of Spiritual and Erotic Longing* edited by Andrew Schelling. First published by Counterpoint Press in 2014. Reprinted by permission of the publisher.

Verses 91 to 107 from *Radhika Santawanam* by Muddupalani, translated by Sandhya Mulchandani, in *The Appeasement of Radhika*. First published by Penguin India in 2011. Reprinted by permission of the publisher.

'At Midnight, Resurrect Our Love' by Pritish Nandy in *Tonight, This Savage Rite: The Love Poems of Kamala Das and Pritish Nandy*. First published by Arnold Heinemann in 1979. Reprinted by permission of the author.

'When My Face Turned Towards His' from *Amaruśataka*, translated by Martha Ann Selby, in *Ancient Indian Literature: An Anthology*, edited by T. R. S. Sharma. First published by the Sahitya Akademi in 2000.

MEN'S WISH TO BE WOMEN

'[Who has the Better Sex?] Man or Woman?' from the Mahabharata, Anushasana Parva Danadharma (12.11-53), translated by Arshia Sattar. Reprinted by permission of the translator.

'Chaptinama' by Jur'at, translated by Saleem Kidwai, versified by Ruth Vanita, in *Same-Sex Love in India: Readings in Indian Literature*. First published by St. Martin's Press (Palgrave-Macmillian) in 2000. Reprinted by permission of the authors.

'Why Should You Go Wandering into the Garden, My Love' by Raskhan, translated by Harish Trivedi. Reprinted by permission of the translator.

'A Mikmaid to Krishna' by Raskhan translated by Harish Trivedi. Reprinted by permission of the translator.

WOMEN ON THEIR OWN

An excerpt from *Nasreen* by K. P. Vaid, translated by Harish Trivedi. Reprinted by permission of the translator.

'Braids Scattered' from *Gāthā Saptaśatī* in *The Cane Groves of the Narmada River: Erotic Poems from Old India*. First published by City Light Books in 1998. Reprinted by permission of the publisher. Reprinted with the permission of the Permissions Company on behalf of City Lights Books.

'I Had a Dream' by Mahadeviyakka, translated by A. K Ramanujan, in *Speaking of Śiva*. First published by Penguin in 1973. Reprinted by permission of The Estate of A. K. Ramanujan.

'Young Women Speak to Their Lovers' from the *Amaruśataka*, translated by Martha Ann Selby, in *Ancient Indian Literature: An Anthology*, edited by T. R. S. Sharma. First published by the Sahitya Akademi in 2000.

An excerpt from *Chittacobra* by Mridula Garg. First published by National Publishing House in 2007. Reprinted by permission of the author.

'Dark One' by Mirabai, in *Love and the Turning Seasons: India's Poetry of Spiritual and Erotic Longing* edited by Andrew Schelling. First published by Counterpoint Press in 2014. Reprinted by permission of the publisher.

'Lihaaf' by Ismat Chughtai, translated by M. Asaduddin. Reprinted by permission of Ashish Sawhny (The Estate of Ismat Chughtai) and the translator.

NOSTALGIA (ON MISSING THE SEX WE ALREADY HAD)
'Bū' (Smell) by Saadat Hasan Manto, translated by Muhammad Umar Memon. Reprinted by permission of the translator.

'Then and Now' by Silabhattarika, translated by R. Parthasarathy, in 'Women's Wisdom Through the Ages', *Manushi* Volume 149, October 2005.

'Kailasam' by Ambai (Dr C. S. Lakshmi), translated by Lakshmi Holmström, in *Fish in a Dwindling Lake*. First published by Penguin India in 2012. Reprinted by permission of the publisher.

SUSPICION AND CONFUSION (WHO ARE WE HAVING SEX WITH, REALLY?)

'Who Was I ?' by Govindasvami, in *Love and the Turning Seasons: India's Poetry of Spiritual and Erotic Longing* edited by Andrew Schelling. First published by Counterpoint Press in 2014. Reprinted by permission of the publisher.

'With the Last of My Garments' by Vidyapati. Ibid.

'What Can I do?' and 'I Made Love' from the *Gāthā Saptaśatī*, in *The Cane Groves of the Narmada River: Erotic Poems from Old India*. First published by City Light Books in 1998. Reprinted by permission of the publisher. Reprinted with the permission of the Permissions Company on behalf of City Lights Books.

An excerpt from *One Part Woman* by Perumal Murugan. First published by Penguin India in 2013. Reprinted by permission of the publisher.

An excerpt from *Cuckold*. Reproduced in arrangement with HarperCollins Publishers India Private Limited from the book 'Cuckold' authored by Kiran Nagarkar and first published by them © Kiran Nagarkar, 1997. All rights reserved. Unauthorized copying is strictly prohibited.

'You Come to Me' from *Adivaraha Sattasai* (1.85), in *The Cane Groves of the Narmada River: Erotic Poems from Old India*. First published by City Light Books in 1998. Reprinted by permission of the publisher. Reprinted with the permission of the Permissions Company on behalf of City Lights Books.

'Sanatan Choudhuri's Wife' by Kamala Das, in *Padmavati, the Harlot and Other Stories*. First published by Sterling Publishers in 1994. Reprinted by permission of The Estate of Kamala Das. Unauthorized copying is strictly prohibited.

'Putting Someone in Your Power' from the *Kama Sutra*, adapted from *The Kama Sutra of Vatsyayana*. First published in Benares by The Hindoo Kama Shastra Society in 1925.

CODA

'Out for Any Shame' from the *Kuruntokai* by Paranar, translated by M. L. Thangappa, in *Love Stands Alone: Selections from Tamil Sangam Poetry*. First published by Penguin India in 2013. Reprinted by permission of the translator.

'Please Mother Get the Cage Out' from *The Cane Groves of the Narmada River: Erotic Poems from Old India*. First published by City Light Books in 1998. Reprinted by permission of the publisher. Reprinted with the permission of the Permissions Company on behalf of City Lights Books.

'I Left Shame Behind' by Manikkavacakar, translated by A. K. Ramanujan, in *Hymns for the Drowning*. First published by Princeton University Press in 1981. Reprinted by permission of The Estate of A. K. Ramanujan.

'Love's Fondness', translated by M. L. Thangappa, in *Love Stands Alone: Selections from Tamil Sangam Poetry*. First published by Penguin India in 2013. Reprinted by permission of the translator.

'Eight Poems for Shakuntala'. Reproduced in arrangement with HarperCollins *Publishers* India Private Limited from the book 'When God is a Traveller' authored by Arundhathi Subramaniam and first published by them © Arundhathi Subramaniam, 2014. All rights reserved. Unauthorized copying is strictly prohibited.

'Miffed with the Patron'. Reproduced in arrangement with HarperCollins *Publishers* India Private Limited from the book 'He is Honey, Salt and the Most Perfect Grammar' authored by Kala Krishnan Ramesh and first published by them © Kala Krishnan Ramesh, 2016. All rights reserved. Unauthorized copying is strictly prohibited.

'The Start and the Finish of Sex' from the *Kama Sutra*, adapted from *The Kama Sutra of Vatsyayana*. First published in Benares by The Hindoo Kama Shastra Society in 1925.

Ambai (b. 1944) is the nom de plume of Dr C. S. Lakshmi who is a Tamil writer, feminist, historian, and independent researcher in women's studies. Her stories have been translated into English in the volume *A Purple Sea* and *In a Forest, A Deer*. She is presently the Director of Sound and Picture Archives for Research on Women (SPARROW) in Mumbai.

Amrita Pritam (1919–2005), the doyenne of Punjabi literature, was a poet and writer. Her best-known works are the poem 'Aaj Aakhan Waris Shan Nu' and the novel *Pinjar* (The Skeleton), which was made into an award-winning film in 2003. In 1956, she became the first woman to win the Sahitya Akademi Award for her magnum opus, a long poem, *Sunehe* (Messages); she received the Jnanpith for *Kagaz Te Canvas* (The Paper and the Canvas). In 2004, she was awarded the Padma Vibhushan, as well as the Sahitya Akademi's Lifetime Achievement Award.

Andrew Schelling (b. 1953) is an American poet, professor, ecologist and translator. His translations include *The Cane Groves of the Narmada River: Erotic Poems of Old India, Love and the Turning Seasons: India's Poetry of Spiritual & Erotic Longing* and *Erotic Love Poems from India: Selections from the Amarushataka*. He has received two grants for translation from the Witter Bynner Foundation for Poetry. Schelling's poetry collections include *A Possible Bag* and *From the Arapaho Songbook*. He is currently a professor at Naropa University.

Āntāl is the only female Alvar among the twelve Alvar saints of South India. The Alvar saints are known for their affiliation to the Srivaishnava tradition of Hinduism. Andal is credited with the Tamil works, *Thiruppavai* and *Nachiar Tirumozhi*, which are still recited by devotees during the winter festival season of Margazhi.

Arundhathi Subramaniam (b. 1967) is an award-winning poet, artist and an eminent writer on spirituality and culture. Over the years she has worked as a poetry editor and curator, and as a journalist on literature, classical dance and theatre. She is the author of four books of poems, most recently *When God Is a Traveller* (Bloodaxe Books, 2014) and *Where I Live: New & Selected Poems* (Bloodaxe Books, 2009). Her prose works include the bestselling biography of a contemporary mystic *Sadhguru: More Than a Life*, and *The Book of Buddha*.

Bhartrihari (5th century CE) was a Hindu philosopher and poet-grammarian. He wrote the influential *Vakyapadiya* (Words in a Sentence), on the philosophy of language. He is considered one of the most original philosophers of language and religion in ancient India.

Bindu Bhatt is a novelist, short story writer, critic, lecturer and translator. Her novel *Akhepatar* was awarded the Sahitya Akademi Award in 2003. Her other significant works includes *Mira Yagnik ni Dayari* and *Bandhani*.

Deepti Kapoor grew up in New Delhi, where she attended college and worked for several years as a journalist. *A Bad Character*, her debut novel, was published in 2014. It received great critical acclaim. She currently lives in Goa.

Ginu Kamani was born in Bombay and moved to the US at the age of fourteen. Two of her short stories from *Junglee Girl* and several of her poems were published in the anthology *Our Feet Walk the Sky: Women of the South Asian Diaspora*. Kamani currently uses her knowledge of herbs, oils, and gardening in her work with woodsmen-artist-farmers in a volcanic rainforest environment in Dominica.

Ismat Chughtai (1915–1991), the grande dame of Urdu literature, was a novelist, short-story writer and essayist who represented the birth of a revolutionary feminist politics and aesthetics in Urdu literature in the twentieth century. Although a spirited member of the Progressive Writers' Movement in India, she spoke vehemently against its orthodoxy and inflexibility.

Jayadeva was a poet of the twelfth century, hailing from today's Orissa. He is most known for his *Gita Govinda*, a work of Sanskrit love poetry and song, based on the love story of Krishna and Radha. This poem, which presents the view that Radha is greater than Krishna, is considered an important text in the Bhakti movement of Hinduism.

Kala Krishnan Ramesh is a poet known for her debut collection, *He is Honey, Salt and the Most Perfect Grammar*. Greatly influenced by Tamil language and literature, Murugan, the beloved God of the Tamils, occupies centre stage in her book which explores the eternal struggle of God, the self and society. She lives and works in Bangalore, and teaches in the Communication Studies department of a college.

K. Satchidanandan (born 1946) has been hailed as one of the pioneers of modern Malayalam poetry. He is a bilingual literary critic, playwright, editor, columnist and translator. He was the former Editor of *Indian Literature* journal and the former Secretary of the Sahitya Akademi. He retired as Director and Professor of the School of Translation Studies and Training at the Indira Gandhi National Open University in New Delhi in 2011.

Kālidāsā was a classical Sanskrit writer, widely regarded as the greatest poet and dramatist in the Sanskrit language. His plays and poetry are

primarily based on the Indian Puranas. Much about his life is unkno Works attributed to him include the popular plays, *Abhijnanashakunt Vikramorvashi* and *Malavikagnimitra*, the epic poems *Raghuvamsha* ; *Kumarasambhava*; and the lyric *Meghaduta*.

Kamala Das (1934–2009) also wrote as Madhavikutty, and later chang her name to Surayya. She wrote novels, poetry and short stories in Engl and Malayalam. She received the Kerala Sahitya Akademi, Sahitya Akade Award, Valayar Award and Kent Award for English Writing from Asi Countries. She was nominated in 1984 for the Nobel Prize in Literature

Kiran Nagarkar (b. 1942) is an Indian novelist, playwright, film and dran critic and screenwriter, writing in Marathi and English. Amongst his wor are *Saat Sakkam Trechalis* (Seven Sixes Are Forty Three), *Ravan and Edd* (1994) and the epic novel, *Cuckold*, for which he was awarded the 200 Sahitya Akademi Award in English by the Sahitya Akademi. He is considere to be one of the most significant writers of postcolonial India.

Krishna Baldev Vaid (b. 1927) is a Hindi fiction writer, literary criti and playwright, noted for his experimental and iconoclastic narrative style His work has been translated into English, French, German, Italian, Polish Russian, Japanese and several Indian languages. He retired as Professor a State University of New York, Postdam. He regards his traumatic experience during Partition as the defining existentialist moment of his life. His works reflect this existentialist nature.

Laurence Hope (1865–1904) was the pseudonym of English poet Adela Florence Nicolson. In 1901, she published *Garden of Kama*, which was published a year later in America under the title *India's Love Lyrics*. Her poems often used imagery and symbols from the poets of the North-West Frontier of India and the Sufi poets of Persia. She was among the most popular romantic poets of the Victorian and Edwardian eras.

Mahadeviyakka, or Akka Mahadevi, was a twelfth century poet-mystic of Karnataka. Most of her poems were dedicated to Lord Shiva. She composed a large number of vachanas, free verse lyrics written in the Kannada language. About 350 extant poems are attributed to her.

Mahendra Bhalla (1933–2015) was a noted playwright and Hindi writer. His most popular play is arguably *Dimaag-e-hasti, Dil Ki Basti Hai Kahan, Hai Kahan*. He was conferred with the Sahitya Akademi Award for Hindi.

Manikkavacakar was a ninth-century Tamil poet who wrote *Tiruvasakam*, a book of Shaiva hymns. He was one of the main authors of *Saivite Tirumurai*. His writings comprise one volume of the *Tirumurai*, the key religious text of Tamil Shaiva Siddhanta. One of the key figures of the Hindu bhakti

revival, his work is a poetic expression of the joy of God-experience and the anguish of being separated from God.

Manjula Padmanabhan (b. 1953) is an author/artist living in the US and India. *Harvest*, her fifth play, won the Onassis Award for Theatre. Her books include *Three Virgins, Getting There* and *Escape*.

Mirabai was a mystic poet devoted to Lord Krishna. She is believed to have been born in 1498 into the royal family of Merta in Rajasthan, and was married to Bhoj Raj of Chittor. Against all convention, she mixed with common folk, singing bhajans and dancing in spiritual ecstasy. About 1,300 verses are attributed to her.

Mridula Garg (b. 1938) writes in Hindi and English. She has published several novels, short story collections, plays and essays. She is a recipient of the prestigious Sahitya Akademi Award and the Vyas Sanman. The Human Rights Watch, New York, awarded her the Hammett-Hellman award for courageous writing.

Muddupalani lived in the mid-eighteenth century in Thanjavur. She was a devdasi attached to the court of King Pratapsimha. She wrote *Radhika Santawanam* in Telugu but was a multi-linguist and also wrote in Sanskrit and Tamil. She translated Tamil saint-poet Andaal's *Tiruppavai* into Telugu.

Perumal Murugan (b. 1966) is a well-known Tamil author, scholar and literary chronicler. He has written six novels, four collections of short stories and four anthologies of poetry. Four of his novels have been translated into English: *Seasons of the Palm*, which was shortlisted for the Kiriyama Prize in 2005, *Current Show, One Part Woman*, and *Pyre*. His *Maadhorubaagan* (One Part Woman) caused great controversy in 2014, but Murugan's freedom of expression was upheld by the Madras High Court.

Pritish Nandy (b. 1951) is an Indian poet, painter, journalist, politician, media and television personality, animal activist and film producer. He was a member of the Rajya Sabha. He has published a number of poetry books, including *Tonight this Savage Rite* with Kamala Das, *Rites for a Plebeian Statue* and *Riding the Midnight River*. He has also translated poems from Bengali and Urdu into English.

Rabindranath Tagore (1861–1941) was a Bengali poet, philosopher, artist, playwright, composer and novelist. India's first Nobel laureate, Tagore won the 1913 Nobel Prize in Literature. He composed the text of both India's and Bangladesh's national anthems.

Raskhan (1548–1628) was a poet who was both a Muslim and a follower of Lord Krishna. Born Sayyad Ibrahim, he is said to have lived in Amroha, India. Raskhan was his pen name in Hindi. *Sujan Raskhan* and *Prem Vatika*

are attributed to him. Most of his poems are dedicated to Lord Krishna.

Roberto Calasso (b. 1941) is an Italian writer and publisher. Apart from his mother tongue, Italian, Calasso is fluent in French, English, Spanish, German. Latin and Greek. He has also studied Sanskrit. He is director of Adelphi, one of Italy's most prestigious publishing houses. He has published twelve novels. *Ka: Stories of the Mind and Gods of India* engages with the fundamental thematic concept of his oeuvre: the relationship between myth and the emergence of modern consciousness.

Saadat Hasan Manto (1912–1955) is the most widely read and, arguably, the most controversial short story writer in Urdu. In a literary, journalistic, radio scripting and film-writing career spread over more than two decades, he produced twenty-two collections of short stories, one novel, five collections of radio plays, three collections of essays, two collections of personal sketches and many scripts for films. He was tried for obscenity half a dozen times.

Silabhattarika was a woman poet of the Classical period in the Common Era known for her Panchali literary style. She is one of the approximately forty women poets who wrote in Sanskrit and to whom a total of over 200 poems are credited.

Sudhir Kakar (b. 1938) is a psychoanalyst, author and translator. He has published twenty books of non-fiction and six of fiction, including *Tales of Love, Sex and Danger, The Analyst and the Mystic* and *The Colors of Violence, Culture and Psyche.* He has co-translated the *Kama Sutra* with Wendy Doniger. He currently lives in Goa.

Tamil Sangam poets, including Paranar, Bhavadevi and Ammuvanar, were a group of poets who wrote from around 300 BCE to 300 CE. Sangam literature is primarily secular, dealing with everyday themes in a Tamilian context.

Tarun Tejpal (b. 1963) is an Indian journalist, publisher, novelist and former editor-in-chief of *Tehelka* magazine. His novel, *The Alchemy of Desire*, was shortlisted for the Prix Femina and won France's Le Prix Mille Pages for Best Foreign Literary Fiction.

Vātsyayāna was an Indian philosopher in the Vedic tradition who is believed to have lived around the second century CE. He is credited as the author of the *Kama Sutra*, the definitive work in Sanskrit literature on human sexual behaviour. It is also a book of philosophy, discussing ideas of virtuous living, love and origins of desire.

Vidyapati (1352–1448), also known by the sobriquet Maithil Kavi Kokil, was a Maithili poet and a Sanskrit writer. Vidyapati's poetry was widely influential in the Hindustani as well as Bengali, Maithili and other Eastern literary traditions.

NOTES ON THE TRANSLATORS

A. K. Ramanujan (1929–1993) was an Indian poet, folklorist, translator, playwright and scholar of Indian literature. He wrote in both English and Kannada. He published works on both classical and modern variants of literature and argued strongly for giving local, non-standard dialects their due. He won a Sahitya Akademi Award posthumously in 1999 for *The Collected Poems*.

Alex Comfort (1920–2000) was a British scientist, physician, novelist, poet, translator, anarchist and pacifist. He is known best for his nonfiction sex manual, *The Joy of Sex* (1972).

Aniruddhan Vasudevan is the translator of Perumal Murugan's controversial Tamil novel, *Maadhorubaagan*, which won the Sahitya Akademi 2016 translation prize in English.

Arshia Sattar's (b.1960) English translations include Valmiki's Ramayana and *Tales from the Kathasaritsagara*. She has a PhD from the Department of South Asian Languages and Civilizations at the University of Chicago and her interests are Indian epics, mythology and the story traditions of the subcontinent.

Charles Brasch (1909–1973) was a poet, critic and translator. He was also a key figure in the development of the creative arts in New Zealand, through his founding and editorship for twenty years of the literary quarterly *Landfall* and his generous patronage of writers, painters and musicians.

Chase Twichell (b. 1950) has published several collections of poetry. She founded the Ausable Press, which is dedicated to publishing poetry.

Denise Levertov (1923–1997) was born, and published her first book of poems, in England. In 1948, she moved to the US and became known as one of the preeminent members of the new American poets, and a staunch antiwar activist.

Edward C. Dimock Jr. (1930–2001) was a professor emeritus in South Asian languages and literatures at the University of Chicago. He wrote and translated extensively in Bengali, and was awarded the Desikottama for lifetime achievement by the Indian government.

Eknath Easwaran (1910–1999) was a spiritual teacher, an author of books on meditation and ways to lead a fulfilling life, as well as a translator and interpreter of Indian religious texts such as the Bhagavad Gita and the Upanishads.

Harish Trivedi (b. 1947) has written on the areas of translation, postcolonialism, Indian literature and world literature. He is the author of *Colonial Transactions: English Literature and India* and the translator of *Premchand: His Life and Times* (2002). He was a professor at Delhi University, and a visiting professor at Chicago and London.

Lakshmi Holmström (1935–2016) was a writer, literary critic and award-winning translator. She has translated the works of major writers in Tamil such as Mauni, Pudumaippittan, Ashokamitran, Sundara Ramaswamy, Ambai, Bama and Imayam. In 2000 she received the Crossword Book Award for her translation of *Karukku* by Bama. She was a Founder-Trustee of South Asian Diaspora Literature and Arts Archive.

M. Asaduddin is an author, translator and critic. His work has been recognized with the Sahitya Akademi Prize, the Katha Prize and A. K. Ramanujan Award for Translation. His published titles include *The Penguin Book of Classic Urdu Stories, Lifting the Veil: Selected Writings of Ismat Chughtai, For Freedom's Sake: Manto* and *Joseph Conrad: Between Culture and Colonialism*.

M. L. Thangappa (b.1934) is a Tamil poet and taught Tamil in the colleges of the Puducherry government until his retirement in 1994. His books include two volumes of translations from classical Tamil poetry: *Love Stands Alone* and *Red Lilies and Frightened Birds. Love Stands Alone* won the Sahitya Akademi award for Translation.

Mani Rao (b. 1965) is the author of eight poetry books, and two books in translation—The Bhagavad Gita, and *Kalidasa for the 21st Century Reader*. Her poems and essays are published in journals including *Tinfish, Wasafiri, Meanjin, Washington Square, Fulcrum, West Coast Line,* and *Interim*, and in various anthologies.

Moussaieff Masson (b. 1941) is an American author. Masson is best known for his conclusions about Sigmund Freud and psychoanalysis. He lives in New Zealand with his family and has written nine bestselling books about the emotional life of animals.

Muhammad Umar Memon (b. 1939) is professor emeritus of Urdu literature and Islamic studies at the University of Wisconsin-Madison. He is a critic, short story writer, and translator. He was editor of the *Annual of Urdu Studies* (1993–20014). He lives in Madison, Wisconsin.

R. Parthasarathy (b. 1934) is a poet, translator, critic and editor. R. Parthasarathy has translated the old Tamil epic, *The Tale of an Anklet: An Epic of South India*. He teaches Indian literature at Skidmore College.

Rita Kothari (b. 1969) is a Gujarati and English language author and translator. In an attempt to preserve memories and her identity as Sindhi, she has written several books on the Partition and its effects on people. She has translated several Gujarati works into English and edited some.

Ruth Vanita (b. 1955) is an Indian author, academic and activist. She specializes in gender studies, lesbian and gay studies and British and South Asian history.

Saleem Kidwai (b. 1951) is a medieval historian, gay studies scholar and a translator. He taught history at Ramjas College, University of Delhi until 1993 and is now an independent scholar. He was one of the first academics to speak publicly as a member of the LGBT community. His other academic areas of interest are Mughal politics and culture, the history of tawaifs, and north Indian music.

Sandhya Mulchandani (b. 1956) is a researcher and writer, and has been associated with the print media for more than two decades. She is the author of several books, including *Five Arrows of Kama: The Art of Love, Sex and Desire*, *Kama Sutra for Women* and *The Indian Man: His True Colours*. She lives in New Delhi.

Tim Parks (b. 1954) is a writer and translator. He has translated works by Moravia, Calvino, Calasso, Machiavelli and Leopardi; his book, *Translating Style*, which analyses Italian translations of the English modernists, is considered a classic in its field and he currently runs a post-graduate degree in translation at IULM University in Milan.

Tony K. Stewart (b. 1954) is the Gertrude Conaway Vanderbilt Chair in Humanities and Professor and Chair, Department of Religious Studies at Vanderbilt University. He is a specialist in religions and literatures of the Bengali speaking world.

Vidya Dehejia (b. 1942) is a lecturer, art historian and curator. She is a professor of Indian art at Columbia University. Her background in Sanskrit and Tamil, as well as knowledge of other modern Indian languages, has proved invaluable in her exploration of the theoretical basis of Indian art.

W. S. Merwin (b. 1927) is a Pulitzer-prize winning poet, and the author of over fifty books of poetry, translation and prose. He is known for the distinctive sparse style of his poems, and his condemnation of the Vietnam War and the destruction of the environment.